MW01073335

WOLF'S EYES

BY

RAE D. MAGDON

Desert Palm Press

Wolf's Eyes
by Rae D. Madgon

© 2014 by Rae D. Magdon

ISBN-13 9781500828707
ISBN-10 150082870X

This is a work of fiction - names, characters, places, and incidents are the product of the author's imagination or are used fictitiously. Any resemblance to actual person living or dead, business, events or locales is entirely coincidental. All rights reserved.

No part of this publication may be reproduced, distributed, or transmitted in any form or by any means, including photocopying, recording, or other electronic or mechanical methods, without the prior written permission of the publisher, except in the case of brief quotations embodied in critical reviews and certain other noncommercial uses permitted by copyright law.

For permission requests, write to the publisher, addressed "Attention: Permissions Coordinator," at the address below.

Desert Palm Press
1961 Main Street, Suite 220
Watsonville, California 95076
www.desertpalmpress.com

Editor: R. Lee Fitzsimmons
Cover Design: Rachel George
Http://www.rachelgeorgeillustration.com

Printed in the United States of America
First Edition August 2014

Dedication/Acknowledgements

To Lee and the wonderful people at Desert Palm Press, without whom the publication of this book would not be possible.

To Linda, whose strength has helped inspire me in countless ways.

To Tory, who has stuck with me through it all.

Thank you.

WOLF'S EYES

Part One:

As told by Cathelin Raybrook, and recorded by Lady Eleanor of Baxstresse

CHAPTER ONE

CLOUDS HUNG IN DARK bundles against the murky-grey sky, casting faint fingers of shadow onto the ground. The brown dirt of the racetrack stretched out beneath me, and the crowd shifted and rumbled in their seats. There was a tiny moving dot of color for each figure, and trying to separate them out was a dizzying task. So many people! This was my first time in Ronin, the capital of Seria, and I was overwhelmed.

Even though it was overcrowded and poorly lit, the Ronin track was still marvelous. The horses tossed their heads proudly, ears flickering and muscles twitching. Voices rose and fell in swells of sound that came like rolling waves, and the noise carried all the way up into the private box where Belladonna, Ellie, Sarah, and I sat.

I felt a soft tug at my arm and turned to see Sarah gripping my sleeve. Her face was flushed pink and her chest rose and fell with excited breaths. "Can you believe it, Cate? We're actually at the Prince's Cup in a private box."

"Not a very original name, is it? The Prince's Cup," Belladonna said before I could answer. She was tall even while sitting down, and her dark, glossy hair and pale blue eyes always drew attention. A few months before, she had been a brooding and unhappy person. Now, she was lighthearted, poetic, and even a bit of a tease. That was my friend Ellie's doing. She sat on my other side with a huge smile on her face.

"Look, Belle, I think I can see Brahms and Corynne!" Ellie left her place beside Belladonna and walked up to the railing. She had always possessed a special bond with the horses. She was *Ariada* —a witch— like me, and her gift was speaking with animals.

Ellie's voice prompted me to look down, and I watched as Corynne D'Reixa and Brahmsian Synng were led out onto the track. Both of them sported Baxtresse's blue and white colors, and they followed their handlers with graceful, rolling gaits. The two horses were siblings, although Corynne was older and more experienced than Brahms. She had won the Prince's Cup five times in three years, but strained her foreleg during her last race. This would probably be her final chance to win the Cup before she retired. Brahms was a few years younger than his sister, and although he was inexperienced, he was also powerful and fast. This was his first year competing, but his odds were higher than any other new horse on the racing circuit.

Belladonna twisted in her seat and rested the tips of her fingers on Ellie's forearm. "Nervous, love?"

Ellie twisted her skirt nervously in her hands and gave Belladonna a cautioning look, although she did not pull her arm away. "Careful, Belle. This box is open. People could be listening." She glanced around to make sure no one was looking at her, but we were far too high for anyone else to hear our conversation.

"No one is going to hear us," Belladonna insisted. "All of the rumors just have you on edge."

'Rumors' was an understatement. Tongues had been wagging about the Kingsclere family for years, but things had only grown worse over the past several months. Luciana, the eldest of Lady Kingsclere's daughters and Belladonna's older sister, tried to bewitch Crown Prince Brendan at his birthday ball, and everyone seemed to know some—but not all—of the details. Ever since Ellie had stopped her, the Kingsclere family was the subject of all the high-class gossip.

Sarah grinned beside me. "Rumors? You mean like the one where Lady Kingsclere was planning to run off with Prince Brendan herself? And the one where Ellie tried to poison the King?"

"Exactly," Belladonna said. "And as far as everyone knows, the rumor that we are actually lovers is just as unlikely as the rest of them." She stood up, folding an arm around Ellie's waist and drawing her close. I had to admit that their connection fascinated me. Love had always seemed fanciful before, something that only existed in storybooks, but I could see it written clearly on both of their faces.

"Rejecting the Prince's marriage proposal only made it worse," Sarah said. That piece of information had sent the aristocracy into an uproar. None of them could figure out why Ellie had turned down the most eligible bachelor in the Kingdom. Since she offered no explanations, they made up their own. Compared to some of the theories going around, the fact that Belladonna and Ellie were lovers as well as stepsisters seemed almost tame.

Ellie blushed bright red. "He knew I would never accept. He only asked to be polite."

"Well, if a Prince ever asks me to marry him out of politeness, I'm definitely going to say yes," Sarah stated. Her infatuation with Prince Brendan was not new information to any of us, but perhaps it was more serious than I thought. Despite being a servant like me, Sarah had met the Prince a few times. Belladonna and Ellie were frequently invited to visit his court. Saving the Prince and the entire kingdom did bestow a few advantages.

I turned my attention back to Belladonna and Ellie. They made a striking picture against the railing, Ellie with her white dress and soft, honey-colored hair, and Belladonna with her broad shoulders and blue eyes. She was tall, with defined muscles that shaped her curves and tapered into the neat flair to her hips. Ellie fit snugly against her side, tucked under one arm. Whenever I looked at them, I felt a strange emotion I could not identify. It was not jealousy, but more like longing. I just knew that I wanted something...

The racetrack grows more vivid around me. I can pick out different smells: sweat and warm bodies, overpowering perfume, and beneath that, fresh, sweet grass. My eyes glaze like I want to sleep, but I do not feel tired. My throat knots and it is harder to breathe.

Rippling bodies surge forward in a cloud of dust. Brown and grey horses drum over the scraped, smooth track. The edges of my sight are blurry, indistinct, as though I am looking in a smudged mirror. The white and blue colors of Baxstresse flicker, flaring bright like a candle flame and then stuttering back.

I recognize Brahms. He has broken early, and he is pulling away. A large black horse in red and gold heaves beside him. Corynne is a head behind. The three leaders pull left, and the red horse swerves sharply to the side. His shoulder catches the round part of Brahms's broad flank. I hear his leg bone snap, smell the fear and blood. A scream rises in my throat...

"Cate, can you hear me? Cate?"

The voice was muffled, like sound traveling underwater. Faces shifted in and out of focus before my eyes. I latched on to the first person that I recognized. "Ellie, what happened?"

"We should be asking you the same question," Ellie said. One of her hands rested behind my head, holding me steady. I suddenly realized that I was sprawled on the hard floor of the private box. My shoulders ached, and I knew without looking that there would be bruises on my side where I had hit the ground. "What did you see? Do you remember?"

I searched for the words to explain. Even though Ellie and I were both *Ariada* , our powers were very different. I could not hear the voices of animals. Instead, I was gifted with the Sight. I Knew things before they happened, and sometimes, I Saw them as well. Although I did not always remember my visions, some of them took me out of my body for a short time. "Brahms," I said in a shaking voice. My mouth was dry, and my tongue felt heavy and thick against my teeth. "Ellie, tell him not to break early. Keep him away from the red horse."

Ellie frowned, but she stood up and left, taking the stairs that led down to the public stands. She was gone without a word. Belladonna offered a hand to help me to my feet. I took it, and she pulled me up. "You really are all right, aren't you?" I noticed the worry line that creased her forehead. Belladonna had never seen me after an intense vision before.

"Oh, Cate does this sort of thing all the time," Sarah babbled, plucking nervously at the sleeve of her dress. Not satisfied, she reached out to try and straighten mine.

I pulled away, shaking my head. I had always Known things, even as a child, but I did not usually collapse to the floor and shout out warnings. I had Seer blood in me, and that was a dangerous thing to admit in a country like Seria, where magic was perceived as a threat. I had learned to conceal my abilities from a very young age.

My visions were also unreliable. I had no idea whether what I had Seen would come true, or only might come true. Most visions only showed a possible future, but some were destined to happen. Sometimes, the Seer could tell the difference. I searched inside myself, but I did not think that it was Brahms's fate to die from a cheap shove in his first race. Ellie would do something to prevent it.

Belladonna pressed a cup of water into my hands, probably from the refreshment table off to the side of the box. I sat up and drank deeply. "Are you sure you're all right? Maybe you should lie down again."

I wiped my lips with the back of my hand. I knew that I should follow her advice and lie down, but I wanted to see the race. Before I could say anything, a choir of trumpets above the track blared the opening theme. I looked down through the gaps in the railing, watching the horses as they loaded into the gates. Brahms was in gate thirteen, an unlucky draw. The red-blanketed horse was in gate six. Corynne was to his right in gate seven. I pressed my lips together and prayed that Ellie had done something, anything, to prevent disaster.

"Here we go," Sarah said, crossing her fingers for luck. Belladonna took back my empty cup and set it aside, helping me to my feet. Her hand stayed tight around mine until I was safely seated again.

The trumpets blasted a second time, the gates swung open, and the horses burst onto the track. Just as they started, the grey sky that had been threatening us all morning finally opened up, and I could hear the harsh drum of rain on the roof of our box. Corynne and the red-blanketed horse took an early lead, their feet pounding almost in unison. Corynne was a nose ahead, but Brahms held back, trying to squeeze his way through the pack and find the edge of the rail.

It happened so fast that I almost missed it. The red horse collided with Corynne's side, upsetting her balance. She faltered for a split second and nearly broke her stride. Falling on the racetrack almost always meant death. My chest ached from lack of air. But somehow, Corynne managed to keep herself upright. She charged forward, kicking up clods of mud behind her hooves. The rest of horses were almost on top of them, but Corynne held her spot, stretching her neck out as far as it would go.

The end of the race was predictable. Corynne held her lead by almost a body length, and then it was over. Brahms managed to pull forward and squeeze into third place while the red horse fell back to the middle of the group. Blue and white flags were raised all around the track, and the trumpeters belted out the winner's march as Corynne trotted her customary lap. We ran from the box in an excited group, hurrying down the steps to meet up in the winner's circle. I hung back a few paces, still shaking and a little weak, but relieved that my vision had not come true.

***

"That could have turned out very badly," Ellie confessed on the carriage ride back to the palace. Prince Brendan had invited our party to stay there for the night. "I talked to Corynne afterwards, and she said it was a deliberate push. But she's an experienced racer. If it had been Brahms..." If Brahms had broken early and taken the lead instead, he might have died.

"It looks like you're good at more than just housework, Cate," Sarah said, trying to brighten the mood.

I turned away and stared out of the window so that I would not have to answer her. I was used to Sarah's teasing, but it still made me uncomfortable. I felt a hand on my knee, and knew without looking that it was Ellie. "She is good at a lot of things, Sarah. Cate has saved me more than once, and not just because of her visions."

"I wish I could have seen her the day Luciana was taken to prison," Belladonna said. "I'm not sure I can picture our Cate bursting into the front hall with a flock of vengeful birds at her back."

"I don't remember much about that day," I mumbled. It was true, although a few hazy details hovered just out of reach. I could remember the harsh calls of the birds and the burning, spiced stench of magic and blood, but the rest was a blur. I was certain that the Sight had come upon me, but Ellie and the others rarely spoke of what I had said or done.

"That is probably a good thing," Ellie said. "What happened to Luciana was no less than she deserved, but it was still gruesome." The warmth of her hand left my knee, but I could still feel the ghost of her touch through my dress. "Sarah is right, though. You did well today, Cate. Your warning probably saved Brahms's life." I did not know what to say, but Ellie continued. "I know you were reluctant to put any bets on the race, but Belle and I wagered a considerable sum of money on both Corynne and Brahms."

That was enough to make me turn away from the window. "How much?"

"A lot. And we want to use some of it to send you to Amendyr."

I was struck dumb. "Amendyr?" I had made up my mind to leave Baxstresse months ago, but I had never considered leaving Seria altogether. Besides, crossing the border was almost impossible with the current unrest between the two kingdoms. All trade had been halted, and news from beyond the forest was even scarcer than material goods.

"I know you were born there, and that you have a Grandmother there. Whenever I asked, you never really knew where you wanted to go, so I thought..." Ellie studied my face and seemed to realize that I did not look as happy as she expected. "Cate? Are you all right?"

I was not all right, and I opened my mouth to try and refuse the generous gift, but no words would come. I wanted to say no, but the more I thought about it, the more the idea appealed to me. Amendyr. My real home. A kingdom where other *Ariada* lived, and where magic was celebrated instead of feared. Maybe my grandmother was still alive. Maybe I could find other members of my family and learn more about my magical gifts.

    "Ellie, I think...I think you're right," I said at last. "It's time to go back home."

Rae D. Magdon

CHAPTER TWO

THERE WERE MANY REASONS that I needed to leave Baxstresse, I thought as I rested against the ivy-laced railing of the balcony. My wandering feet had taken me away from everyone else and out through one of the palace's many doors. This secluded spot happened to overlook the gardens. Since it was too dark to see more than silhouettes of the flowers and the trees, I stared up instead. Stars winked in the black fabric of the sky, and a soft wind played over my face.

Behind me, the Prince's dinner party was still going on. I could hear laughter and the scraping of silverware from outside, but I was not a part of that world. Even though some of the richest, most powerful people in Seria were my friends, I was still a servant. I was also a foreigner and magic burned in my blood. Serians took one look at my curly red hair and freckles and knew that I was from Amendyr, even though I had no accent. I would miss Ellie and my other friends, but this was not where I belonged.

I was started from my thoughts when a voice spoke behind me. "So, you decided to escape as well?"

My breath caught, and my head snapped over my shoulder. "Oh...yes," I said to the man standing there. He had a neat little black beard and very bright eyes. Warmth and energy flowed from him. He was *Ariada* , like me. "I felt stifled in there."

The man smiled. He wore gloves, but he removed them and let them hang from his right pocket. His hands were soft, not calloused from work. Like his beard, the rest of his hair was tidy and well groomed. "The nobles can be tiring. Sometimes, I sneak out of dinner parties, too." The stranger's clothes were made of fine material. He certainly looked like a noble. If he was a commoner, why was he here?

He read the question in my face and said, "My name is Cieran. I am the King's magical advisor."

That explained the energy I felt from him. Cieran and his wife, Cassandra, were the liaisons between the King of Seria and the magical community. They also protected his son, Prince Brendan, from any magical threats. Magic was not outlawed in Seria, but many non-magical people, especially nobles, were afraid of it. It was easier for them to pretend that *Ariada* did not help their crops to thrive or repair the trading roads that held the kingdom together.

"My name is Cate," I said, offering him my hand. To my surprise, he stepped forward and touched my forehead with two fingers instead. A shiver started at the base of my spine, rippling along my back. My bones began to hum, and I felt warm.

Finally, he stepped back. "Ellie tells me that you are going to Amendyr."

Impulsively, I touched my forehead where his fingers had been. Nothing seemed different. I wondered what Cieran had done, but decided not to ask. "Yes."

"Good. I must confess, Miss Cate, that I had a motive for following you out here besides escaping the dinner party."

Other questions pushed the strange touch that he had given me to the back of my mind. "What do you mean?"

"Your friend Ellie confided in me today. She told me that you See things before they happen."

For some reason, I was not afraid of admitting this. Maybe it was because Cieran was also *Ariada*. "Yes," I whispered.

"That is one of my abilities, too. I have Seen something of your journey to Amendyr. I want to give you a task, a warning, and a blessing."

My mind spun. A task, a warning, and a blessing? Things that came in threes were usually either very good or very bad. Whatever Cieran wanted from me, I sensed that it was important. "What is the task?"

"You will ask any powerful *Ariada* that you meet to tell you about Umbra, the last of the High *Ariada* . Do you remember the chain that Luciana Kingsclere wore when she tried to bewitch the Prince?"

I shivered again. This time, it was unpleasant. I did not know which subject disturbed me more—Luciana or the strange necklace that she wore around her neck. It had been a simple piece of jewelry with three circles—a golden coin with a silver ring in the middle and a golden dot in the very center. It almost looked like the iris and pupil of a metallic eye.

I could picture it hanging below the dip in her pale throat without closing my eyes. She never took it off, not even with the rest of her clothes.

Cieran went on, and I forced the memories down. "I believe that it was a focus object, made for Umbra centuries ago to store some of his magic. I would like to find out more, but information on the magical history of Amendyr is scarce in Seria, and since Ellie broke the chain, there is no way to study the object itself."

"How will I let you know if I learn anything?"

"I will speak to Ellie about that," Cieran said. "So, will you ask about Umbra if you meet a magical scholar in Amendyr?"

Asking a history question did not seem dangerous or difficult to do. "Yes, I will," I assured him. "I'm sure I will be able to find someone."

Cieran smiled at me, and his face suddenly looked much younger. "Thank you. I know I haven't explained very much, but I only see glimpses..." I understood. It was difficult to describe things you had Seen to other people. "Now, I will give you the warning. It may seem like common sense, but when you go into the Forest that separates Amendyr and Seria, do not talk to strangers or leave the path."

I gave Cieran a curious look. My mother had given me the same warning over and over again as a child, and hearing it over a decade later almost felt silly. "All right. I know what sort of creatures live in the Forest. I grew up there."

"I'm sure you do, but it never hurts to be careful. I grew up in Amendyr, too, although I lived in the South." I studied Cieran closely, trying to see if I could detect any Amendyrri in his appearance. He looked like a pureblooded Serian. "My parents knew that I was magical from a young age and had no idea what to do with me. They sent me to live with some acquaintances in Kalmarin." The great walled city on the cliffs was the capital of Amendyr, and the most magical human city in the world. It rested along the southern coast, watching the sea from its high perch. I had never been there, although it was a secret dream of mine.

"I have always wanted to see Kalmarin. What is it like?"

"I haven't been there for many years. It's hard to travel to Amendyr, but I have a feeling that you will see it for yourself someday. Now, I need to give you my blessing. Let me be the first to wish you every happiness and joy for what you will find."

I was surprised. "Happiness and joy for what?"

Cieran's eyes were half-lowered. He would not explain, but I guessed he knew more than he was telling. "I cannot read every detail of your future, Cate. You have to live it yourself."

I began to ask him more, but a figure appeared in the doorway behind Cieran's head, and I saw Ellie motioning me over. "Cate, are you out here? Come look," she said in a loud whisper. Then, she noticed Cieran. "Oh, hello, Cieran. I just wanted to show Cate something. Do you mind if I..."

"Of course not, my dear." Cieran ran his fingers over his small, pointed black beard. "Take her inside. Your friend Cate and I were just discussing her journey to Amendyr."

Cieran took my arm and passed me over to Ellie, who hurried me back inside with a gentle but insistent hand. "There, Cate, see?" she said, pointing to the crowded dance floor.

As a large man with a monocle moved to the right, I saw Prince Brendan with a girl in his arms. They were gliding over the dance floor, but I could see nothing exceptional about them. I turned back to Ellie. "What did you want to show me?"

"No, look closer." I tried to reclaim my sleeve from Ellie's persistent tugging, but then Prince Brendan twirled his partner, and I finally saw what she had been trying to tell me. Sarah was dancing with the Prince. With her hair up and a beautiful dress, I had not recognized her until I saw her from the front. I was speechless.

"Doesn't she look lovely?" Because she could not tug my sleeve, Ellie squeezed my hand instead. This time, I let her. "Sarah always said she wanted to dance with the Prince." Sarah did seem to be having a wonderful time. Her face was glowing as she looked up at him, and her eyes were filled with stars. I knew that look. Another impossible romance, although Ellie and Belladonna had managed it somehow.

I noticed the scandalized faces of the noblewomen surrounding us. A few started whispering to each other. They looked like a group of fat hens, clucking and bobbing their heads. "Which is more offensive?" I asked in a soft voice, so that only Ellie could hear. "A servant falling in love with a Prince, or two noblewomen who happen to be stepsisters falling in love with each other?"

"The stepsisters," Ellie whispered back. "Besides, I was a commoner before my father married Lady Kingsclere."

"But you were a rich commoner," I argued. "You were almost a noble."

"Blood means a lot to these people."

"You grew up on your own estate, with your own horses and

parties and family heirlooms, and even a pianoforte."

Ellie tossed her hair. "Fine, but Sarah is in love with a man, at least." A shadow crossed Ellie's face that I almost missed. I studied her thoughtfully. I knew that Sarah had shared Belladonna's bed before Ellie's arrival at Baxstresse. Ellie seemed very pleased that Sarah was interested in someone else. She could be very possessive about her wife.

"Belladonna is in love with you." The name felt strange in my mouth without putting a 'Miss' in front of it. Technically, I was still her servant, even though I was their guest at a fancy dinner party. "Besides, Sarah would never try and steal her friend's lover."

Ellie sighed, brushing aside a strand of golden hair that spilled across her cheek. "I know. Sarah is harmless, except when she gossips and snoops."

I snorted, remembered that I was at a party, and quickly looked around to see if anyone had noticed. Fortunately, no one seemed to be paying attention to us. "You know," I suggested, looking around the room for Belladonna, "maybe you two could go out on that balcony. You can still hear the music out there." I spotted her on the other side of the room, talking to a tall man with grey hair. She had a bored expression on her face. I gave Ellie a little shove. "Go."

Smiling again, Ellie took my advice and went over to Belladonna without any more encouragement. They spoke for a moment, leaving the grey-haired man alone as Ellie led Belladonna out onto the balcony that I had just left. Their faces were flushed.

Slowly, I made my way over to the double doors opening out onto the balcony. After making sure that no one was watching, I peered through the crack. Ellie was tucked in Belladonna's arms, one cheek resting against her shoulder. Belladonna's hands were on Ellie's waist. The music struck up again inside, and they started dancing. I backed away and turned back to the crowd, not wanting to intrude on their privacy.

The image lingered with me as I stood in front of the door to make sure that no one disturbed them. Ellie always said Belladonna was an excellent dancer, and that she wished they could be partners when they received invitations to balls and parties. A piece of me felt lighter when I realized that I was giving them that special moment. Ellie and Belladonna were very lucky. I could only hope that Sarah's ill-fated romance escaped disaster, too.

Rae D. Magdon

CHAPTER THREE

BREAKFAST WAS DELICIOUS, BUT the trip home from the palace was miserable. Long carriage rides made Sarah sick. She had been ill on the way here, but persevered without complaint because she was determined to see the race. On the way back, heartbroken after leaving the Prince behind and with nothing to look forward to, she felt even worse.

Since we were so many of us, Sarah, Ellie, Belladonna, and I were squeezed together in the back of the carriage. Belladonna sat on the far right. Ellie was practically on her lap, but she did not seem to mind. Sarah was near the left door so she could make a quick exit, and I was in between her and Ellie.

When we finally passed Whitechapel, Ellie began giving me secretive looks, pressing her lips together and shifting in her seat. Since I was on her left, this made me shift as well. "Ellie, what is it?" I asked, nudging her leg with mine.

"I have a surprise for you."

"A surprise? What kind of surprise?"

Ellie smiled. She had a sweet smile and a pretty pink mouth that made her look charming and innocent. She still had a touch of farm girl in her, even though she was a Kingsclere now. "A helpful surprise. I talked to Prince Brendan today."

Hearing the Prince's name made Sarah look up from her small metal bucket. Ellie had thought ahead and borrowed one from the palace for the journey home. "What about Prince Brendan?" she asked, hope lighting her pale face.

Belladonna's eyes squinted open. She had been dozing with her face pressed against the cool carriage window, but our conversation had roused her. She tried to swallow back a yawn. "Why are you all yelling?"

"Go back to sleep, dear heart." Ellie stroked Belladonna's hair and kissed her forehead. Belladonna's mouth twitched into a relaxed smile, and she rested her head back on the seat.

"What were you saying about the Prince?" Sarah repeated, but Ellie too was busy stroking Belladonna's face to listen. She traced an affectionate finger over one dark eyebrow.

"Mm, what?"

"You were talking about a surprise," I said.

"Oh, I asked Prince Brendan to grant you official Serian citizenship papers before your trip. He agreed, thanks to your 'exemplary service to the Kingdom at large.' I know that any you might have had were lost long ago."

"Exemplary service?" I stammered. "But Ellie, you were the one who..."

Ellie shook her head. "We all stopped Luciana together, but it doesn't matter. You're free to move between the two kingdoms whenever you want. I also found a copy of your Amendyrri citizenship papers. They were in the old records, so that probably means your mother applied for citizenship years ago. Her death might have stopped the process."

I was surprised. I had lived at Baxstresse for so long that I had forgotten all about my citizenship papers. It was even difficult for me to remember my mother's face. I often tried, but time had blurred the edges, and the colors were all washed out. I wasn't sure whether I looked like her or not. Despite everything, she had left me one last gift.

Sarah looked pleased, and she hurried to fill my silence. "That's good news, Cate. So, you're really going to do it? Go to Amendyr?"

I nodded. "Yes. I am."

"Isn't it dange—" Sarah started, but the carriage hit a bump, and she had to stick her head back in the bucket.

Ellie and I winced at the choking and groaning noises. "I also got you a personal letter from the Prince," she said to distract us both. Sarah surfaced again, looking very pale. Her lips were wet and her eyes were dull. "That should help you cross any border."

I was touched by her thoughtfulness. "Ellie, you didn't have to..."

"Prince Brendan was glad to do it, and so was I."

Sarah looked back at us. Her face was a little brighter. "He is very kind, isn't he?"

"Yes, Prince Brendan is a very generous person," Ellie said. That made Sarah even more cheerful.

I lowered my head. Ellie knew the Prince better than I did. I had only said a few words to him in the past. He had interviewed me after Luciana's plot was uncovered, I had offered him tea once, and we said quick hellos when we saw each other after that. My hellos included a curtsey and a "Your Majesty," but he had not been conceited about it. "He does seem nice. He's just…"

Sarah finished my thought. "From a different world than us. I know."

"All of us are from different worlds," Ellie said. "Fate has a curious way of twisting people's lives together."

It certainly did. A year ago, I never would have imagined escaping Luciana's torture, and the relationship between Belladonna and Ellie was too far-fetched even for a dream. But here they were, sitting next to each other. Their hands were linked comfortably in Belladonna's lap. Maybe in another year, I would look back and wonder why I ever doubted that Sarah could capture the heart of a Prince.

I tried to remember what the Prince's face had looked like when they danced. I could only recall that he was smiling. Maybe I should worry less about Sarah. She was certainly more experienced with relationships than me, no matter what the result of her ill-advised romance turned out to be.

* * *

I am running. Running through the tall grass. The forest is alive with pale, golden beams of sunlight. They dance over the fallen leaves and the dust in the road. But I do not follow the road. I weave through trees, and a twin shadow weaves beside me. My lungs burn, but it is a good hurt. Everything is right.

The shadow remains a few breaths ahead. My feet fly over the grass, but as fast as I chase, the stranger is faster. It darts along the bank of a clear river, using the noise and smell of the water to stay just out of reach…

I left the dream slowly. First the sunlight went away, then the trees and the river, and finally the twin shadow. I strained to see closer, but the two dark eyes of the face—and it was not a human face—were already beginning to disappear. I was left alone, curled into a ball on my new mattress. It was too soft, but I would never tell Ellie. She had spent so much time trying to make my room comfortable after she and Belladonna regained control of Baxstresse. It was supposed to be compensation for the miserable broom closet we had been forced to share as servants.

The room was cold, but I did not want to relight the fire. Baxstresse was always cold at night. Cold lived in the stone walls and the grey floors. Sometimes, I wondered if the cold was really there, or only in my heart. But while I slept, I had felt the glow of warmth for just a moment. I wanted to go back to that place, to the forest and the trees and the river where I was not so alone.

Remembering the dream made me think of Ellie. We were both *Ariada* . She would understand when I explained that those eyes were waiting for me. I pulled my arms through the sleeves of my nightgown, sitting up in bed and searching for my slippers with my feet. Once I was dressed, I left the lonely bedroom and the unlit fireplace behind, going up the servants' stairway to the second floor of the manor. Because I had gone to bed after supper, I did not expect Ellie to be asleep. She was probably writing by candlelight, scratching things in her journal. Belladonna had become her wife because of a journal, Ellie told me, and so she wanted to write one herself.

I walked silently beneath the stained glass windows that lined the second floor hallway. St. Eugiers stared down his nose at me, his golden sword raised to behead a great, coiling black dragon. The Serians were obsessed with their Saints and their rules. What to do and not to do was chiseled in stone. In Amendyr, we worshipped the Maker in much simpler ways. I passed him with only a brief glance, staying far to the right side of the wall so that I would not wander near the library door. Ellie loved it, but the library had never been one of my favorite places to visit. It held bad memories. That was where Luciana had so often cornered me.

Finally, I reached Ellie and Belladonna's room. I lifted my hand to knock, but a soft noise made me pause, and I listened at the door. I could hear soft, muffled sobs and hushed voices coming from inside. Was Ellie crying? I hurried to open the door, but what I saw made me freeze. I had to clutch at the doorframe to keep my balance. Ellie was crying, but in ecstasy. Her head was thrown back, her golden hair tossed over the pillows. She sobbed openly as Belladonna's hand worked between her legs with steady, rocking thrusts. Both of them were naked, moving and shifting against each other.

I tried to turn away, but I was entranced. My only sexual experiences had been forced on me. Thinking about Luciana still made me dizzy and sick with fear, but the intense connection I was watching seemed so different than what I had endured. I was not sure what I had expected lovemaking to look like, but it was not this. Not passion and heat and an endless joining of lips. I could see the need in Ellie's flushed face and in the smooth muscles that ran along Belladonna's naked back.

One of Ellie's knees hooked around Belladonna's waist, and the bare sole of her foot slid down along her calf. Belladonna's hand pushed up along her thigh, grasping her hip, pulling her deliberately into each thrust. I gasped, ducking a little further back in the doorway. I could hardly imagine willingly making myself so vulnerable to someone else's touch, but at the same time, I felt a strange, throbbing emptiness in my lower belly.

It took me a few moments to realize that they were speaking to each other, sometimes barely breathing the words, sometimes nearly screaming them. Belle called Ellie her rose, her sweet girl. "Let me have you," she coaxed in between kisses, sliding her lips down along the column of Ellie's throat and biting into her shoulder.

A soft whimper broke in Ellie's throat, but she tilted her chin back for more. She was obviously feeling pleasure, not pain. Even if I had not been sure, I could read the words she mouthed back in answer. "I love you."

That brought the end crashing down. They stiffened and shuddered, clinging tight to each other. Ellie's fingers clutched at Belladonna's shoulders, and the solid grip that Belladonna had on Ellie's waist tightened until it looked almost bruising. But finally, they collapsed into each other, still joined and breathing heavily. The sheets were wrapped around their legs, binding them together. Two halves of one soul.

I backed out of the doorway as fast as I could and ran, too embarrassed and awestruck to remember why I had come. The dream was pushed to the back of my mind, but only for the moment. I was consumed with what I had witnessed.

Back in my room, I could not un-see the private moment. A small part of me felt guilty for stumbling upon something so personal. I was ashamed and fascinated. The two of them had looked beautiful together. I raised a hand to my face, and my fingers came away wet. I had not realized that I was crying and I had a startling thought as I brushed aside my tears. I wanted that beauty, too. Not with Belle or Ellie, but with someone else. Someone of my own. Someone who was waiting for me. For the first time in my life, I dared to imagine a lover. Once, many months ago, I told Ellie that I could never bear to let anyone else touch me after the pain Luciana had caused. She had taken me in her arms and told me that I was not abnormal or damaged, but only now did I truly believe her words.

Tuathe. Two-souls. Really, just one soul in two bodies. I had not believed in that since I was a child listening to fairy-stories. With my parents gone and Luciana tormenting me, how could I think about another half? Now, I had seen *Tuathe* for myself. Ellie and Belle were more than ordinary lovers. And I craved. I hungered for that connection. I longed to be whole.

But I was afraid. What if I had no other half? What if I found my other-heart and then lost her? I thought that it would be a 'her', but how would I know? I had so many questions. I wanted to talk to Ellie, but just thinking about her made me feel embarrassed. I had seen her naked. Emotionally naked, not just physically bare. I had witnessed something so private, so intimate and beautiful. I did not want to intrude even more. Instead, I climbed back into my bed and stared at the ceiling, trying to fall back asleep. It was no use, and I spent the rest of the night tossing and turning until the first soft blush of dawn finally crept through my window.

CHAPTER FOUR:

LEAVING BAXSTRESSE WAS NOT as heartbreaking as I expected. On the day of my departure, my friends woke before first light to see me off. The morning was cold, but the sun rose quickly, and soon a golden blanket of light covered the grass and drove away the chill. Summer had not left yet, and the fields were still tall. I realized, a little sadly, that I would not be here to see the harvest this year.

With a pouch of Amendyrri coins and paper Serian notes stuffed in the right pocket of my traveling dress, and a heavy pack over one shoulder, I waited before the carriage. Matthew, the stable master, sat on the driver's box, and his faithful horse, Sir Thom, was hitched at the front. Ellie had offered to let me use the matching pair of carriage horses, but I had refused. She, Belladonna, Sarah, and Mam the cook stood side by side in a solemn line, not sure whether they were happy for me or worried about me. Secretly, I was worried, too, but I would never tell. They might try and convince me to stay.

Ellie was the first to say goodbye. "Oh, Cate, I'm going to miss you," she whispered fiercely, flinging her arms around me and squeezing tight. I endured the hug, but gasped for breath beside her head. "Write to me as soon as you stop for the night. Do you promise?"

I gave her a confused frown. "How could we send letters? I would be gone days before yours got to wherever I was staying."

Ellie pulled away and gave me a secret smile, the kind she reserved for very clever thoughts. "Oh no, we aren't going to send each other letters. You and I are going to keep a journal." She placed a leather-bound book in my outstretched hand. It was small enough to fit in a pocket or bag, easy to carry from place to place. "This was a gift from Cieran," she explained. "It is a two-way journal. I have a matching one in our room. Everything you write in your journal will appear in mine. Instant letter delivery."

The words 'our room' made me blush, and I tried not to remember what I had witnessed between Ellie and Belladonna several nights ago. "Thank you," I said, eager to end my train of thought.

Ellie passed the journal from her hands to mine, and then leaned against Belladonna's side. "Do you have your citizenship papers, Cate?"

I rolled my eyes. "You gave them to me last night. I haven't lost them since then."

Ellie opened her mouth to scold me, but Belladonna smiled and dropped a kiss on the crown of her golden hair. "Stop fussing, Mine." I caught Ellie's shiver, and my embarrassment flared up again.

I was still glancing shyly at them when Sarah swooped in from one side and wrapped me in a tight, one-armed hug. Her other hand was hidden behind her back. "I have a present for you, too."

"You do?"

"Well, Loren helped me with it." The old washerwoman and seamstress had lived at Baxstresse longer than any of us. She was a permanent fixture of the manor. With a flourish, Sarah whipped out her arm and produced a blood red cape. "To keep you warm. Ellie told me it would be colder in Amendyr."

The cape was beautiful. The gold stitching along the seams shimmered, and the ripples in the fabric almost made it look alive. I hurried to put it on, still holding the journal in my right hand. As I reached behind to un-tuck my hair from the neck, I discovered a hood. "Oh, this is beautiful!" I did a quick twirl to show off my new present. Ellie and Belladonna smiled in approval, and Mam clicked her tongue in a motherly way.

"So beautiful you're looking, Cate." Mam rested a large hand on my shoulder. She was Amendyrri, like me, and she had helped care for me after my mother's death. She knew that Amendyr was a wild place, especially lately. Ellie and Belladonna were well-read, and they had heard of the dangers, but some things needed to be experienced before they could be understood. As I leaned in to hug Mam, I realized that she was carrying a basket. I lowered my chin to study it. "I've got some sweetcakes and bread here for you. Good for traveling, they are. You never know what they'll be serving at them inns along the road, 'specially across the border."

"Oh, thank you, Mam," I murmured, my eyesight blurring. The generosity of all my friends was touching. Warm tears rolled down my cheeks. "Thank you all..."

The rest of the goodbyes were a blur as Belladonna, chivalrous as ever, helped me into the carriage. "Best of luck," she said, and closed the door behind me.

"Ready?" Matthew called over his shoulder, looking back at the carriage even though he could not see inside.

"Yes."

Sir Thom began plodding down the road. Staring out of the back window, I caught one last glimpse of my friends' smiling faces as we pulled out of the gravel drive and began the journey.

***

The five days I spent traveling west to the Amendyrri border were uneventful. By the time we reached an inn (or, on one night, simply a farmhouse) I was too tired to do anything but sleep. We passed Southwood and Felbrook, and finally reached the long stretch of trees that marked the border between Seria and Amendyr.

We met our first patrol of rangers an hour after we started on the sixth day. They were dressed in Serian uniforms. I could just make out the sword and plumes coat-of-arms on their shields through the frosted glass of the carriage window. Their armor was lightweight, mostly leather, and easy for maneuvering in the forest. One of the three men, the tallest, stepped from the side of the road and blocked the path. The cry of "Halt!" was a little too forceful, and I flinched at the noise.

I heard Matthew hop down from the driver's box. I imagined him tipping his straw hat, but he was not in my line of sight. "Mornin' to ye, sirs."

"I'm sorry, sir," said the tallest ranger. I opened the carriage door a crack to watch what was happening. "No one is allowed to cross."

I opened the carriage door wider, reaching for my traveling pack. "Excuse me, I have some papers here. Just a moment." The three men watched me open my bag and begin digging. All of them looked young. They were probably fresh out of training. Finally, I found the papers that Ellie had given me. "Here," I said, holding up my prize. "Serian citizenship papers, Amendyrri citizenship papers, and a special note of permission from the Royal Court."

The tallest ranger stepped forward. He flipped through the papers, stepped back, and began whispering to the others. After thirty seconds of quiet discussion, the tall ranger turned back to me. "We've got orders not to let any horses or vehicles through, but seeing as you have your papers, and...well, I suppose we could escort you through with the carriage and make sure it comes back to our side. We're mostly trying to stop people coming in to Seria from Amendyr. We don't see many going the other way."

I had heard rumors about tightened security at the border, but this was more than I expected. "What am I supposed to do when I get to the other side?"

The ranger to the left kicked his boot in the dirt of the road. "You could hire a cart, Miss, but I would turn around and go home. Amendyr isn't the safest place right now."

"Why not?"

"The Queen," one ranger began, but another interrupted him.

"There's a lot of unrest. It just isn't safe. Are you sure you want to cross?"

"I need to go." I was surprised how firm and confident my voice sounded. I knew that I needed to go to Amendyr. It was where my future awaited me. "Thank you for offering to escort us."

Matthew glanced at me. A shadow clouded his cheerful brown face. He did not like the idea of leaving me on the other side of the border without a carriage. However, he did not protest. He hopped back up onto the driver's box and urged Sir Thom into a slow walk while the Rangers followed us.

A few minutes later, the carriage stopped again. Our three rangers talked with a second group. Their faces were distorted through the frosted window-glass, but I could see their mouths moving, shifting dark holes against their pale skin. The first three rangers left and the new group escorted the carriage. We were passed from one group to the next for two or three hours, moving slowly so that the rangers could keep up on foot.

I was just dozing off, lulled by the rocking motion of the carriage and the steady plodding of Sir Thom's hooves, when I heard a loud crack. I nearly tumbled from my seat. The smell of burning meat seeped through the edges of the door. I started coughing. "What is that?" I pressed my face against the glass, trying to see outside.

A huge fire towered just a few hundred yards to the side of the road. Thick smoke swirled up from the leaping flames, drifting off into the grey afternoon sky. Large, twisted black lumps were piled on top of each other in the center of the blaze, and even though I squinted, I couldn't make out what they were…

The carriage shuddered to a stop, and my stomach lurched along with it. Bodies. The black lumps in the middle of the fire were bodies. There had to be at least twenty or thirty corpses there, all piled on top of each other. I threw open the carriage door and fell to the ground, catching myself on my hands and retching violently. I had not eaten breakfast, so there was nothing in my stomach to throw up. I felt Matthew's hand on my back, holding me steady as I shivered. One of the rangers hurried over and gathered my hair at the nape of my neck. I took several shaky breaths, keeping my eyes closed. "What…is that?"

"Refugees, Lass," said a rough voice behind me. "They've been tryin' ta cross fer months now." I balanced myself on my knees and looked at the ranger who was holding my hair. He was an old, grizzled soldier with a scar across one eye. Long grey hair was pulled back behind his head. He looked more experienced than the three youngsters we had seen before.

"But…they're being burned? Why?"

"Oh, the fire ain't what killed 'em. The Forest did. We just find the bodies. Gotta get rid of 'em somehow. Too many to bury."

"Cate," Matthew whispered in my ear, "we should turn 'round and go home! It ain't safe here."

"No." The word cracked, so I cleared my throat and tried again. "No. I need to get to the other side. Take me through."

"But Cate!"

"Take me through." The old soldier looked surprised, and so did his companions. "Matthew, if things are this bad, if there are refugees dying when they try to cross, I need to find my family on the other side and make sure they're all right."

Matthew helped me to my feet with new understanding. "Right, Miss. I'll help ye back to the carriage." He straightened his back and held his shoulders proud. Matthew had no children of his own, but he felt a deep commitment for family. My journey was no longer a young girl's whim to him. I realized, suddenly, that he had called me Miss. Maybe he meant it as a term of respect. It had not been said unkindly.

The rangers watched as I returned to the carriage. The thick, biting smell of cooked flesh stung in my nose. I closed my eyes against it and prayed that my grandmother, who had always been stubborn, had not left her old house and tried to cross the border. Or, a darker part of my mind thought, met an even worse fate.

Rae D. Magdon

CHAPTER FIVE

WE DREW UP TO an old army post just before sunset. It was not much more than a pile of crumbling stones with three tilted towers, but at least we would be out of the elements. The soldiers there offered us food and drink, and Matthew accepted their hospitality. I ate a bit of traveling bread from Mam's basket. After that, I scratched a quick message to Ellie in the journal to let her know I was safe and tried to fall asleep on my small cot.

I dream of the brown eyes again. They are so familiar, hovering over me without a face. I reach out to touch them, but they back away. I sit up. I am not resting on a cot, but on a bed of leaves. I am back in the forest. Stars are scattered across the sky, pricks of light in the black velvet. They are everywhere.

I can even smell in the dream, earth and trees and young spring grass. And hear! I can hear the whirring of flying insects, the chirping of hidden frogs. The sounds are unbelievably clear. Water is running somewhere nearby. Maybe it is the same river.

"Close your eyes." A woman's voice, low and coaxing. Soft, invisible fingers press my eyes closed. Somewhere, a wolf opens its throat and sings to the moon. My muscles twitch at the call.

When I opened my eyes, no one was there. My hand reached out, clutching at the empty air, but I was alone. I shuddered at the bite of cold air on my bare arms. My cape had fallen onto the floor beside me. I groped for the edge and pulled it back around my shoulders. What did these dreams mean? They were like, but also unlike, the visions I had experienced before. I could not make sense of them.

I did not fall back asleep that night. The long hours were too quiet, and I was relieved when Matthew came in to wake me. After a quick breakfast, we set off again with an escort of three more rangers. These were hardy, experienced men, the core of Seria's military force. They were not the same as the group of youngsters who had first stopped us just outside of Seria. I was amazed that the rangers would take such an interest in me. It made me wonder what the letter from the Prince had said.

When thinking about a border, people usually picture a thin line on a map. In reality, the border between Amendyr and Seria was very wide. It stretched on for miles of empty space. There were watchhouses and small stone fortresses hidden among the trees, tiny wooden relief huts, and through it all ran the narrow, lumpy road with its large, winding curves. Finally, we reached the farthest outpost. There were no Amendyrri soldiers, only more Serian rangers. When one of them knocked on the carriage door, motioning for me to step out, I voiced my concerns. "Where are all of the Amendyrri guards?"

"In the south, quelling the uprisings," the ranger answered. "Lots of scuffles and town-burnings goin' on, there are."

"They know we take care of things here," added another. "We don't want nothing coming in to Seria, what with the Queen…"

The third guard glared at the other two. He obviously did not approve of talking. "Fair travels, Miss," said the first, looking chastened.

I thanked him and the others and turned to Matthew. In a fit of emotion, I rushed into his arms. Matthew had always been kind to me. When I felt a tear on my nose, I knew that I was not just crying for Matthew, but for Ellie, Belladonna, Sarah, Mam, and all of my friends. Baxstresse was not my home, but the people that lived there were part of my family. I would never forget.

"Ah, there now, lass," Matthew said awkwardly, patting my head. "There now."

"Thank you so much," I whispered. "Tell them I give my love. I will be back."

"A'course you will, Miss Cate. Now, off with ye. Go find that gran'mum a'yours." I kissed his whiskery chin and watched as he climbed back into the carriage. I continued staring long after the rangers, Sir Thom, and Matthew had disappeared into the trees. Then, I turned the other way and started off.

***

My steps were light and easy as I walked along the road. My cape kept me warm and I could smell autumn coming. The seasons arrived early in Amendyr, rolling from west to east. My traveling pack bounced against my shoulders as I gazed up at the familiar tall trees. Mam's basket was still in my right hand. Once I got to the next village, I could hire a cart to take me where I wanted to go.

I was born here, near the border, and I had seen the great Amendyrri forest before, although my memories of it were dim. Of course, only Serians called it the Amendyrri forest. Here, we just called it the Forest. I knew that if I chose a tall tree and climbed to the top, I would be able to see the purple-blue shadows of the Rengast Mountains against the skyline.

Not many people traveled along the edge of the Forest at this time of year, so I was surprised to see a dark, hunched figure come out of the trees and step onto the road. I stared curiously, squinting to see better. As the dark outline became a human shape, I realized that it was an old woman. If she was going to the outpost I had just left, she would not get there before nightfall. Perhaps she was lost.

I called out and raised my hand in greeting. "Arim dei." In Amendyrri, arim dei actually meant 'pleasant sun', but it was like the Serian 'hello'.

"Arim dei," the old woman said. She held a knotted wooden stick in her right hand. Long silver hair spilled out of her black hood, and her eyes were bright and pale. I was surprised and a little frightened by them. Her left hand was hidden in her cloak. She looked friendly enough, but I knew that people and things in the Forest were not always what they seemed. I checked her fingers quickly, making sure that she had five and not six. I counted the correct number and sighed with relief. At least, I thought, I had not discovered a Rijak. The malicious forest dwellers sometimes took human form to lure people from the road.

"Thank you kindly." The language that I had grown up with came easily to me. I was glad that Mam and a few of the other servants had conversed with me enough to keep me fluent. "Are you traveling to the outpost? You won't get there before sundown. They aren't letting anyone through."

The old woman took a step closer, examining me with great

interest. I shivered under the scrutiny. "Ah, well, aren't you a pretty one? No, I live here. But you, where are you going?"

I smiled. "Just to the nearest town. I need to hire a cart so I can visit my grandmother."

"And why are you in such a hurry?" she asked, gesturing with her stick. I was not surprised at her questions. Amendyrri could ask and answer questions until the daylight was gone.

"Well, I don't want to be caught out after sundown. The Forest is dangerous at night."

"Dangerous," the woman murmured. "Only dangerous if you don't know what's waiting for you in the darkness. But what have you got in your basket?"

"Traveling cakes and some wine. A friend made them for me." I thought of Mam and felt a wave of homesickness, but it quickly passed.

"Where does your grandmother live, girl?"

"Several villages over, on the edge of the forest beneath three large oak trees." At least, she used to live there. For all I knew, she had died or moved away. I hoped she had dug her heels in and stayed. Nothing short of physical force would have moved her from her tiny cottage at one time.

I noticed the old woman studying me and allowed myself to be inspected, making sure that my hands were in plain view. She had probably already counted my fingers, but it was good to be sure. "And what a beautiful red cape," she complimented, eyeing the fine material. "Someone must have been hard at work making that for you."

"Yes. Another friend." I glanced nervously at the sky, even though it was still blocked by the leaves. The sunlight was fading quickly.

"Oh, you will be having a while yet before dark," said the old woman. "You walk like a child off to school, so serious minded you are. Travel easy. See the flowers, listen to the birds. Leave the road for a while. There is still light left."

"I should—"

"Absorb all that life has to offer you. Enjoy the moment."

I smiled and nodded, deciding that this strange woman was probably a little touched in the head. What would it hurt to stop and watch the birds for a moment, anyway? As I looked up into the branches of a slender ash tree, watching the jerking hops of a red-breasted robin, she threw her left hand out of her dark cloak. A sharp smelling powder flew from her fingers, covering my face. I sneezed, blinked my eyes three times, and collapsed into the dust.

***

I came to my senses in a dark, wet place. The steady sound of dripping water rang in my ears, but I could not see. Hard, unyielding stone pressed into my back. Was I in a cave? I tried moving my arms, but the muscles held stiff. Every inch of my body was cold, an unnatural cold that froze me down to my bones. My abdomen ached terribly, as though someone had sliced through the muscle with a knife.

"Arim dei," said a voice, cruelly echoing its earlier greeting. It was the old woman. This time, I felt the searing bite of magic crawling over my skin. It mixed with the chill and ate away at my flesh. I wanted to scream, but the sound would not escape my throat. Where am I? Help me.

"No one will help you," the old woman said. It was as though she could read my thoughts. Maybe she could. She was *Ariada,* even though I had not been able to sense it before. Her footsteps grew louder, and even though I could not see, I knew she was standing in front of me. A cold, dry hand stroked my cheek. I tried to flinch away, but my body would not obey my commands. "Soon, pretty one."

Soon what? My mind screamed. Who are you? What are you?

"I am Mogra, a Daughter of Lyr. I control nature. I twist its laws. You are needed. Soon, you will be a part of the greatest army of monsters ever created in Amendyr!"

I knew one of those names. Mogra was a sorceress that lived in the Forest. When she was younger, she had been fond of kidnapping children to eat. Many mothers used Mogra to threaten disobedient boys and girls, but nothing had been heard of her since she had stolen the son of a visiting noble several years ago. Some people even denied her existence.

Mogra's hand drifted lower on my body. There was nothing sexual in the touch, but thoughts of Luciana's unwelcome hands made my stomach twist. My heart throbbed desperately inside the cage of my ribs until I thought they would burst. She stroked a strip of skin that was especially sore, just above my hipbones. The pain made me cry out in my head. She heard and laughed. "That spot will be painful for a long time, girl. I had to sew the wolfskin into you with my magic thread."

That was the first time I realized what Mogra had done.

No. Please, no. Anything but...

"You are an animal. You will forget your name, your friends, your whole identity. Your thirst for blood will consume you. No part of you will remember what it means to be human."

I wanted to deny her words, but the strip of flesh around my belly burned with pain. I knew what I was. What I would become. Soon, hair would sprout all over my body, and my teeth would sharpen to daggers. I would burst out of my old flesh and transform into something terrible. I was cursed, infected. But maybe there was some hope left. My thoughts had not deserted me. I did not crave blood and death. Perhaps Mogra had not finished casting her spell. For now, at least, I was still human.

CHAPTER SIX

IT COULD HAVE BEEN minutes, hours, or even days later when I stirred again. This time, my sight was painfully clear even in the dark. I had been right before. I was trapped in a cave. It was furnished with shelves, a large table, and cruel metal cages. I was trapped in one of them, and the stone of the cave itself made up the fourth wall. The other cages were empty, but I did see a torn set of clothes on the floor.

So, I had not been the first prisoner here. But how did I know, aside from the clothes? The smells, I realized. Strange smells, smells belonging to other people. The scent of their fear lingered. Then the scent changed, and I turned to see the witch coming from a dark hole near the back of the cave. Searing claws of magic hooked into my flesh when I saw her face, and I flinched against the stone.

"Ah, my new pet. Are you feeling the change yet?"

The change. It had not been a nightmare. Mogra had turned me into a Wyr. Since the beginning of time, there had been stories of humans that could become wolves. When the full moon rose, they went mad and tore through anything they found in their lust for blood. "No," I whispered.

Mogra peered at me through the metal bars. There was another blistering flare of heat, and my muscles froze. I could not move. Satisfied that I would not be able to run, the witch opened the door to my cage. For an old woman, she was surprisingly strong as she lifted me off the floor and carried me out into the cave. The chill grew worse, and so did the blistering pain.

Once I was out of the cage, she laid me on the stone table and began examining me. She checked my eyes, peeling back the lids. Her twisted fingers probed my palms. She combed through my hair and pushed back my gums to look at my teeth. I emptied my mind, trying to surrender to white, cold nothingness. Luciana taught me that skill, but it did not work this time. *You are a monster*, my mind screamed. The words pounded through my head, and I could not think anything else. *You are a monster. You are a monster.*

As she started to check the aching strip of skin between my hips, a strange scent filled the dark cave. It was heavy and unfamiliar, but clearly alive. Was it some kind of animal? My ears twitched, picking up a soft scrape off to the right. It was a quiet noise, but I heard it clearly. So did the witch. She stopped her examination and turned to look.

A sleek shadow burst out of the darkness, leaping directly at Mogra. She shrieked and stumbled back, collapsing to the cave floor beneath its bulk. The magical bindings around me loosened, and blood flowed through my muscles again. I cried out, relieved that I could move. Before I could climb down from the table, rough hands grabbed my arms and dragged me away. The echo of Mogra's screams bounced from the walls of the cave. "An attack! Help me!" Grey bodies flew everywhere, all thick fur and white teeth. They were wolves. An entire cave full of wolves, tearing and snapping at each other.

Whoever was holding my arms kept dragging me forward. Fresh air blew across my face, and I saw a faint circle of light hovering before my eyes. We were near the entrance of the cave. I did my best to stumble toward it. Together, my rescuer and I made it outside, but I was blinded by the sun and could not see who, or what, had found me. My head spun from the sudden brightness. Heavy breathing and pounding footsteps echoed behind us in the cave, and I felt warm bodies beside me.

"Come," said a hoarse voice from somewhere ahead. "Faster!"

I stumbled several times, almost losing my pack, but sure hands always set me on my feet again. As we ran, my sight improved. There were at least three, maybe four people in heavy leather and fur helping me along. I was herded through tall trees that reached up, up, up into the sky, my bare feet crunching over leaves and grass and stones. We had left Mogra's cave far behind.

After several minutes of running, I staggered and gasped for air. The strangers did not seem to be tired at all. I forced myself to keep going for as long as I could, but when I finally fell to my knees and begged them to let me stop, a pair of strong arms lifted me from the ground and carried me. With my cheek pressed against a warm chest, a woman's chest, I felt the air slide over my bare skin. We ran faster than I had known a person could run, if this woman was a person at all.

The rest of our journey was a blur. When my surprise and fear began to fade, I realized that I was wrapped in a rough blanket. The woman pressed a cup against my lips, and I drank deeply, letting out a grateful sigh in between gulps of water. The cup was pulled away, and I looked into the face of my rescuer. She was very tall, with broad shoulders and narrow hips. Her dark, shaggy hair hung around her face, and her large brown eyes seemed impossibly familiar. She lifted the cup again. I took another sip.

"Better?" she asked in Amendyrri.

I nodded my head. "Thank you. Who are you?"

"My name is Larna. You are safe here."

Larna set the cup on the ground. Her shoes and outer garments were made of stitched fur and leather, obviously handmade. As she leaned forward to adjust the blanket around my shoulders, her woolen undershirt lifted, and I noticed a thin strip of fur around her waist that was not a part of her clothing. I reached out to touch, but reclaimed my hand before it made contact. "Did she capture you, too?"

"Yes," Larna answered. I looked around and realized that I was in a camp, surrounded by other men and women. We were not alone. They were all dressed like Larna, and many of them were watching me with sad expressions on their faces. "We are the Farseer Pack. All of us are Wyr, little sister."

"Am I...?" I trembled, fearing the answer. "I can't be...I never want to hurt anyone...I..."

"Hold still." Larna's hand settled on my shoulder, and my heartbeat slowed down a little. "You are a Wyr now, but you are not a murderer. You must understand. You are having a choice. If you learn to control your other body, you will not be killing anyone." Her face softened for a moment. "When I was alone and afraid, the pack helped me. They can do the same for you."

I collapsed against Larna's shoulder, sobbing with relief. My humanity was not gone. I could reclaim it. I was still afraid, uncertain about the future, but this strange woman had offered me a sliver of hope.

"Come," Larna said in a warm voice. She held most of my weight, helping me to stand up. I did not notice where we were going until I felt the grass beneath my feet change to smooth wood. We were climbing up a short set of steps. Numbly, I looked up to see the door of a small cabin. Shelter. I allowed her to lead me inside. It was small, but also dark and cool, and much more comfortable than a cave.

Larna showed me to medium-sized pallet in the corner. My muscles screamed as soon as she lowered me on to it. I was already weak from lack of food, and our frantic escape had drained the last of my energy. "Here, rest." Her warm hand rested on my forehead, and I closed my eyes. For the moment, at least, I was safe.

***

My body relaxed as I floated in and out of sleep. Who was this woman who cradled my head so sweetly? The soft voice that whispered in my hair, who did it belong to? My eyes fluttered and I saw Larna's face above mine. A smile spread across her lips, and the recognition made my heart warm. "Are you all right? You were asleep for a long time, little bird."

"My name is Cate," I tried to say, but my voice was weak and hoarse.

Larna's eyebrows lifted in surprise. "Cate? You wouldn't be having an Amendyrri name as well, would you?"

"Cathelin," I croaked. My throat was filled with rings of fire. It hurt to speak. There was something achingly familiar about Larna, but I could not remember what it was, even though I desperately wanted to. The pounding ache in my head distracted me, and I was tempted to fall back asleep. I closed my eyes and let my breathing slow down.

Soft fingers stroked my face, cupping the curve of my cheek. "No, dinna go back to sleep. Try and stay awake."

I forced my eyes open again, but only with great effort. "Was I really asleep for that long?"

She nodded. "Long enough that we were worried you might not be waking up again." I did not question why she was so concerned about me, a stranger that she had just rescued. Perhaps she was just a caring person, or perhaps she simply did not want to see her efforts to rescue me wasted. A sharp pain in my stomach interrupted my thoughts. My muscles were trembling and weak, and I could not remember the last time I had eaten.

Larna must have seen my discomfort in my face, because she stepped away from the pallet and opened one of the cupboards along the wall. As I studied the rest of the cabin, I noticed that my pack was

36

sitting at the foot of the bed. I had no idea how I had managed to keep it with me during my escape. It seemed more likely that one of my rescuers had managed to snatch it from the cave. When Larna turned around, she was holding a loaf of bread in her hands. She carried it back to the bed and offered it to me, along with another cup of water. "Here, try this. Eat it slowly."

The salted bread was simple, but nothing had ever tasted so good before. Despite Larna's advice, I finished it in a few seconds. "Thank you." After the bread and water stayed down for a few minutes, Larna allowed me to have some fresh cheese. It was gone in a flash. I sank back on the pallet and let my strength come back.

"Do you feel well enough to stand? If you are, I will be taking you outside."

I flexed the muscles of my legs to test them. "Yes, I think so." Without being asked, Larna offered me her hand. I took it, and little sparks leapt over my skin. Suddenly, I noticed that I could smell her. She smelled of the woods and smoke and warmth. A dark scent. It was clean and good.

Larna held still as I leaned forwards and breathed her in, forgetting that it was strange. It was almost as though she expected it. She wrapped a careful hand around my waist and sniffed lightly at my hair. I was surprised, but only because the action did not feel as awkward as it appeared. It was almost like a greeting. After we had learned each other's scents, both of us felt more comfortable. I was too surprised to wonder why. Our short getting-to-know-you moment ended, and Larna helped me to my feet and walked beside me towards the door.

Outside, there were clusters of small huts in all directions. We were in a little village. There was a clearing in the middle of the huts with a good-sized fire and cooking pit. Several people were seated around it with bowls in their hands. The light of the fire was dim and the sky was dark, but I could see their faces clearly. In fact, every detail was sharp and focused.

A well-muscled man with thick shoulders and wild white hair braided down his back sat in the middle of the group. My eyes were drawn to him instantly, and he lifted his hand and waved to us. Larna waved back and left me to go sit down beside him. As I stepped closer, I noticed that the man's face was beginning to show age. His body looked sturdy and strong, but his eyes and skin gave him away. For an old man, he was powerfully built. I hung back, intimidated by the group of strangers.

"Come here, little bird," Larna called, motioning me over.

I tripped forward, wide-eyed and hesitant. I could not forget that all of these people were Wyr. They could probably tear me in half. But Larna did not seem dangerous. In my short time with her, Larna had been gentle and kind. What had she told me? *You must understand. You have a choice.*

Something made me approach the fire in a curved half-circle instead of a straight line. I obeyed without question. It was a little like Knowing, but there was no magic here, only instinct. Maybe it had something to do with the change. When my feet took me to Larna and the old man, I lowered my head. Some strange voice was whispering to me, explaining what I needed to do. This man was the leader. I could see it in the set of his muscles and the way he held his chin. I needed to look respectful.

"Welcome, little sister," the old man said. His voice was surprisingly strong. "I am Jana Farseer. I am Alpha here." He moved closer to me, catching my scent, and I did not move. I could smell him, too. He was different from Larna. Jana Farseer was like rocks and moving water. I had never paid so much attention to my nose before.

"Thank you. Alpha?" I repeated his title as a question.

"I am the leader. You will be staying with us until you have recovered from Mogra's magic. Then, we will be teaching you how to run with your new blood."

Everyone around the fire watched me. The stares made me nervous, but they were not unfriendly. "You forgot to ask her name, Farseer," said one of the company.

"Cate. I mean...my name is Cate."

"Arim dei, Cate. My name is Yerta." Yerta was medium height, with wiry muscles and soft grey eyes. His face was thin, but not sharp. He and I scented each other, and then he shook my hand. That simple human custom made me relax a little. "You are welcome here."

Larna noticed my muscles loosen and touched my hand. I looked up into her eyes and grew dizzy all over again. "It is overwhelming at first. Soon, you will be knowing everyone and feel at home with the pack. They can become family, if you let them."

"I need to stay here?" I was grateful that the Farseer pack had rescued me, but I did not want to stay here for the rest of my life. I needed to find my grandmother and eventually return to Baxstresse.

"We will not keep you prisoner," Farseer said, "but it would be wise to stay for a while. We will teach you to run, and help you when you go into your half-shape. If you leave, you might be hurting someone by mistake."

That had been my first thought after the change. I did not want to hurt anyone. "What is half shape?"

"Half-shape is between man and beast. It is the shape a Wyr takes at full moon, when they fight, or when they are in great pain."

I asked the question that had nearly driven me mad in Mogra's cave. "Will I kill in half-shape? Will I lose myself?"

"You might kill if you needed to defend yourself, but not because you are in that shape. Humans kill without it. Your conscience will not be leaving you."

I breathed a sigh of relief. I was still confused and overwhelmed, but not as frightened now that I knew I would not lose my mind.

"Our wolf forms and half-shape are not curses," Larna said. "If you train your mind and body to use them, they are becoming tools. Do you understand?"

"Yes." And I did understand, but not about half-shape or tools. I understood that I was no longer human, and my life would never be the same again.

Rae D. Magdon

CHAPTER SEVEN

I JOINED THE WYR around the fire for the next hour. A few strangers came and left the conversation, but Farseer, Larna, Yerta, and most of the group stayed. Not all of them introduced themselves, but I could separate their scents, and I tried to remember them. Perhaps names were not as important to Wyr. I did manage to match a few names to faces, and repeated them to myself so I would not forget.

They told me a little about their lives. Farseer explained that Mogra had been collecting travelers in the Forest for almost seven years. He had been one of her first victims, but managed to escape before she could enslave him. As the years passed, he tried to free others. The pack was over forty strong now, with a few children among them.

"Sometimes, the witch sends her dogs to hunt us, but we are faster, stronger, and smarter. They are rarely finding us," said Goran, a Wyr with a dark beard and a heavy forehead.

"Her dogs?" I frowned. Coming from Goran's mouth, it sounded like a curse.

"The Wyr she puts under her control," Yerta explained. "Her magic is strong, but they are mindless. She has to command them. We can think for ourselves."

"Be quiet, *Pekah*," Goran snapped. He did not appreciate being interrupted.

I tried to ease the tension. "But aren't they still dangerous?"

"They would be, but we are clever, and we know the forests," Jana Farseer said. "It is sad that you call your brothers dogs, Goran. You were nearly becoming one of them yourself. The witch clouds their minds."

Goran looked shamefully at the ground, but I was surprised that Farseer had not scolded him for snapping at Yerta. Surely he did not deserve such rude treatment.

"Is that all she does? Send the other Wyr after you? You're a threat. It seems like she would try harder to get rid of you."

"She has an army to build," Farseer continued. "People are going missing in the Forest all too often."

"They say," a thin woman beside me said, "that she might be working with the Queen. That she has sent her monsters through the Forest and up into the Rengast Mountains to find the Rebels." The rest of the small circle frowned at her, and the unfortunate speaker also lowered her head.

"Kera," Farseer rumbled, warning her to be silent with his eyes.

"The Queen? Rebels?" This was the second time I had heard both of those things mentioned. I still did not understand what had happened to Amendyr in my absence, and no one seemed willing to explain. Kera did not enlighten me. She glanced away guiltily instead.

Larna pressed a heavy hand to my shoulder. "I think I should be taking you to bed, Cate. You are tired."

I recognized Larna's change of subject for what it was, but did not feel comfortable enough to insist on an answer. With my belly full of cooked meat and my head filled with more questions, I allowed Larna to lead me back to her small hut. My body was drained, but my mind was racing. So much had changed so quickly. Ellie would never believe what had happened to me. I gasped, suddenly remembering my journal. I had not written in several days. Surely Ellie would be worried about me.

"Cate? Is something wrong?"

The concern on her face took me by surprise. It was touching. My cheeks grew warm. "I was supposed to contact one of my friends before now. She will wonder where I am..."

"You are a Wyr now. Friends might not be staying your friends any longer. Family will not understand." Her eyes darted to the ground, and I sensed there was more she was not telling me. "I know from experience."

My heart clenched in my chest. Was Larna right? Would Ellie, Belladonna, Sarah, and Mam reject me? "No," I said confidently. "My friends love me." They had shown that love countless times when I lived at Baxstresse, and I knew that it would not vanish just because I was Wyr.

Larna frowned. "Send your friend a message, if you must, although

I dinna know how you'll be doing it, but do not be telling her where we are. Many humans hate Wyr. If they knew where our camp was, they wouldna hesitate to burn it."

My first instinct was to tell Ellie where I was anyway, but some deep part of me knew that I needed to stay here. Ellie would try and bring me back to Baxstresse. Now that I thought about it, I had no idea what part of the Forest I was in anyway. "Fine," I said. Larna's face brightened. I wondered if my staying pleased her because she wanted to protect the pack, or because she did not want me to leave.

That night, in Larna's small room, I thought about what to write to Ellie. I was not afraid of rejection, but I was worried that she would come to fetch me. Eventually, I decided on a pleasant slant of the truth. My letter started: *'Oh, Ellie, the most amazing thing has happened.'*

I told her everything, but I kept my fears to myself. I described how Mogra had captured me, how she had changed me into a Wyr, and how the Farseer pack had rescued me. I did not tell her that the belt around my waist still ached, or that I was terrified of losing myself when I shifted. Hearing those things would only worry her. Those were private thoughts, ones I needed to examine on my own before I shared them.

I also wrote about Larna. I did not notice it at first, but her name crept into my letter more and more frequently as I kept writing. "Perhaps it's not so strange," I said to myself as I set down my quill. Larna had been the one to carry me from the cave when my body gave out, and her face was the first thing I had seen when I opened my eyes. Reading over the letter before I signed it, I realized that I sounded slightly infatuated. I had only known Larna a little more than a day, but I could not help wondering what would happen if I followed Farseer's advice and stayed here longer.

Impulsively, I added a line to the end of my letter. *'How long did it take you to fall in love? When did you know?'* I closed the journal and hid it beneath the mattress of my cot so that no one else could find it.

***

Larna was not in her hut the next morning, so I ventured out on my own to wander the camp. The early morning sun warmed my face and hair and made shining, moving patterns over the leaves. The grass felt soft under the soles of my bare feet. Others were moving about outside, carrying empty sacks or small stone knives. For Wyr, daytime meant working to find food. Perhaps Larna was already out hunting. A small group was working to raise another hut off to my left, but she was not among them.

Near the fire pit, which was still black from the night before, a silver-haired woman with strong bones in her face was mending a pile of clothes. Her thin fingers moved quickly with the flashing silver needle. Finally, something normal and calming in my unsteady world. I never would have imagined that something as simple as sewing could make me so happy.

I approached the woman cautiously, in the same non-threatening half circle from the night before. "Arim dei," I said, keeping my eyes a little lower than her face. I had no idea where these new silent rules came from. I was a new member of this pack, and I did not want to offend anyone.

The woman's face broke into a smile as she saw me. "Arim dei, Cate. You are feeling better, little sister?"

I blushed, surprised that she knew my name, but it should have been obvious. A new face in a pack of forty was hard to miss. I was probably the talk of the camp. "Yes, thank you. May I help you?"

I spent the next few hours helping with the pile of clothes. The woman's name was Seppea, and she told me a little more about life in the Farseer pack. "I felt trapped at first. I did not want to be staying away from my village, my family. But Wyr need the pack. It is in our blood. Pack is family."

Seppea's words were hauntingly familiar. I was conflicted about staying with the Farseer pack, but I had little choice. I could not leave and look for my grandmother until I learned what it meant to be Wyr. The last thing I wanted to do was lose control of the change and hurt someone by mistake. Besides, staying meant that I would be able to spend more time with Larna. She fascinated me, although I did not fully understand why.

After we worked our way through the pile of clothes, Seppea and I shared a meal of salted meat and bread. It was a simple meal, but I was grateful for it. As I swallowed my last mouthful, I saw another Wyr standing off to my left. He was tall and reedy, with sharp shoulders and grey eyes that seemed strangely familiar. When he saw me, he changed direction and headed for us in a straight line. Something about him made me want to take a step back.

I was not the only one. Seppea looked uncomfortable as he came to a stop beside the fire pit. "Arim dei, Hosta." The man nodded to her, but did not speak at first. Instead he turned and looked at me. His gaze made me shiver, although I did not understand why.

"So, you are the new female," he said, studying my face.

I was not sure how to respond at first. His tone made me uncomfortable, and I did not like being referred to as a 'female'. It made me feel like breeding stock. Eventually, I fell back on politeness. I was not eager to make enemies of my rescuers. "Hello, my name is Cate." I was careful not to challenge Hosta with my body language, but I did not go out of my way to be submissive, either. When he stepped closer, I held my ground. I had to carve out my place in the Farseer pack sometime. They had been receptive so far, and I was beginning to feel more confident.

"Cate." Hosta spoke slowly, tasting the word in his mouth. His smile was very wolfish, even on his human face. He seemed to realize that I was uncomfortable. "And are you from Seria, Cate?" he asked, sounding much more polite.

I took in a breath, trying to ease some of the tightness in my chest. My foreboding feelings were no excuse for rudeness. "I lived there for over ten years, but I was born in Amendyr."

"Well, this place might not be what you are remembering. Strange things are happening in Amendyr. It never is hurting to be sure of your friends in times like these."

"The pack is your friend," Seppea said.

"Of course," Hosta replied smoothly, "but trust is hard to be coming by, and the kingdom is full of dangers."

Seppea gave Hosta a sharp look, but not before my curiosity got the better of me. Everyone had been dancing around this subject since I returned to Amendyr, and I wanted a straight answer. Perhaps Hosta would be more forthcoming than the others. "What dangers? Does it have something to do with this Queen everyone whispers about?"

Hosta's eyes narrowed. "It is best not to say her name, and best not to say the witch's name, either. Speaking evil's name can summon it, and we are not rebels here."

I was not sure whether his words were a warning or a threat. I looked at Seppea, hoping she would explain further, but she shook her head and remained silent. Even though she was older, I knew from instinct that Hosta held a higher rank among the pack. She disapproved of his actions, but was unwilling to challenge him. I tried one last time to get the information everyone seemed determined to keep from me. "If no one will speak about how Amendyr has changed..."

"Amendyr has not changed," Hosta insisted. "It has always been a wild place. This is no different. Arim dei, Cate. Seppea." And then he walked away without another word. His sudden departure left me feeling even more unnerved than his arrival.

"Hosta has been here for six years, almost as long as Farseer," Seppea said, noticing the uneasy look on my face.

"That long?" I continued watching Hosta's retreating back. Soon, he had melted out of sight amongst the trees. It was like he had never been there at all.

"He has a brother, Yerta. They were captured together." I realized why Hosta's grey eyes had seemed familiar. They reminded me of Yerta's. Now that I thought about it, their bodylines were also similar, although Hosta was taller.

"I can see the resemblance," I said, but it was an understatement. They looked so alike that I was shocked I had not realized it sooner. Even their body types matched, although Hosta was taller. The biggest difference was in their demeanors. Yerta was halting and shy, and Hosta was anything but. "I wish Hosta was a little more like Yerta. At least he's friendly."

Seppea shrugged and turned back to her needlework. "Yerta is friendlier with strangers because that is his place."

"What do you mean, his place?"

"He is *Pekah*. That is his role," Seppea said, as if that explained everything. "Hosta is a leader. He can be off-putting, but Farseer is trusting him."

So I needed to trust him, too. That was the unspoken message. "And the Queen? Why didn't he want to talk about her?"

"No one is wanting to talk about her," Seppea said. "Hosta was right, little sister. It would be best if you forgot everything that was said. This is no rebel camp. We dinna want any attention from forces greater than we are."

I looked at Seppea, telling her that I understood without words. We returned to work in silence, but I was still not satisfied. Eventually, I would find someone willing to explain how the kingdom had changed during the past ten years. I needed to know what had happened to my home.

***

When Larna returned to camp just before nightfall, I was waiting inside of her hut. She smiled when she came in and saw me, pausing only to close the door before heading in my direction. We came together cautiously, unsure of our boundaries, but wanting to touch each other. She put a hand on my shoulder, and I pressed my side against hers as we re-learned each other's scents.

"Arim dei, little bird."

I smiled back at her. Her smell was already becoming familiar to me. "Arim dei, but I'm afraid the sun isn't out anymore."

Larna released my shoulder and stepped back. My chest ached a little when she broke our contact. "So, were you finding a way to send a message to your friend?" she asked, almost too casually.

I had to keep my eyes from drifting over to my cot. My magical journal was hidden beneath the mattress. I could tell that Larna did not like the idea of communicating with the outside world, and I wondered why she was so resistant. "Yes, I did, but I haven't heard back yet."

Larna's dark eyes narrowed at me, and her smile disappeared. "You found a way to send a message and expected to hear back right away?"

I decided to keep the journal to myself a little while longer. "Not right away, but I did tell her what happened to me."

"Well then, I wish you better luck than I had. Maybe your friend is as nice as you say." The look of suspicion on Larna's face was replaced with one of sadness, but she concealed it quickly. "Most humans are fearful of Wyr, even in Amendyr. They do not take the time to understand us, and few villages beyond the forest will trade with us."

I could tell that Larna was discussing a very sore subject with me, but despite my better judgment, I was curious. "Why are humans so afraid of the Wyr? Everyone here has treated me with kindness, and I'm an outsider..."

"You are not an outsider," Larna insisted. "You are one of us. There is a reason Seppea calls you little sister. Pack is family, and all of us would die defending each other."

I felt uncomfortable at the thought of complete strangers dying for me, and I wondered what the Farseer pack had done to inspire such fierce loyalty in Larna. From the sound of things, she had no other ties to the world outside of the Forest.

Larna picked up on my hesitance. "Dinna worry, little bird. Everyone is friendly here. We accept everyone who joins us, and we are all working together to make the pack strong. Once you are getting to know everyone, you will feel at home here." She paused, glancing out the small window beside the door. Beams of fading daylight stretched across the floor of the hut, but they were almost gone. It was nearly nightfall. "There is a singing tonight. Would you be wanting to go?"

"What is a singing?"

"Just what it sounds like. All of us meet outside and sing to the night sky."

A blush stole across my cheeks. I had never been much of a singer, even though my grandmother had taught me many of Amendyr's old songs. "My voice is not the strongest," I said, about to refuse the offer, but the hopeful look on Larna's face changed my mind at the last moment. I did not want to disappoint her. "But if you promise not to laugh at me, I'll go."

Larna gave me a happy smile, and I knew I had made the right decision. "Dinna worry. It is not that kind of singing, Cate. You will need to be changing."

My eyes went wide. Changing? During my short time with the pack, I had still not taken my other shape. The thought terrified me. Changing would prove that I was a Wyr, not a human. If I stayed in human shape, I could pretend that I was still the same.

Larna noticed my nervousness. "You should not be afraid." Her thumb stroked my cheek, and her brown eyes looked down at mine. "Only your body will be changing, not the rest. The humans are wrong about us."

Something in her voice reassured me. I had to face this new part of myself sooner or later. Perhaps it would be best to do it now and get it over with. "All right. I'll try."

"Good. The wolf is a part of you now. It is a bad thing to hide it inside yourself. It could be coming out and hurting someone later."

I knew that Larna was right. If I did not learn to control this, it might take control of me instead. Even though I was afraid, I was determined not to become the monster that Mogra had tried to make of me. "How do I change?"

"First, take off your clothes."

My mouth fell open, and my blush flared up again, creeping down my neck and spreading above my collarbone. My pulse hammered along the side of my throat, and each freckle on my cheeks burned like a small spark. "But...why...?"

Larna stroked my cheek. "I will be doing the same, little bird. You canna be a wolf in human clothes. They do not fit. For Wyr, bodies are not hidden."

I bit my lip, but at the same time, I could not deny that I was very curious to see what Larna looked like without her clothes. I imagined that the sleek strength in her arms would run the entire length of her body. My lower belly began to ache again, but this time, I knew it was not because of the wolfskin belt. I had caused this reaction myself.

Larna backed away to give me more space and began pulling her shirt over her head. She kept her eyes directly on mine as she tossed it onto the floor. Her breasts were small and high, and the tips stiffened to hard points. Was she cold? Excited? My gaze moved down. Her soft brown skin stretched tight over smooth sheets of muscle. I turned away as she began tugging at her pants, too shy to keep watching her. It felt wrong to admire her body so intently when I still did not really know her.

With my back to her, I stripped off my own shirt, pants, and underthings and left them in a pile on the floor. I crossed my arms over my breasts, almost wanting to cup one hand between my legs and hide myself. I felt Larna's burning eyes on my back, but did not turn around.

"You may be staying turned around if you want."

I thought that was best. I knew that if I turned and saw Larna completely bare, the sight would haunt me forever.

"Close your eyes." Larna's voice covered me in a blanket of warmth. I felt safe with her. My arms fell to my sides, relaxing. "Pull skin into muscles. Pull muscles into bones." My skin felt alive and tingling. "Think of your breathing. Slow and deep. Now, imagine running. Running through tall grass, through trees. Think of smelling. Think of chasing."

All of these thoughts should have crowded my head, but instead, they wove together into a picture that I could touch and smell and taste. I was running through the high grass, brushing the earth with my paws. My paws? I opened my eyes and stared down at my hands. I still had fingers, but my skin seemed to be shifting, changing. The nails sharpened, and a dark shadow crept down past my wrists. I was shocked when I realized that it was a soft, downy layer of fur.

My heart thumped frantically in my chest, and I fell to my knees, shivering as I tried not to panic. "Dinna fight it," Larna said. She dropped to the ground beside me and put a reassuring hand on your shoulder. "Just follow the call." At first, I had no idea what she was talking about, but then I felt the pull. The ache. The need to surrender myself to the swelling power inside of my chest.

I howled and gave in. My muscles curled and stretched and rippled. Even my bones ached. Every part of me seemed to be coming alive. There was warm, humming magic in my blood. I wanted to move, wanted to stretch out my legs and run. I could smell Larna beside me, and her energy touched mine. We would run together. I was not afraid anymore.

When I opened my eyes, there was a sleek grey wolf beside me. She was covered in dark, bristling fur. I knew that it was Larna even though I had never seen her in this shape. The scent was the same. I tried to move closer, but stumbled on my new legs. It took me a few moments to figure out how to move four of them at the same time. That was when I truly understood. I was a wolf. I was a wolf, but I was still Cate. My body had changed, but my words, my thoughts, had not been taken away.

Larna lifted her head and gave me a soft nudge with her nose. I twitched my ears at her. I could hear everything now, even the shallow sound of her breathing. When she glanced toward the cracked door, I walked toward it. My steps were hesitant at first, but after a few steps, I gained more confidence. I could move in this body. It was different, but it was mine, just as my human form had been. Larna nudged the door open, and we left the safety of the cabin together.

There were more of us in the forest. I could sense them, but I could not see them. When I reached them, they surrounded me. I found myself in the center of a tight circle. Black, twitching noses and warm breaths pressed in on all sides. They were learning my scent, and this time, it did not feel strange or uncomfortable. It was as natural as shaking hands.

One of the wolves tilted its chin up to the sky, opened its throat, and howled. The cry poured out of two mouths, then four, then all. Everyone was singing together. I lifted my head and sang to the sky with them. I was a small part of something large and powerful and old. With Larna beside me and the pack around me, I felt connected.

CHAPTER EIGHT

MY LIFE FELL INTO a routine over the next few weeks. Larna usually left early in the morning to go hunting. I woke up after she left and went outside to find Seppea, Yerta, or one of the other Wyr. They would find somewhere for me to work for a few hours, sewing, cooking, even building and repairing the huts. Many members of the pack came to say hello to me or worked with me. Most of them were very friendly. I was quick to remember faces and smells, but names came more slowly.

Many of us ate lunch together. Sometimes, Larna got back in time to join us. Other days, she did not get back until late in the evening. I always greeted her with a hug. Every day, I found myself growing more and more attached to her. When she left to hunt or patrol the Farseer territory, I felt a strange, gnawing restlessness that I could not explain. My hands twitched because I wanted to touch her skin.

I could not talk about this with Larna. It would have been too much, too soon. Our friendship was still so new, so fragile and vulnerable. I hardly knew anything about her yet, and I did not want to upset the balance. When she did come home, I ran into her arms and hugged her. She would stroke my back and murmur in my ear. "See? I told you I would be coming back to you safe, Catie." And then I would smile as we held each other tight.

It was not long before Ellie wrote back to me in my journal. The first paragraph demanded to know exactly where I was.

'Cate,

Where are you? All of us are sick with worry. When I sent you off to Amendyr with my blessing, I thought you would find magic and adventure, but this wasn't at all what I had in mind. Obviously, I've been living too much in my books. I should have listened more closely to Mam when she said that Amendyr was dangerous.'

Once Ellie had expressed her shock and worry, she moved on to questions. Most of them were about Wyr. I still did not know very much about them myself, so I had difficulty answering her.

'When I told her, Belladonna's first instinct was to go to the library. By the Saints, I think she would live there if I did not make her come to bed.' I blushed at that part. *'She read all about Wyr and tried to explain the different ways they were made. What I want to ask you is how it feels. How do you change? Are your senses stronger? Do you feel different? Does it hurt?'*

Ellie's instincts were right. I did feel different, and my changing senses were occasionally overwhelming. It was not easy to adjust to hearing and seeing so clearly, or easy to obey the strange, unspoken social rules that I felt compelled to follow. The change did not hurt my body, but sometimes the wolfskin belt fused to my waist ached. I wanted to pull it off. The skin around it was still swollen and puffy, but Larna had checked it for me and said it did not look infected.

As I read the rest of the letter, my eyes stuck on a few sentences. *'You asked me when I knew I was in love. The deepest part of my heart knew the moment I saw Belladonna's face. The rest of me did not catch up until several months later, when I read her diary. After that, it took me a week to realize that I could not live without her. I knew it was love because every moment I spent with her was better than the moment before. I wanted to share every single part of my future with her. Forever.'*

That answer struck a chord in me. It described exactly how I felt. *Tuathe.* Two-souls. That was what Ellie and Belladonna were. The more familiar I got with Larna, the more I wanted to know. It was like a craving. I just wanted more of her time, more of her attention, more of her. But was I really in love with her? I was afraid of the answer. I still knew so little about her. What if it was too soon? What if I was too shy, too damaged for love? What if Larna did not want me?

'I have no idea if you are in love with Larna or not,' Ellie wrote, *'but you sound like an infatuated schoolgirl. That is very unlike you, Cate. If someone has finally turned your head, it must mean they are extraordinarily special.'*

I wrote Ellie a long letter back. I told her about Jana Farseer and Seppea, and about changing. Larna had been practicing it with me on nights when she returned to camp early. It was not hard to change into my wolf form anymore. I had to think of things that a wolf would think of, running and hunting and smells that a wolf knew. Then, I pictured myself turning, and my body followed. It was easier if I was running. It was much harder to change back into a human. I had to think of human things. On my third time, I discovered a trick that helped a little. I thought about kissing Larna. I needed human lips to do that. When I pictured it, I had lips again.

Larna came in just as I signed my letter. "What are you writing, Catie?" she asked, staring curiously at the journal. I gripped it a little tighter in my hands, debating whether or not I should confess. Larna had been nothing but kind and accepting toward me since my arrival, and I liked to think that we were growing closer, but I remembered how somber she had become when I last mentioned writing to Ellie. She had made her loyalty to the Farseer pack and her distrust of humans very clear then.

Eventually, I decided to tell her the truth. "I was writing another letter to my friend. Don't worry," I added before she could protest, "I still haven't told her where I am. You were right. She would come after me if she knew."

Larna snorted. "Probably with torches," she muttered.

"Ellie isn't like that," I insisted. "She doesn't care about what I've become, and she's only worried about my safety. Why would you judge her when you don't even know her?"

Larna gave me a guilty look, hanging her head and folding her hands in front of her. She sighed. "I am sorry. You are right. I canna be judging someone I have never met. If you like her, your friend is very kind to be sure."

I could tell that her apology was sincere, but it did not satisfy me. I wanted to know why Larna was so protective of the pack. It seemed to me that a large group of Wyr could defend themselves from almost anything, and she had no reason to fear invading humans. "Larna, why do humans frighten you? I was one once. So were you. If we couldn't shift, we would be exactly the same."

"That is why I am afraid of them. I grew up in a normal village, with a normal family and a normal life. But one day I went to the Forest, and came back...different."

Memories of Mogra stole over me, and I thought I could smell water, rock, and rotting flesh in my nose. I breathed out sharply to clear out the stale air in my lungs. "Farseer said that the witch made all of us.

She captured you, too?"

Larna nodded. "Aye, but she was not keeping me prisoner long. Farseer and the pack rescued me. We were fewer then. I stayed for a little while, learned how to run as a wolf, but I was missing my old family." The small muscles around her eyes tightened, and I could see the tension there. "They were not missing me as much."

I was horrified. "So, they just abandoned you?"

It took Larna a while to answer me. She did not speak often, but when she did, she chose her words carefully. "They were afraid. They called me monster and told me never to come back. My mother told me she wished I had stayed dead like she thought. So I stayed here, with my real family. The Farseer pack accepted me. I have a place here. A role. They take care of me, and I take care of them."

I could not remain seated any longer. I set the journal aside and stood up to give her a big hug. I buried my face in her shoulder and let my hands run up along her back. We held on longer than usual, but neither of us wanted to let go. "Your family shouldn't have abandoned you," I mumbled into her shirt.

"No. They shouldn't have. But you are right, too. I canna be afraid of everyone who is not a member of the pack." She stared down at me and forced a weak smile. "Perhaps I will meet your friend one day, and she will change my mind."

"Her name is Ellie."

"Ellie," Larna repeated, testing the name. "Be you writing about me to this Ellie of yours?"

I pulled out of her arms, but not before she gave me another squeeze. "Yes. After all, you saved my life."

Larna gave me a small smile. "I am glad you were all right."

"Ellie and her wife are glad, too."

Larna's dark eyebrows shot up. She looked very surprised. "Her wife? I thought they were not allowing things like that in Seria."

I grinned. "They don't, but why does it matter? They are very much in love."

Larna was quiet for a moment. I noticed that she was studying me thoughtfully. I could not read her brown eyes, but I loved looking at them and trying. There was something vulnerable in her face as she said, "If I were after looking for a mate, it would be another woman." The last few words were almost a whisper, but I heard them clearly.

My heart flew up into my throat. "Me too," I whispered back.

Larna rocked from one foot to the other, her hands buried in the pockets of her leggings. I chewed on one corner of my lip. She looked adorable, like a nervous child. I had never seen this side of her. Apparently, she was not strong and silent all the time. There were hidden depths to her that I had not uncovered yet. "I am glad you told me about your friend. I was not knowing if a Serian would judge me."

"I am not a Serian," I reminded her. "I was born here. But even if I wasn't, I would never look down on you for that. Perhaps you're the one who is a little too quick to pass judgment."

Larna pulled one of her hands out of her pocket and rubbed at the back of her neck, scratching her short, dark hair. "Aye, perhaps you are right about me. I still have much to learn before I will be matching Farseer's patience."

"Well, I think you're on your way. At least you seem willing to change your mind, and you listen when other people talk." I could only hope that Larna would not judge me when she found out that I was *Ariada* . Although I was back in Amendyr now, some of my Serian habits lingered. I did not consciously decide to hide my seeing from Larna and the rest of the Farseer pack, but I did not tell them, either. In Seria, such things brought only trouble.

Larna glanced at the journal, which was still lying on the table. "Would you be telling your friend Arim Dei for me, Catie?"

"I will," I promised. "I already told her all about you."

"Not everything, I hope." Larna watched me, considering something. Then, she opened her arms for another hug. I gladly gave it to her. Hugs from Larna were my new favorite thing. Her body was tall and strong and just right against mine. "I was after telling the truth before. I would like to meet your friend someday."

The corners of my lips curled up. I always seemed to smile around Larna. "I think both of you would like that."

***

Not surprisingly, my secret was discovered soon after. It was not dramatic, like the vision at the Prince's Cup. I did not see pictures and collapse to the ground. It started when Larna told me that she needed to chop wood. The bad feelings came immediately. "Do it another day," I suggested, not wanting to get into a long discussion. "It will probably rain later anyway."

Larna looked at me strangely. "Little bird, there be no clouds in the entire sky. It is a good day to be working outside." I walked over to the door of our cabin and looked out, disappointed to see that the sky was a clear, pale blue. There was no sign of rain, and Larna looked excited at the prospect of fresh air. Given the choice, she would always rather be outside working.

I tried something else. "I wanted to spend the day with you. Maybe you could help me practice changing? We were both too busy yesterday."

"That is a good idea. After I bring in the wood, we can do whatever you like." She gave me a beautiful smile, but it did not soothe me.

"I have a strange feeling," I tried to explain. "A feeling that you shouldn't go out."

Larna laughed. "I have those feelings every morning when I am needing to work hard, but work does not do itself." I realized that she was not going to take me seriously and dropped the subject. Perhaps it was only a feeling. People had feelings all the time. Not every emotion I had was connected to my gift. Besides, there had been no bright, blinding vision. I was still sitting upright in my chair. But this did feel curiously like Knowing.

The unpleasant feelings lingered for the next few hours. I distracted myself by cleaning everything—the bed, the table, the floors, even just outside the door. I helped cook lunch with some of the others and read a new letter from Ellie in our journal. Apparently, Sarah and the Prince were also writing letters. I was amazed. That strange piece of news was enough to distract me until I heard a pounding on the door.

"Who is it?" I called out as I got up from my chair.

"Seppea. Let me in, Cate."

I could hear the urgency in her voice, and a sharp stab of fear pierced my chest. I hurried to open the door for her and stepped aside to let her in. "Is Larna all right?" I asked as soon as she entered the hut. "What happened to her?"

"There was an accident. A tree was rotted inside, and the wind pushed it over. It almost fell on Larna and Goran. They moved away in time, but it could have been crushing them both!" My stomach sank, and I knew that this was what my feelings had been trying to tell me. Seppea's eyes focused on me like hot beams of light. "How did you know that I came here about Larna? You were asking before I even mentioned her name."

I bit down nervously on one corner of my mouth. Confronted directly, I could not lie about my gift. "I knew this morning that something would happen if Larna went out today. I hoped that I was wrong."

"You knew?" Seppea was surprised, but not skeptical. "Are you *Ariada*?"

"Yes, I am."

Strangely, I was relieved to admit it to her. I had kept my powers a secret for so long, and talking about them openly made me feel as though I was casting off a heavy weight. I was even more relieved when Seppea took my hand, but that feeling quickly vanished when she said, "We will go and tell Farseer. He should know about these things." She led me through the door, and I followed reluctantly. "Why were you not telling us that you Saw?"

I dragged behind her, a little nervous about revealing my secret to the leader of the pack. "I tried, but Larna didn't listen when I told her to stay."

Seppea rolled her eyes. "She would have if you explained that you were having the Sight. You are in Amendyr, Cate. We understand magic here." She was right, of course. Living in Seria for so many years had changed me, but now, I could be myself again. "Your family has seer blood?"

"Yes, but that's all I know."

"Can you heal as well?"

"I'm not sure. I can clean wounds..."

Seppea snorted. "Anyone can clean wounds. So, you are having no idea what kind of magic you use?"

"None." Under her barrage of questions, I felt like even more of an outsider than usual.

Seppea stopped at last, and I stopped behind her, almost falling on top of her. She whirled around to face me. "We will be asking Farseer if you can study with our shaman."

My eyes grew wide. "You have a shaman?" I had heard of shamans, of course. They used powerful magic to do all kinds of things, but I did not know how they were chosen or what sort of secrets they studied.

"Aye, a good one. She's getting on, and could probably use an apprentice. She will be helping you, even if you are an oracle of some kind."

"What's the difference?"

"Between an oracle and a shaman? A shaman is talking with spirits to know the future, to heal the sick, to control nature. They know the magic of the soul. An Oracle uses signs to ask questions of the future. They read the stars, the leaves, even the lines in your hand. Both can be using visions. Have you ever had visions?"

A thought struck me. "Wait...how do you know so much about magic?"

Seppea smiled. With her thin face and her narrowed eyes, she looked strangely like a wolf, even though she was in her human skin. "Many of us in Amendyr use magic. I make things." So, that explained how Seppea got through her work so quickly. It also explained where some of the enchanted clothing and armor in the camp had come from. "Now, stop staring at me like a gaping fish and go in."

I realized that I was still frozen in front of her, and that we were standing in front of Farseer's tent. Two firm hands pushed between my shoulder blades and sent me stumbling in. I staggered forward. My pupils grew larger in the dark, and I could make out two familiar figures. Jana Farseer was sitting inside, and Yerta was with him. Both of them smiled at me.

"Arim dei, little sister," Farseer said. "Was that Seppea outside I was hearing?"

"Yes." The entire story spilled out of me. The tree that had almost fallen on Larna and Goran, how I had known about it, and several other things that Seppea was not aware of, like my visions back in Seria. I explained that my family had always been different, but when we left Amendyr, I decided to hide my gifts.

My voice trailed off into the dark tent, leaving me feeling empty. Farseer shifted in his seat. He stood up from the three-legged wooden stool that he had been using, resting his arm on the table. He studied me with curious eyes, examining my face carefully. I clenched and unclenched my hands.

"Well, Cathelin, I think you had better be after paying a visit to Kalwyn." The name was ancient Amendyrri, and it meant, quite appropriately, 'one who knows'.

"Kalwyn?" I asked. "Is she a shaman?"

"Aye. I canna say how old she is, but she has lived longer than my father and perhaps his father before him."

"If she is older than Farseer, she must be a thousand," Yerta said.

Farseer growled, but did not seem angry. "Quiet, young pup. I can still pin you in less than three seconds."

"He could, too," Yerta whispered loudly, winking at me. My nervousness started to go away.

"Kalwyn makes her home in the Forest. She is not Wyr, but she hates Mogra, and the witch willna come near her. She will be knowing what to do with you."

"When will I go? How will I get there?"

I had so many more questions to ask, but Farseer said, "Larna will be going with you. You two are friends, yes? I canna be sending you out alone. You do not know the Forest. Go and tell Larna to come see me. I will be writing a letter for you to give to Kalwyn." I stood in place, still smiling because Larna would be going with me. "Cate? Go," Farseer prodded, not unkindly. I had to stop myself from running out of the tent at a full sprint.

Larna was both pleased and a little disappointed when I explained everything to her, not because I was *Ariada*, but because I had not felt safe enough to tell her. "You, a shaman? I canna…" she started, still absorbing what I had said. "Well, I thought you were having a magical look about you. I mean, not magical…well…"

"I know what you mean," I said, trying to make her feel better about her stammering. "I'm sorry I didn't let you know. It's habit. In Seria, everyone is afraid of magic."

"Perhaps a little like how I am afraid of humans?" Larna asked, reading more in my words than I had intended.

I gave her a guilty shrug of my shoulders. "Maybe."

"I am trusting you, Cate, magic or not. *Ariada* make the pack stronger. I willna think of you any differently. In fact, I am admiring you all the more." She made a face at me. "I dinna want to be like the Serians, anyway."

I laughed. "They are a little stuck up, aren't they? My friends excluded."

"Only a little. Anyway, I am glad for you, little bird." My cheeks flushed. I was beginning to like that special-name more and more.

"I'm glad, too. So, will you take me to see Kalwyn?"

"Aye, I will be taking you. I have not been after seeing Kalwyn in a long time. I was hurt out on the hunt, and she healed me. It is a noble art to be learning, surely." The thought of Larna being hurt unsettled me, but I was glad that she did not mind walking me to my first lesson. I would be glad of her company, perhaps more than I wanted to admit.

Rae D. Magdon

CHAPTER NINE

KALWYN'S SMALL HUT WAS crammed with bottles and books and baubles of all sorts. They were stuffed into cupboards, tossed carelessly on tables, and flung across the furniture, including three wobbly-legged chairs. Her living quarters were so strange that I could not help staring. There was a finely carved hourglass on a stand next to the entrance, and my hand almost knocked it over as I reached to close the door behind me. There were detailed anatomy sketches of Liarre, the half man, half beast tribes that lived in the west, tacked on the walls in one corner, and a cage of brightly colored lizards in another. Whoever this Kalwyn was, she certainly enjoyed collecting things. I stepped forward into the room and looked around.

"She knew you were coming," Larna said. "This place is cleaner than I have ever been seeing on a visit."

I moved aside a tiny chest with my foot, and a strange humming noise buzzed reproachfully from inside. I did not open it. A simmering brown pot spat and fizzed over the fire. No smell came from whatever was inside, but the scent of the room itself was overpowering—dust, paper, and old wood with lots of oil. It reminded me of a library. Underneath everything else, I could catch the familiar, warm smell of magical energy.

The scent of magic grew stronger, and I looked up to see an old woman in a dull green coat step out from the maze of stacked books. She carried a walking stick with one hand, and it nearly knocked over a tall, thin wire that spiraled in the shape of a corkscrew. "Well then, let's be having a look at you," she said, not bothering to introduce herself or ask my name. She grabbed my chin in a wrinkled, firm hand and pulled it closer to her face. Her grip was surprisingly strong. "Of course, I should have guessed. I knew your grandmother."

I was surprised. "My grandmother? I mean, my name is Cathelin Raybrook, and I—"

"Yes, yes, I know all that. You should be hearing that your grandmother fell asleep two years ago, child. She passed comfortably." My mouth went dry, and a stinging tightness grew in my throat. I thought I had prepared myself for the possibility, but her loss was still a blow, even after so many years. She had helped raise me, and it was difficult to imagine her dead.

"Thank you for telling me," I said scratchily. Kalwyn produced a cloth from somewhere in her robe and passed it to me. As I wiped at the soft tears that rolled from my eyes, Larna wrapped a strong arm around my shoulder. When my tears slowed down, I handed the cloth back to Kalwyn. "Thank you. I'm sorry for that."

"It is wise to grieve, but you came here for a reason. I will be dealing with you more in a moment." She turned to Larna. "Now you, young pup, be taking that pot off the fireplace, if you please."

"Surely, Grandmother," Larna said politely. She seemed to respect Kalwyn. I watched her back as she walked towards the fire, but Kalwyn tapped my hand with her stick sharply. I pulled my hand back in surprise, almost wanting to suck on my fingers like a scolded child.

"Stop making cow eyes," she barked. I blushed fiercely, although my face was still a little red from crying. "Go to the kitchen and get a bowl."

"Where is the kitchen?" I managed to ask, trying to push thoughts of my grandmother and Larna out of my head.

"Over there." She gestured to her right with a twisted hand, and I looked toward a doorway with a strange tribal mask perched above it. I wrinkled my nose at its twisted eyes and mouth. "Oh, don't you be minding him. He always looks unpleasant. Good for warning me about guests, though."

I felt magical energy coming from the mask, but decided to save my questions about it, and the rest of the house, for later. My mind was too full already. I went to the kitchen, which turned out to be just as crowded as the first room. There were no dirty dishes or crumbs on the floor, but clean dishes were shoved haphazardly into wobbly stacks, and cleaning rags and empty sacks lay scattered around the room. I found a bowl near the sink and carried it back into the first room.

"Ah, good. Give it here, girl." I handed it to her, and she took it with both hands, shuffling over with a hop-step to the pot. She looked rather silly for a powerful magic-worker. She did not look like a shaman at all, more like an eccentric old collector. She certainly did have a lot of things in her house.

Involuntarily, I reached out to touch a strange crystal shaped into three pronged spikes. "Leave it be, child. Now, come to the fire." I joined Kalwyn and Larna at the fire. Cupping the bowl with two hands, she dipped it in the pot and scooped some liquid. She held the bowl out to me. The liquid inside looked clear. "Dip two fingers in, your second and third. Then, stir the bowl seven times to the right."

While she held the bowl, I dipped my second and middle finger. The potion felt ordinary, almost like warm water, but when I started stirring to the right, the surface began to shimmer and glow with golden ripples. I made seven circles and took my fingers out. "Ah yes," Kalwyn said, mostly to herself. "She is having the touch." I rubbed my two fingers and thumb together, bringing the potion near my nose. It had no smell, but now that I could feel it, the texture was more like oil. "You have come here to be trained, yes?"

I looked up, startled. "Yes. Jana Farseer sent me."

"Why?"

"I had a vision. I Know and See things before they happen."

A rapid burst of questions followed. "Are you seeing pictures, or can you read the sky and stars? Or do you just have feelings you cannot explain?"

"I see pictures. I smell and hear them, too. Sometimes I have feelings."

"Are you often right?"

I thought about that. "Yes. If what I See doesn't happen, it still almost happens...if you understand what I mean."

Kalwyn nodded. "Are you skilled at healing wounds?"

"I have never tried."

"Do you often remember what you See?"

"Not always. Sometimes I don't know that anything has happened to me. Someone else has to tell me what I said."

"Common in the young ones. We can be solving that problem." Kalwyn tapped her fingers on the jacket of a book that rested on the wooden table. "Learning magic and the ways of a shaman is not easy, child." I noticed that her eyes, which were a pale blue, seemed to grow brighter. Her white hair fell about her shoulders in thick, spilling strands.

Instead of looking odd, she was an impressive sight. "Magic is a responsibility. You have to choose what to tell, when to interfere. You are having power over others that most do not even realize. Magic can do great good, but it can also do great harm."

"Please," I said, surprising myself with my eagerness, "I want to learn."

Kalwyn nodded, took a seat on one of the three-legged stools, and gestured at Larna with her stick. "I will start with her, young pup. Off with you, there is food in the kitchen." Larna's eyes brightened, and she wandered towards the kitchen door. I could not help staring after her as she went. "Sit," Kalwyn said, interrupting my silent pleasure. I sat in the chair across from her. "Listen. Long ago in the western lands, where the world began, there lived seven brothers. The Maker gave them gifts at birth, and as they grew, each one proved to be different than the others.

"The first son was a wizard. He used words of power to call water from the sky and sea, to shake the earth, and make fire and wind from nothing. And so it was that he controlled the elements, and even man, because man is made from the elements. And so it was that many followed him. Some made crops grow and villages thrive, and some burned these villages to the ground, for magic is only as good as its user.

"The second son was a shaper. He could take flesh in his hands and twist it, breathe life into stone, and create creatures beautiful and terrible to behold. And so it was that he controlled magical beasts, and even man, for man is created just like every other creature. And so it was that many followed him. Some made the gentle stone giants and the mermaids in the sea, and some made the demons of black fire and the goblins under the earth, for magic is only as good as its user.

"The third son was an enchanter. He could forge objects with strong enchantments and make all manner of magical things. And so it was that he controlled the many objects of power in the world, and even man, because man is nothing without the tools he makes. And so it was that many followed him. Some made magical swords to aid the light, and flutes and harps to soothe the animals, and some made evil weapons to kill or curse, for magic is only as good as its user.

"The fourth son was an oracle. He could read the movement of sky and leaves to understand the secrets of the world. And so it was that he had great knowledge of patterns and signs, and even man, for man is a follower of patterns. And so it was that many followed him. Some used their knowledge to help good kings and warn of disaster, and some used their knowledge to cloud men's minds, for magic is only as good as its user.

"The fifth son was a druid. He could speak with the animals and trees and lived with the mountains and streams and valleys. He could call on them all for aid, and even man, for man is one of the beasts. And so it was that like his eldest brother, he knew of nature and its many secrets. And so it was that many followed him. Some used the secrets of the earth to make the forests bloom and care for the animals, and some used them to poison and kill and destroy, for magic is only as good as its user.

"The sixth son was a necromancer. He could see ghosts, speak with the dead, and even bring them back to life. And so it was that he could call men back from the brink of death and even beyond its gate. And so it was that many followed him. Some used their powers to heal those almost gone, or put the walking dead to rest, and some used their dark energy to raise corpses and twist the laws of nature, for magic is only as good as its user.

"The seventh child was a shaman. He—or, as some say, she—could travel into the otherworld to talk with the ancient spirits and learn of the future. And so it was that the seventh child learned all they could and sailed far away from the western lands to Amendyr. And so it was that many followed that child. Some used their visions to bring wisdom to their kingdoms and villages, and some used their powers to turn men's minds to wickedness, for magic is only as good as its user.

"You are a daughter of the seventh child. You have been called, Cathelin Raybrook, to be a shaman. Your grandmother was a shaman, and so was your mother, although she was not fully trained. Magic is in your blood, but it will only do as much good, or as much harm, as you command it to do."

And then there was silence. As I re-examined the story that Kalwyn had told me, I realized that I could remember word for word what she had said. Perhaps it was magic, or perhaps the story was just enthralling, but I knew that I would be able to repeat it exactly if she asked.

"Teach me," I said. "Teach me to be a shaman. I want to know like my grandmother."

"That is where the word Shaman comes from, acha. To know." I flushed pink when I realized that she had called me 'acha': student. Kalwyn had accepted me.

***

My first lessons were not in shamanism, but in history. For the rest of the day, Kalwyn told me more about Amendyr's past than I had ever read in any book. She told me of the High *Ariada* at the king's court in Kalmarin, who had fallen and allowed half of Amendyr to be seized by the Serians. I learned of the great enchanter, Grath, who had made the Red Lion Shield that the kings and queens of Amendyr had carried into battle for centuries. Grath had invented sorcerer's chains for his wizard brethren and had made many objects of power like the pipes of Nemoth and the silverglass mirror.

Kalwyn spoke of Lyr, the powerful shaper who had been corrupted by his own creations, making more and more monstrous creatures until they eventually killed him. He had been the first to call demons, and he had made the Liarre, which were named for him, in a bizarre magical accident while trying to fuse animals and humans together. He had also been the first to create a Wyr. It was his path that Mogra was following.

I asked Kalwyn about Ellie, who could speak to animals. From my description, she told me that Ellie probably had some untrained druidic powers. I was eager to share everything I had learned with her, but by the time Kalwyn reached a pause in the lesson, the sun had already set.

Larna, who must have been listening at the door, entered during the break in our conversation. "Cate and I should be after getting home."

Kalwyn smiled. "Take her home, then, young pup. Make sure she sleeps. Next time, we will be learning about the spirit world." My head spun. The spirit world? I had still had so much to learn.

I must have mumbled a goodbye to Kalwyn, because Larna led me from the small cabin by the hand and out into the night. I was grateful for my Wyr blood, because it made traveling in the dark much easier. I did not stumble, and I always seemed to know which direction we were going. Larna did not let go of my hand, sending a pulse of warmth through me that kept my face hot for several minutes. This time, I did let her take my pack, and she carried both over one shoulder by the straps.

"Did Kalwyn teach you many things, little bird?" she asked, seeming genuinely interested and not just polite. I did not blame her. Magic was fascinating. I had sensed no magical energy from Larna, but I was not an expert in the subject. Maybe she practiced it herself and I had no idea. If she did have any powers, she must have used them to read my mind, because she said, "I am knowing almost nothing about magic, but I find it interesting. I find you interesting."

My face flushed even hotter. I was glad that it was dark and my blush was not too noticeable. Night-seeing was different than day-seeing. I was less aware of color and more aware of movement. "It is interesting. Magic, I mean," I stuttered. "It...it feels like a great weight has lifted. I can talk about it now. Are you sure you don't mind coming with me?"

Larna squeezed my hand. She must have heard the insecurity in my voice. "No. But how are you feeling about your grandmother?"

My good mood faded a little. "I miss her. I hadn't seen her for several years, but I have good memories of her. I'm glad that Kalwyn told me what happened, though. It's better than not knowing, and I did feel bad about staying with the pack instead of looking for her."

"I know how it feels to be losing family," Larna said. Her face looked even darker among the shadows. "Surely your grandmother would have been proud of what you are doing with Kalwyn. Take comfort in that."

I was too shy to say anything else to her as we walked back that night, and camp was not very far away. We moved as humans because we did not want to leave our clothes and packs, but I could tell that we were still moving faster than I had been able to travel a few weeks ago. My body had changed. Although my thoughts never completely left Larna, I began thinking about Kalwyn's parting words. She would be showing me the spirit world tomorrow. I needed to rest well that night, but I knew that I would probably dream of Larna's eyes.

Rae D. Magdon

CHAPTER TEN

THROUGH MY HEAVY SLEEP, I felt a strange tingling. I was blossoming outward, swelling inside my skin, stretching to the low ceiling of the hut. My muscles burned. Flesh rippled and crawled around my bones. I started scratching, trying to gouge out whatever was inside of me.

A large, square hand caught my wrists, stopping me from tearing at myself. I noticed warm, wet blood leaking from the cuts on my skin, but as soon as they opened, I felt warm fire knitting them back together. I could not see it, but I could feel it in the dark. Squinting up, I could only make out a black shape above me. It was Larna. I knew her scent. But something about her smelled...different. A heavy musk surrounded her, a primal scent sharp with magic.

There was a flash of silver, and I saw two eyes above me. They were like, and unlike, Larna's eyes. I imagined that I could see a reflection of the moon in them. It was a heavy grey moon, and my heart felt the pull. Larna helped me up from the bed. I followed her, naked, out of the front door. There was no one else outside, but the strange smell was everywhere. I realized what was happening. "Half shape?"

"It is time."

"The others?"

"Running."

So we were alone. I was glad that no one but Larna would see me naked and afraid. I had become a wolf several times now, but I had never taken this form before. I was frightened. Would it hurt more than the usual change? What if I lost myself? What if I never came back? But Larna's fingers squeezed tight around mine, and my breathing grew steadier. Together, we looked up to the sky. The moon was a flashing white disc, almost painful to watch. My heart beat heavily in my ears. I imagined that I could hear Larna's heartbeat too as she held my hand.

My shoulders broadened. My back rippled with muscle. My arms became tough, knotted ropes, and my legs were tree trunks. Everything swelled and ached and burned. I lifted my heavy head to the sky and howled. My voice was not my own. It was deep and resonating. Beside me, Larna howled too. From around the forest, there were answering calls. Some were close by, others miles away.

I turned my head to look at Larna. Beside me was the most beautiful and terrifying creature that I had ever seen. She had coal black fur and familiar brown eyes. Her coat had a wiry layer on top and a downy soft layer underneath. Her body was long and tight, and the sheets of muscle were sleek like a hunting dog's. She stood on two legs, and her small black nose was dainty against the rest of her long head.

My claws shifted in the dirt. My legs twitched. I wanted to run. I wanted to feel my blood rushing. I wanted the warmth of Larna's body against mine. I wanted Larna inside of me, taking me. These thoughts excited and frightened me. Larna's ears perked up. She pushed her head forward, asking without words. 'Play?' There was something in her face that reminded me of a puppy. I could not mate with Larna yet. I was not ready. Play seemed like a good idea.

I realized with a fierce joy that my mind had not left with my human body. I could still reason and analyze and make decisions. The urges were just stronger. The last of my fear dissolved.

I nipped Larna's ear and crouched down as she swiped at me with a large paw. She chased me all the way through the camp, and we crashed through the forest trees together, heading for the river. My senses blossomed open. I could see in colors I had never imagined, could smell in a thousand threads. My ears picked out each tiny noise, and through it all, I felt Larna pressed close beside me. The world around me was wild and beautiful, and I was no longer afraid of the forest or myself.

We ran around tree trunks, crashed through the river, and leapt over the grass. The two of us tussled and played, darting in circles and howling up at the moon. Our voices blended together, and it was the sweetest sound I had ever heard. My heart pounded, and the rush of my blood made every inch of my new body tingle. We ran until we exhausted ourselves and crumpled back into our human shapes, resting on the ground and drawing in heavy breaths of the cold night air into our burning lungs.

When we climbed back to our feet, the evening was calm and still beneath the full moon. Silver threads of light from the stars wove to the ground in soft beams. It was a beautiful night, but Larna was even more wondrous to me. She looked lean and powerful in the faint glow. I walked close beside her, our arms just touching. I was still tired from changing into my half-shape, but my heart was happy and full. We wandered beneath the treetops together, not following a set path on our way back to camp. Instead, we made our own way, drawing close to save heat.

"Cate," Larna said, as if she wanted to ask a question. Her voice was like a deep river. It had many currents, and hearing her speak made me shiver. She noticed and wrapped her arm around me. That simple gesture touched me. Belladonna was always doing that sort of thing for Ellie, and Ellie always found little ways to surprise her, too.

"What is it, Larna?"

"Nothing." We smiled at each other and she blushed. Dancing around our feelings was silly. We both knew it. Her brown eyes reflected the moon like dark glass, almost glowing. "Little bird." Her face drew closer. My heartbeat doubled. I melted as she wrapped her arms around my waist and bent her head. I forgot to breathe. Finally, she kissed me. My lips twitched, smiled, and relaxed against hers. My eyes stayed shut. I knew that hers were closed, too. For the first time, I realized that we were both naked. Strangely, I was not embarrassed.

It was my first kiss. Luciana had not been interested, and I had not wanted to kiss her. Not knowing what to do, I just held still, feeling Larna's mouth over mine. It was warm and soft like the rest of her. Larna did not move either. We stayed like that for a long second, not moving an inch. We pulled apart, only a breath between us, and kissed again. "That was my first kiss," I whispered against her mouth. Larna looked surprised, then pleased. Her dark eyebrows lifted on the pale curve of her forehead. "I never loved anyone enough to kiss them before."

"Is that meaning what I think?" Larna whispered back. Her pale cheekbones were dusted with twin spots of pink, barely visible in the silvery light.

"That I love you? I think so. I want to find out."

Larna's kiss had given me strength. I wanted another, and so I threaded my fingers through the short hair at the back of her neck, drawing her lips back down to mine. Our second kiss was just as good as the first one. Larna did not have to tell me that she loved me back with words. The hand on my side, her thudding heartbeat, and her warm lips said everything. It was just as Ellie had said. Every moment was better than the one before.

***

"How can you be loving me when you are hardly knowing me?"

It amazed me that Larna could think of such a deep question so early. The sun did not shine through the open windows yet, but it smelled like morning. Larna's voice did not sound hesitant or afraid. She seemed curious, almost hopeful.

I reached across the small table where we sat and rested my hand on top of hers. She let me keep it there. "But I do know you," I said. Larna looked at me with thrilling brown eyes. She waited for an explanation. It took me a moment to find the words. "I know that you are honest. I know that you are brave. I know that you are stubborn..." She laughed and gave me a mock glare, nudging her shoulder against mine. "Let me finish! I know that you are stubborn, but you listen to me anyway. I know that you care for me. And I also think you are very handsome." That made her eyebrows lift, but she accepted the compliment. "The rest of it, your favorite color and that sort of thing, will come later. But I do want to know."

Larna smiled, teasing a lock of my hair with her left hand. Her fingers toyed with it gently. "My favorite color is red." My face turned exactly that color. Larna's hand moved down to stroke my cheek. My heart pounded harder. Her fingers were so soft.

"Have you ever felt that two people can fit? Maybe as friends. But maybe as something else? They are tied together by something invisible, something..."

"*Tuathe*." Larna guessed the word that I was afraid to speak. "Yes, I have been thinking of things like that before. From stories." Both of us were too shy to say more, but the thoughts hung heavy between us. We could sense them.

"My grandmother told stories. I wish I could see her again."

Larna let go of my hair, but kept looking at me. "Tell me more about her?"

"I will, but only if you tell me something about your past." Larna frowned. She always seemed uncomfortable discussing the details of her life before she joined the Farseer pack. If she needed time, I would give it to her. I was grateful for the trust she had already placed in me. "Or something about you, things you like."

"I like you." Larna's frown became a charming smile, and my heartbeat raced faster. "I like swimming. I like to be making things with my hands. I watched the tradespeople in the town I grew up in, the basketweavers and the blacksmiths and the woodcarvers. I enjoy making any sort of thing." And she was strong enough for the work, too, I thought. I admired her broad shoulders and the long muscles of her arms.

"Did you build this hut?"

"I helped," Larna said modestly. "A group of us were putting up most of them together. What do you enjoy, Cate?"

I thought about it for a moment. "I know how to mend and sew, but I don't enjoy it much. I can cook and clean, too. You know, I worked as a servant for so long that I have no idea what I like to do."

"You were a servant?"

"Yes, in Seria. My mother worked for one of the noble families there, and when she died, I took her place. It wasn't a very good life. I worked for a lady and two of her daughters. One of them was kind, and she married my friend Ellie, but the other..." I swallowed, unsure how much of my past I wanted to reveal. "She was cruel to all the servants, especially me. Until Ellie came to live there, she went out of her way to make me as miserable as possible."

A worry line creased the middle of Larna's forehead. "Why?"

"I'm not sure. I don't know if she was born evil, or if something made her that way. She wore an enchanted necklace for a long time. Maybe that had something to do with it...but it doesn't matter. She's in prison now. She can't hurt me anymore, especially now that I can grow claws." I lifted my hands and wiggled my fingertips, trying to lighten the mood.

Larna caught one of my hands and threaded our fingers together. "Aye, you'd be able to take care of her now. I think you're almost ready for your first hunt. Maybe you'll be liking that more than cooking and sewing. They are important tasks, but not much fun. You are needing a few more interesting hobbies."

Suddenly, I realized how much I was missing in my life. I had left Baxstresse behind for a reason, and it was time to start trying new things. "Will you really show me how to hunt? I want to learn something different."

Larna smiled. "I will show you whatever you wish, as long as it is not interfering with your magic lessons. Hunting is exciting, but magic is a part of you."

"You feel like a part of me, too, Larna." Sometimes, it felt like Larna and I were moving too quickly, and other times, everything between us felt incredibly right. I almost regretted speaking until Larna smiled back, showing a row of neat white teeth.

"And you are a part of me."

***

In fairytales, the suffering, the longing, ends when the two lovers find each other at last. But that is only in stories. At Baxstresse, I ached for someone to complete my soul. Now that I had found Larna, I discovered the sharp, persistent pain of waiting. The hardest part was just beginning.

Our touches were cautious. Even our kisses were careful. Knowing she was just across the room, but so far away, left me cold at night. I wanted Larna to return to her bed, where she belonged. With me. But I did not know how to ask. I knew that Larna was waiting for me. At any moment, I could ask her to make love to me, to take what belonged to her. She would accept. But could I give her what she wanted? What she deserved?

I warred with my doubts constantly. What if I disappointed her? What if it was too soon? What if I made a mistake? I did not think that Larna would hurt me, but sometimes, thoughts of Luciana rose to the surface. I worked hard to shove them down.

Perhaps some of it was guilt. Wanting a quiet, tender lover would have been easier on my conscience. But that was not the lover that haunted my dreams. I wanted Larna to have me roughly. I needed her to consume me. Mark me. Claim me. Lose herself in her own need and hurt me a little. Then, I would remember how Luciana had hurt me. That was not what I wanted with Larna at all.

Other times, I thought about Ellie and Belladonna. I remembered the scene I stumbled upon months ago. How tender they had been with each other. The whispered words. The joy and sweetness in their kisses. Would it be like that with Larna?

She had no idea, of course. I was not ready, so she would wait. Larna's thoughts and feelings were not hard to interpret. She was wonderfully simple. I was the one who had become a jumbled mess. I was ready and not ready at the same time, and I ached with wanting.

I hated myself for holding back. My heart urged me to take Larna in my arms and forget everything but her. Knowing that the decision was mine made me sick. Sometimes, I cried myself to sleep, hiding my face in my pillow so that Larna would not wake up and see. Just as often, I woke in the middle of the night, pulsing and close to release with my hand clutching between my legs, waiting for my lover to make me hers while she slept on the other side of the room.

Part Two:

As told by Cathelin Raybrook, and recorded by Lady Eleanor of Baxstresse.

CHAPTER ONE

THE MESS IN KALWYN'S house surprised me all over again the second time I visited. She was standing in the same place where she had waved goodbye to us last time, and it was almost as if we had never left. When she saw us, she said, "Ah, it is the new shaman and the young pup. Come in, but step careful. There are a few things on the floor."

'A few things' was an understatement. Objects were piled and scattered haphazardly around the room. It took some effort to make my way into the front room without stepping on anything. "Good morning, teacher," I said once I had found a safe place to stand. "Am I going to visit the spirit world today?"

Kalwyn smiled. Her face became a netted crosswork of brown wrinkles. In the center were her two black-button eyes, and they glinted cheerfully at me. "What was I saying before? Yes, acha, I will show if you will learn."

"I want to learn."

Larna squeezed my shoulder. "Of course you do." She dropped a kiss on my head, and my face went bright red. Larna and I shared simple touches, but neither of us knew what they meant. They just felt right. Our hugs, our kisses, our linked hands...we were more than friends, but not quite lovers yet. We hung somewhere in between. "Is there any heavy work for me, wise one? I am wanting something to do while you teach."

Kalwyn thought for a moment. "The roof is needing repairs. But I only be letting you fix it to keep you out of trouble! I am not too old for work."

"Of course not," Larna said. I felt the vibration of her voice against my side. "But too old for climbing about on roofs, to be sure."

Kalwyn went to show Larna where the damage was, and where to find her supplies. They left me alone in the cluttered house, and I looked around to occupy myself. The first thing my eyes settled on was the hourglass I had nearly knocked over during my first visit. A long golden rope snaked around its glass body. Perched on top was a miniature golden dragon, its wings stretching out in flight. I realized that the golden rope was actually the dragon's tail, and all of the sand was in the bottom half of the hourglass.

"Ah," Kalwyn said from behind me. "You found that, have you?"

I jumped back, clutching my hand to my chest. My heartbeat seemed unnaturally loud. "I was just looking at the hourglass."

"That is a very special hourglass." Kalwyn picked it up, turning it on its side. The grains of sand inside it did not move. When she flipped it upside down, they did not run back toward the top. I stared at it, confused. "My mother gave it to me, and her mother gave it to her."

"How much time does it measure?"

"It doesna measuring time. It knows when the dragons be returning."

Kalwyn set the hourglass back in its place, and when I reached out to touch it, she did not stop me. It felt warm in my hands as I picked it up. No matter which way I turned the hourglass, the sand did not leave the bottom half. "I thought all of the dragons were gone."

"Not gone, just sleeping," Kalwyn said. "When it is time, the sand in the hourglass will be flowing up to the top."

"How soon?"

Kalwyn shook her head. "How would I be knowing, acha? The hourglass is stopped. Now, we will be using the deadeye." With her dark green folds flapping, Kalwyn shuffled over to a chest of drawers. She began rummaging around while I tried not to stare. After a lot of muttering, she pulled something out and held her fist up in triumph. "Ah, here!"

In her hand was a glossy black stone. It was a round oval, about the size of an egg, but flat and thin. There was a large hole through the center. Kalwyn peered through the gap, and I could see her tiny black eye glinting in the empty space. She was looking at me, but did not seem to see me. She took the stone from her eye and offered it to me.

"The deadeye is very powerful. Dinna be looking through it yet," she scolded as I held it up to my eye. I lowered my hand and clutched it in my palm instead. The stone hummed with energy. It was warm against my skin, just like the hourglass. "There be many ways of talking to the spirits," Kalwyn went on. "Most of them do not use voices. They are sending you feelings."

"What is a spirit? Do we turn into ghosts after death?" I did not like the idea of lingering in the Forest of Amendyr for eternity. Perhaps it was foolish, but I had always pictured some kind of afterlife with my family and friends.

"Only the Maker is knowing what happens to the soul after death. A spirit is only magical energy left behind when a person passes."

I tested the weight of the deadeye in my palm. It was lighter than it looked. As I squeezed, the surface became warmer, and the stone pulsed in my hand. "It feels like it's moving," I whispered, amazed that an object could be so responsive to my touch.

"Lift it. See." I obeyed and lifted the black stone to my right eye.

Thousands of shimmering shapes flickered along the walls, under the chairs, around my legs. They were everywhere, like white water, faintly glowing. Some were just tiny dots in the air, floating alone. Some formed faces and the shapes of bending arms. Two or three looked like full people with clothes, moving around.

"The stronger the magic was in life, the more is being left behind," Kalwyn explained. "Powerful *Ariada* are gathering the energy into shapes, even bodies. Weaker energies are only that—energy."

I watched, fascinated. "Do they remember who they were?"

"In a way. They sense other magic, and they come when they are called. You can be using their energy to increase your own powers."

"I want to talk to them," I said, still peering through the deadeye. The small sparks of light seemed to feel me watching. They swirled around my legs and arms, and I felt warmth and light crawl over my skin. I was filled with energy, but it was not frightening or unpleasant.

"Not yet," Kalwyn clucked. "Give me the stone, acha."

Reluctantly, I lowered the stone. My skin was still warm as I placed the deadeye back in Kalwyn's hand. She tucked it away in her robes. "It is important to know where your power comes from as a shaman. Someday, your energy will be added to what you saw. Now, we will be singing. It is one way shamans draw from the magic around them, just as the wizards use their words of power."

My heartbeat hammered faster. Singing? In front of someone else?

I could carry a tune, but the thought of anyone hearing my voice made me nervous. I wished I had been born a wizard instead. Surely reciting words of power was less humiliating. "I really have to sing?" I asked, shifting my feet uncomfortably.

"You grew up in Amendyr. Sing the winter song."

I sighed. At least it was a song I knew. That made me feel a little braver. All Amendyrri children learned the old songs growing up, but I still did not want to sing. "It isn't winter yet," I protested weakly.

Kalwyn whacked my arm, and although the blow was far from painful, I gripped it sulkily. "Sing!" she ordered. So I sang.

The high wind blows down from the mountains
The tall cliffs climb out of the sea
The sharp wind blows up from the ocean
Come sit by my fire with me
The cold wind blows over the moorland
A white blanket covers the Sweep
The stars in the sky have grown dimmer
So rest in my arms now and sleep

"You," Kalwyn declared, "are a baby. Afraid of a song…" She rolled her eyes. It was not as nice as a 'good job', but it did make me smile. "Now, I will be teaching you tone sets. Sing after me."

After that, we did not sing words. Instead, I learned patterns, combinations of notes that would draw magic closer to me. They started simply. Each pattern only had three or four notes. Then the range got bigger.

Kalwyn made me hold the deadeye and watch while she sang. The white sparks of magical energy gathered around her in a swirling, humming cloud. She sang a mournful half-step, and one of the human shapes came and took her hand. I wondered if she could feel its fingers lacing with hers. "So, you will practice?" Kalwyn asked, glaring at me suspiciously. I was certain she could read my mind. I did not want to practice where other people could hear me, especially Larna.

I resigned myself to my fate. "Yes. I'll practice."

"Good. Next, I will teach you dances."

I almost fell over.

***

The leaves were tinged with red the next morning when I stepped outside. Winter was finally coming, and the scents of pine and wood smoke were strong in my nose. Even though I could feel autumn in the trees, I was only a little cold. The red cape that Sarah had given me kept off most of the chill. Seppea had helped me repair it after my escape from Mogra's cave, and the stitching was so fine that I could barely tell where it had been torn.

My hair tickled my neck as the wind blew it over my shoulders, but the cape's hood blocked the worst of the gusts. I walked along the border of camp, not heading anywhere. I just wanted to be outside, where I could think. Larna was still sleeping inside of our hut, but I decided to let her rest, hoping that some distance would bring me a little peace. I craved her company like nothing else, but wanting her so much frightened me.

A twig cracked behind me, and I glanced over my shoulder. I saw nothing. Lifting my nose, I tried smelling instead. The scent of Wyr was nearby, but that was not unusual. I was still near camp. I had only taken a few steps when I heard the sound again. This time, I knew someone was following me. I thought of turning around and returning to my hut, but whatever was stalking me stood in the way. "Come out," I said, my voice shaking.

I stepped back when Hosta emerged from behind a tree. He was in his human form, but seeing him made me feel uneasy. "Did I startle you?" He spoke smoothly, as though he was concerned, but there was something unsettling in his black eyes.

I avoided the question. "Sorry. I wasn't expecting company."

He took another step closer. I held my ground, refusing to let him back me farther into the woods. "I saw you walking alone. I wanted to make sure that you were all right." Goosebumps rose over my skin, but I was not cold. I recognized the emotions on Hosta's face. It reminded me of Luciana, and I felt sick. My chest tightened, making it hard to breathe. "Do you need a coat?" Hosta offered, reaching to take off his. "That cape doesn't look very warm."

I shook my head. "No, thank you." He reached out, perhaps to say something more, but I hurried past him, walking quickly back the way I had come.

I was so distracted that I slammed right in to something solid and warm. My legs buckled, and I fell backwards onto the grass. My heartbeat slowed down when I saw Yerta's concerned face peering down at me. It surprised me that he could look so different from his brother, even though their features were similar. Maybe it was their expressions. He reached down to help me up, and I bent to brush myself off.

"Did I startle you?" The words made my heart jump. That was exactly what Hosta had said moments before.

I decided to lie. No matter how I felt about Hosta, he had not actually threatened me. "No. I was just looking for Larna."

"I haven't seen her this morning. I thought you were staying with her?"

"I am," I said, turning away to end the conversation. "I apologize for running into you. It was my fault."

Yerta smiled. "Pretty girls running in to me every day? I should be so lucky." I blushed, flattered instead of unnerved by the compliment, and started walking back the way I had come. Before I could get too far, Yerta called after me one more time. "Cate, have you seen my brother? I need to find him."

I turned back and pointed into the trees, gesturing in the direction that Hosta had gone. Yerta headed into the forest, waving a hand to thank me as he went. Once he was gone, I continued my short walk back to Larna's hut. Yerta and Hosta looked so similar. They even said many of the same things. Why did Hosta frighten me so badly? Why did Yerta seem so kind? My thoughts were jumbled, and running in to Hosta had brought back unpleasant memories.

It did not take me long to reach the safety of the cabin, and I forced my stiff fingers to open the door. It was colder than I thought, cold enough to make my hands slow and turn my breath into a silver cloud until the warmth coming from inside washed over me. Larna was sitting up in bed, waiting for me. She stood up and walked over to meet me as soon as I closed the door. "Cate? Did something happen?"

"Nothing that matters," I said. Larna pulled me against her chest, and the warm circle of her arms drove out the last of the autumn cold. I felt bad for worrying her, but I was grateful for her closeness. "It was silly. Someone startled me outside, and it reminded me of a bad time in the past."

Gently, Larna pushed me away from her, and I was sad until I realized that she had done it so that she could see my face. Her brown eyes were soft and warm, and I lost myself in them. "Will you tell me about it? When you feel ready?"

I was grateful that Larna did not push me. Talking about Luciana was difficult, even when I unburdened myself to people like Ellie, who had been there and suffered some of the same abuse. Luciana was no longer a part of my life, but traces of her shadow still lingered.

I ran my fingers down the side of Larna's arm and gave her a smile. Once I gathered my courage, I would tell her everything. "Yes. I'll tell you about it when I'm ready. I promise."

Rae D. Magdon

CHAPTER TWO

"TELL ME THE CARD," Kalwyn said, holding up a thin sliver of paper between us. It seemed like a silly child's game, or the cheating trick of some wandering fortuneteller, but telling Kalwyn what picture was on the card took a great deal of concentration and effort.

I looked through my other eye. The deadeye was a shortcut, a link between two planes, but with Kalwyn's help, I could see the white sparks of magic without it. They gathered at my fingers, around my eyes and mouth. I thought I saw the ghostly form of a man standing by Kalwyn's chair. It was an imprint of someone who had lived here long ago, the last residues of his magic. I had already seen him twice before. The man smiled and made wavy lines with his fingers. Then, he began to fade.

The sparks against my skin hummed, and my mouth twitched into a smile. "Ocean."

Kalwyn nodded. "Good. You are better at cards. Have you practiced singing the tone-sets?"

I had, but only a little. Kalwyn insisted that all shamans sang, but I was not so sure. I did not like the sound of my voice. I refused to sing in front of anyone but my teacher, especially Larna, and I desperately hoped that she could not hear from outside.

Kalwyn noticed my glazed eyes. "You did not," she guessed correctly. I blushed. "Were you studying your history, then?"

"Yes. I think I remember most of the names, but there are so many..."

"You must know history," Kalwyn insisted. "You must be learning of the High *Ariada* and Kalmarin. They are your past. You are their future."

Her words triggered a memory. Suddenly, I recalled my long-ago conversation with Cieran and the promise I had made to him. Surely my teacher counted as a magical scholar, no matter how strangely she behaved. "Kalwyn, what do you know about Umbra?"

Kalwyn looked surprised, but she composed herself quickly. "Where were you after hearing that name?"

"Cieran, the magical advisor in Seria...but you said it, too. I remember now. It was on the first day I met you."

Kalwyn sighed. "Umbra was the last of the High *Ariada*. Not a good man. No, not good. He was trying to steal dragon magic by draining a hatchling. When the magic was released, there was too much for any human to hold. The wizards could not control it. Many died."

"I've heard that somewhere before," I said, trying to remember. I knew that someone had told me that story as a child. Maybe my mother, or even my grandmother.

"It is a children's story. Well, what happened after is a children's story. The Prince of Amendyr went to the hatchling's mother, Feradith, because she had cursed the land with a drought. He offered his life for his kingdom, and she let him live. Instead, she went and ate all the wizards. That was the end of the High *Ariada*."

A vivid image flashed in my mind, a circle of gold ringed with silver. "A necklace. Was there a necklace in the story? My friend, Ellie...her stepsister had a necklace. It looked like an eye, and I think it might have belonged to—"

"Slow down, child!" Kalwyn gave me a reproachful look. "I am not understanding. You go too fast."

The entire story came out in bits and pieces: Luciana, Prince Brendan, the sorcerer's chain, and Cieran's guess about where it had come from. Kalwyn seemed very interested when I described what the pendant looked like. "Maybe it was once belonging to Umbra. I am not remembering anything about a chain in the story, but the burning magic in it could be some of the hatchling's stolen power. Human magic fades, but dragon magic lasts for centuries and stays bright and strong."

My face fell. "But the chain was destroyed. How will we know?"

"Maybe we will never know," Kalwyn said, but I could see unspoken thoughts behind her eyes. "Gather your things, acha. Next time, we will be looking through some of my books. Maybe we will find something to tell your friends in Seria."

***

My lessons with Kalwyn were postponed one day when the Farseer pack decided to take me on my first hunt. It was very informal. Larna remembered that I had expressed an interest in trying new things, and asked if I wanted to come. "As long as I won't be in the way," I said, a little nervous.

"Of course not, little sister," Farseer said. We were in a small group of twelve, gathered by the large fire pit. "Larna told us you were wanting to come. Now that you have been through your first half-shape, it is time."

I regained some of my confidence, but I was still not sure if I could kill another animal. It was not the same as butchering a hog. I would be using my claws and teeth instead of a knife. I did not feel nervous again until the hunting party started stripping. They were casual about it, chatting together as they unbuttoned shirts and kicked off pants. Larna noticed my burning cheeks and stepped in front of me, blocking my view. I cast my clothes away quickly and started the change before anyone could look.

Shedding my human body and shaping myself into a wolf was not difficult. I thought about it, and it was. My fur stretched from the strip sewn into my hips and covered me like a warm glove. My muscles curled into a comfortable, four-legged shape, and I dropped to my hands and knees until they became paws.

The others around me followed, changing their shapes like wind-blown clouds. It was smooth and easy. We all looked to Farseer, whose wolf form was large and brown with silvery scars on his flanks. I felt Larna's dark shape to my right. She was panting, eager to find prey. Yerta was on my left. He gave me a friendly nudge, and I wagged my tail.

Then, as a unit, we felt a new presence touch the edge of our group and turned our heads together. A thirteenth member to our hunting party came from the southern edge of the camp. He was already in his wolf body, which was just as lean and angular as his human one. I recognized his scent, even though I had never seen him under the change's magic. It was Hosta. My muscles stiffened. Larna noticed and placed herself between us automatically.

The other wolves greeted him politely, with open mouths and wagging tails. He and Farseer sniffed, but Hosta kept his tail low, not offering any challenge. Apparently deciding that Hosta could come,

Farseer padded off into a clump of trees to the west, and we all followed him.

I watched every movement of Larna's sleek black body, not wanting to miss any instructions. She had to teach me without words. I observed how she rolled her steps so that she did not make any noise among the leaves and tried to copy her. When she tested the grip of the earth with her claws, I did the same. We communicated silently, but effectively.

Soon, I felt a change ripple through the group. Farseer lifted his head and sniffed the air, turning right, and then left. Finally, he made a quarter circle and went on. Soon, I smelled it, too. A herd of deer had been here not long ago. Farseer began a brisk trot, and we all followed, forming a triangle. Larna stayed near the front at Farseer's right, and I made sure to keep close behind her.

It took us almost an hour to track the deer. They were moving through the forest slowly, grazing and stripping the bark from the trees. Suddenly, Farseer stopped. He held stiff, almost like a pointing dog. His head was thrust forward, his eyes locked on a target. An older stag limped near the back of the herd. He was a giant beast with a majestic set of horns. In his prime, he must have been an impressive sight.

Larna brushed by my side, leading me off to the right. Hosta took another group off to the left. I knew instinctively that we needed to make a half-circle. Like two pincers, the right and left groups would close in once Farseer burst out of the trees. I was not sure how I understood what was happening, but the strategy was obvious to me. Larna showed me how to lower my shoulders and move silently so that the leaves did not catch against my fur. She demonstrated how to tell where I was by smelling the ground, judging our distance.

Everything happened in a blur. Farseer charged out at the back of the herd, sending the large brown bodies hurtling forward like a living river. Their hooves shook the ground. Leaves fell from the trees. Larna started running, and I followed a breath behind her. Our chests rose and fell, and our hearts pounded together. I saw the second group closing in from the other side, cutting off the stag's path to escape. He reared on his hind legs and turned only to find Larna's gleaming white teeth waiting for him. He tried to strike with his hoof, but with a neat clip of her jaws, she moved the deer in the direction she wanted.

It was almost like a game. The stag kept surging forward, trying to break through the circle, and someone would block him. Then, the mighty beast ran for me. I knew it was my turn and peeled my lips back from my teeth. I caught his throat in my jaws and felt sweet blood burst on my tongue. I did not know how to grip, though, and he shook his large, shaggy head free.

Farseer ended it, grabbing hold of the stag's head and pulling him to the ground. I watched, euphoric and tormented at the same time, as the creature's eyes glazed. White specks of foam came from its mouth, and its eyes rolled in terror. Larna gave the creature mercy and tore out its throat. Blood matted the black fur of her chest and stained her mouth.

We ate to regain our strength while the kill was still fresh. Farseer took his portion first. Everyone seemed to know when to approach the steaming body and which part to take. I thought that I would be last, but Larna nudged me forward after eleven of the rest had eaten. Yerta had not taken his portion yet. I looked at him for reassurance. With his tail hanging low, he settled on the ground, waiting.

The taste of food made me forget my confusion, and I ate until my stomach was stretched. I wanted to lie on the ground and sleep after gorging myself, but I only had time to rest while Yerta ate. We started moving again, trailing the herd and searching for another kill to bring back to camp.

***

"You did well today, Cate."

Larna and I were curled up together at the edge of the cook fire. Most of the camp was outside, even though the evening was cool. It was near dark, but the fire gave us some light. The smell of cooking meat was strong, and I felt myself growing hungry again even though I had already eaten at the kill site.

I knew that Larna had more to say. "But?"

"But I was noticing that you became upset when Hosta was near you."

"He does not like you, Larna," I whispered, keeping my voice low. We were sitting by ourselves, but there were other small groups near us. I did not want anyone to overhear. "I have seen him look at you with…hatred in his eyes."

Larna laughed and shook her head in dismissal. "Surely not," she said. "He is part of the pack, Cate. We are all good to each other here. Hosta and I are both respected by Farseer. We are Betas."

"Betas?" I asked, trying not to feel hurt that Larna had not taken my concerns seriously.

Larna raised her eyebrows. "I have not named the rankings for you? You are knowing them already in your blood, since you are following our rules. Farseer is Alpha. Hosta and I are Betas. We are young, strong. We are an example for the pack." There was pride in her voice, but not for herself. I knew from experience that she was proud of the Farseer pack as a whole, and cared about them far more than she cared for her own ambitions.

"Could he be jealous of you?" I asked, trying to think of a reason for his behavior.

Larna thought for a moment. "Well, I have only been here four years. He has been here for six. But perhaps he is a little jealous..." She gave me a meaningful look.

"Because of me?"

"You are young and beautiful, one of the only unmated Wyr in the pack. I think that he wants you. It irritates him that you are showing an interest in me. Dinna let it upset you. He will get over it, and I am sure you will be getting along better."

I doubted it, but I knew that arguing with Larna about the pack was a pointless exercise. Because Farseer trusted Hosta, so would she, and it did not matter what I said to try and change her mind. "But his brother is so nice," I sighed. "Why does Hosta have to be so disagreeable?"

"Yerta is the *Pekah*. He has to be nice."

That word, *Pekah*. Where had I heard it before? I finally remembered. On my first night by the fire, Goran had snapped it at Yerta like an insult. "What does that mean?"

"*Pekah*? It means last. Every pack has one member that is the lowest. Yerta's role is sometimes underestimated, but we are needing him. *Pekah* keep the pack together."

I was surprised at the casual way Larna described Yerta's position. Apparently, she was not upset over the fact that the others snapped at him. I had never witnessed Larna treating him with anything less than respect, but she had never stood up to defend him, either. With the amount of power she commanded, she easily could have stopped the bullying. "That's why he is mistreated sometimes? Just because the pack needs someone to berate? It doesn't seem fair."

Larna shrugged. "Living in a pack is not always fair. Yerta has a good life here. He is still one of us. We would never really hurt him, and we would give our lives to defend him. That is the purpose of the pack. But someone has to be last, or there can be no first. Then, we would have no leader."

I did not like it, but some part of the Wyr in me understood. Larna had been right before. Even though I did not know the names of the pack's ranks, I had instinctively sensed which Wyr were leaders and which were followers. "Is that why Yerta ate last at the kill?"

"Yes. And it is why Hosta and I were eating after Farseer. But think about it, Cate. We made sure he was fed, just the same as us. We are his family. I am respecting his role, just as he is respecting mine. And you should be respecting Hosta's." Larna reached up to stroke my cheek with her knuckles. My skin grew warm, and I forgot about Hosta, and even about Yerta. Larna's eyes drew me in. "You might be his equal sooner than you think. If you become my mate, you can eat with me."

Her voice made my body quiver, but I was not thinking about eating food. I hungered for something else. "I want to be with you," I whispered, burying my face in the curve of her throat. Her long arm hooked around my waist, pulling me close. "But I'm not sure when the right time will be."

"You will know," Larna whispered back. I hoped that she was right, and that our time would come soon.

CHAPTER THREE

KALWYN'S 'LIBRARY' WAS NOT really a library at all. It was more like an explosion of paper, leather bindings, and ink. There were books piled together, scrolls shoved in drawers, and broken quills everywhere. Nothing was organized. As I scanned the mess before me, I began to reconsider one of the first thoughts that had occurred to me upon entering Kalwyn's house. Perhaps Belladonna would not have wanted to visit this library after all. It might have driven her mad.

"I still am not knowing what you are looking for," Kalwyn called out as she re-entered the room. The large stack of books in her arms muffled her voice.

"Neither do I. Hopefully, we'll recognize it when we see it."

We had already spent the morning browsing through some of the less-dusty magical texts. So far, there was nothing about Umbra, and the High *Ariada* were only mentioned briefly. "It's like there is a missing chapter of history," I mumbled to myself. Every time I thought we were on the brink of discovering something useful, we reached another dead end.

As I bent over the page of a yellow book, my quill fell out from behind my ear and clattered to the floor. I bent to pick it up and noticed a scroll shoved beneath my chair. One of us must have shoved it there during our search to clear some room. I pulled it out and unrolled the parchment. It was a rough sketch with faded, blotchy text, and underneath it was the caption, "U__ra and t__ __gh Ariad_ _____ the Hatchling". Not even a complete sentence, but it was enough. The picture did not need words. Thirteen people stood in a circle, all wearing hooded robes. Signs of power decorated the sides and base of a stone table. The corpse of a baby dragon lay on its flat surface. I could guess why the signs had been drawn in red ink. The wizards had probably used the dragon's blood.

"I think I found something," I said, but the happy feeling of success had already faded. I did not want to look at the picture any more.

I handed the scroll to Kalwyn. She held it close to her nose, her black eyes squinting as she craned her neck forward. Then, she gave it back. "See the one behind the table? Look at his chest, acha." I obeyed and saw that one figure stood out from the rest. He was drawn in darker lines than the others. On his chest, above his heart, was a three-ringed circle.

"Put it away," I said, not understanding why I felt so uncomfortable.

"Aye, but you will take it with you when you go. It is only a drawing. It has no power over you, Cathelin." Kalwyn rarely called me by my full name, and I looked up in surprise. "You must be brave."

"I'm not very brave if a simple drawing upsets me this much," I said, a little embarrassed.

Kalwyn was not impressed. "You are braver than you think, and you have learned much during the past few months. Do not be dismissing yourself so quickly."

I knew that there was no arguing with my teacher. "Are you sure that I can take this?" I asked, holding up the yellowed parchment. When I got back to camp, I would copy it into my journal so that Ellie could show it to Cieran. I was no artist, but it was the best I could do.

"Yes." Kalwyn fussed as she tried to put a piece of wrapped bread in my pack. "You will take it. And some food." She was forever trying to give me food when we were not studying, and often claimed that I was too thin. "Some for the young pup, too, but she is not needing the energy."

"Larna always has plenty of energy," I murmured. My thoughts began to wander, and the disturbing images of the robed figures and the baby dragon were quickly replaced by memories of Larna. I pictured her messy black hair, her uneven smile, the powerful line of her body. My heart raced a little faster. Even when I was sad or afraid, thinking of her made me happy again.

I snapped back into focus when Kalwyn said, "Here, take this, too."

She handed me my pack, and set something heavy in my hand. I shifted the weight of the pack so that I could see what she had given me. It was the golden hourglass I had admired so many times on my visits. The sand was gathered in the top half, hanging in suspension, and the tiny dragon coiled possessively around its curve.

"Why are you giving this to me? I can't take it."

"You will be needing it," Kalwyn said. I tried to protest, but she frowned at me. "I am the teacher. You will listen to me." I knew that I would get nowhere arguing with Kalwyn. It was easier to simply take the hourglass. "Here, I have one more gift for you. Taking three things on a journey will be bringing you good luck." I did not know what journey I was going on, but decided not to ask questions. Kalwyn held out the deadeye. A string was threaded through the hole in the middle and tied in a knot at the back. She draped it over my head, tugging the hood of my red cape out of the way.

"Won't you need this?" I asked, concerned.

"You will need it more, acha. Now, go find that handsome woman of yours."

***

"Does it ever bother you, being the *Pekah*?"

Yerta and I were eating lunch together, since Larna was away from camp for two days. She and some of the others had taken a cart and gone to trade with a nearby village. The trip did explain where some of the items in the camp came from, like the salt used to store our meat, but I was worried for her. I knew that being around humans mad her nervous.

Yerta looked up at me, obviously surprised by my question. A flash of something—distrust? suspicion?—crossed his face, but he hid it quickly. "There is always a *Pekah*. Without a last, there can be no first," he said, choosing his words carefully.

I frowned at him. "That is exactly what Larna told me." I missed her very much, and hoped she would make it back tonight in time to fall asleep with me. Even though she still had not joined me in my bed, I enjoyed spending the evenings with her. Her presence calmed me and excited me at the same time, and being apart from her was surprisingly difficult.

"Sometimes it makes me upset, but it is not bad. The pack needs me. I am making sure no one is too serious. It is like a job," Yerta tried to explain.

"It still does not seem right." The pack's treatment of Yerta offended my sense of fairness, perhaps because of the many years I had spent as a servant. That time seemed so distant, and so did the silent, terrified girl who had suffered so much at Luciana's hands. I was a different person now, but I had not forgotten..

"My brother and I lived in a human village once," Yerta said. His tone was guarded, but his words were revealing. "Outcasts are tormented there. Anyone who is different. Here, I am part of the pack. I have a family. I have a role."

Even though I still did not understand, Yerta seemed genuinely happy. I decided to drop the subject. "I am only just learning what it means to be part of a family. I haven't had one in a very long time."

"I am happy for you, little sister." Yerta gave my leg a friendly pat. Then, he hesitated, glancing over his shoulder to make sure that no one else was nearby. He leaned forward, forgetting the rest of his lunch. "I...am wanting to apologize. For my brother. I know that he is watching you."

"He is," I admitted, relieved that someone else had noticed. Larna was completely oblivious, and after the gentle rebuke she had given me last time, I was reluctant to bring the subject up again. Hosta normally made himself scarce whenever she was around, but he had been my shadow during the past few days. Unsettled by his silent attention, I spent most of my time at Kalwyn's hut in order to avoid him. I had only returned here for lunch.

"I have told him to give you space. Let me know if he is still following you."

"I will." It seemed a better option than telling Larna. She would not want to hear ill of another member of the pack, especially without any proof. I still did not know what Hosta's motivations were, and part of me did not care. I just wanted him to stay away from me.

***

I woke to the smell of water. It had rained the night before. Even though I was inside the hut, the smell of damp earth lingered in my nose. I was still adjusting to my stronger senses as I opened the door and stepped out onto the wet grass. The scent of the storm hung somewhere over the treetops, and it was overpowering.

It was still early, and the rest of the pack had not stirred from their own huts. I felt strangely alone, but it was a peaceful sort of isolation. I squinted up at sky, trying to see through the leafy forest canopy. Grey patches of cloud blocked the morning sunlight that usually made dancing patterns on the forest floor. A lonely morning songbird called out twice before flying to another tree.

When I turned to go back inside, I nearly ran into Larna. She was standing in the doorway, and she caught my wrist when I stumbled back, trying to help me keep my balance. The unexpected touch startled me, and I gasped, instinctively pulling away. "Oh," I murmured once my brain had caught up with my eyes. "It's only you. I'm sorry."

"Shhh…" Larna pulled me close to her chest, and I relaxed against her body, my heartbeat drumming at double speed. She smelled warm and clean and good. Her familiar scent reminded my body that it was not in danger. I looked up into her face, my cheek resting just above her breasts. Close to her heart. "I frightened you," she said, sounding disappointed.

I would have shaken my head, but I did not want to move away from Larna. "It was nothing."

"Why? Sometimes when I touch you…" Her forehead tightened, and her words trailed off. "Are you afraid of me?" Larna's voice did not break, but I could hear the tightness in her throat.

"No." I wrapped my arms around her, holding her as tight as I dared. It was a strange and wonderful surprise to feel tall, strong Larna melt in my embrace. "No, I promise. I could never be afraid of you." Larna had already rescued me once. She was so different from Luciana, who hurt people because it brought her pleasure. It made me angry that Luciana still had such a hold on me, even in the forests of Amendyr.

"Then why?"

Larna's dark eyes were so concerned that I had to tell her something. And I could never lie to her. I pulled away from her warmth and sat down in the doorway. Larna sat next to me. "Do you remember when I told you about my life at Baxstresse? The cruel daughter of the lady I worked for?" I did not want to say her name. It was hard to even think it. "She used to…"

"I can be after guessing," Larna said. A shadow crossed her face. "You dinna have to—"

"I do have to." This time, tears rose in my own eyes. They rolled down my cheeks before I could stop them, leaving the line of hair that touched my face wet. "Larna, I'm not…innocent. If you don't want to be with me, I can leav—"

Larna had been stunned into silence when I started crying, but my guilty admission shocked words back into her. "Of course I want to be with you, Oh, sweetling, here...Softly, Cathelin, softly..." She held me tight in her arms, and I felt my heart tearing and stitching itself back together at the same time. The tears passed quickly, only a light storm, and I was left trembling against her. She kissed the top of my head and murmured, "I never meant to make you cry, little bird."

"The past made me cry. You make me happy and safe."

"Cate, if I make you feel safe, tell me. Was she hurting you?"

"Yes," I blurted out before I could change my mind. Larna said nothing as she held me, only kissing my hair again and rocking me softly. Her loose white shirt was stained with wet patches. Neither of us cared. "I was fourteen. It lasted five years."

"Five years?" I could not see her face, but I could tell from Larna's voice that she was shocked. "Five years," she repeated in disbelief. "Not many would be as strong as you after that."

"I'm so ashamed. I wish I was a virgin for you," I confessed in a low whisper. I was not sure that Larna heard me, even with her sharp ears. "You should have been the one..."

Larna tucked her fingers under my chin, tilting my face up. I wanted to look away, but I could not seem to tear my eyes from hers. "But you are," she whispered, drawing comforting circles over my back with her hand. "You are a virgin, Cate."

My face was hot with shame. My lips trembled. I could barely speak. "But she—"

"She forced you. Little bird, your innocence is something that canna be taken against your wishes. Only given. Like your heart."

The truth of what she was saying slowly dawned on me. I started crying all over again, and buried my face back in the folds of Larna's damp shirt. "You...you think that I'm..."

"You are my moon and stars and sky. And if you choose to give that gift to me, I would be honored. But that is your choice. No one else can be making it for you. Besides, only Serians with their silly rules worry so much for innocence. Taking a lover, or even several, does not change you or make you worth less. Only a fool would think so. You are still Cate. If you took someone else to your bed willingly before we met, I would not care at all, as long as you are mine now and you love me."

Larna did not know it, but my choice had already been made. I was relieved that she did not hate me because of my past with Luciana. The idea that I could still be a virgin had never even occurred to me. It was too wonderful and frightening to consider all at once. I tucked it at the back of my heart to examine later, when I was alone. But deep inside of me, a small piece of my soul that I could hardly remember stirred to life again.

Rae D. Magdon

CHAPTER FOUR

I AM RUNNING, WEAVING through a cluster of sharp-needled pines. Another wolf is following my scent. She is still too far back to see me in the dark, but she can smell me. I push myself faster. A clawing, aching need deep in my lower belly almost overwhelms the sharp burn in my lungs, but I know that I cannot stop. Not yet. I want her, but she has to catch me first.

Roots and earth move under the pads of my paws. I race around a thick tree trunk, changing direction. The other wolf closes the gap between us. I can hear a river ahead of me, and I change course, heading toward it. The water will hide my scent, but she is so close behind me that she might be able to follow me by sight.

My strength is fading when I reach the bank of the river. Part of me wants to stop running and let her catch me, but it is too soon. A lean silver body flashes through the trees. I leap into the river, holding my nose above the water as I swim for the opposite bank. I hear a splash behind me as I haul myself on to dry land, scrambling up the bank. The other wolf is swimming after me.

The urge to stop running grows stronger, but I charge forward, water flying from my fur. The other wolf has crossed the river. Within a few moments, she is on me, her teeth gripping my throat. Her jaws do not close in a death bite. Instead, she bends her head, forcing me to lower my body to the ground. Instinctively, I roll onto my back, revealing my soft, vulnerable belly...

A rippling heat consumed every inch of my skin, and I howled as I returned to my body. My eyes darted around the small wooden cabin. My heartbeat was heavy and quick, as though I had been running in a short burst. My lips parted in a silent scream, and my body vibrated with need. I stumbled to my feet. Something was wrong. Something was happening to me, and I had to find Larna. My muscles thrummed with energy, and I wanted to run again.

I burst out of the cabin and ran down the steps, unashamed of my nakedness. My flesh burned even in the cool night air. My heart pounded in my head, and its echo throbbed between my legs. Slickness and heat ran along my inner thighs. "Larna," I called, not caring who heard me in the dark. "Where are you?" There was no answer. I raised my chin, trying to pick up her scent. It was thicker than usual, and once I found it, I was off, tracking her deep into the forest. I did not notice the leaves beneath my naked feet, or even the moon above me. I was completely fixated on Larna.

I found her with her back against a slender ash trunk. She arched her spine, tossing her head back as she fought off half-shape. Her muscles twitched, rolling beneath her skin, and her teeth were gritted tight. One of her hands was cupped between her legs. Her breath came in short gasps, and I felt my own breath quicken as I watched her. I longed to hurry over to her, to shove her fingers aside and...and...another wave of heat crashed over me. I yelped, almost losing my balance. Larna looked up, seeing me for the first time. Fear and hunger shone on her face.

"Leave, Cate," she ordered, her voice cracking. "Walk far away until it passes."

I did not move.

Larna bared her fangs at me, her eyes clearly more wolfish than human. She growled low in her throat. "Fight it! I am not wanting it to happen like this..." The desire to run swelled in me again, twice as powerful as before. My legs shook, and I turned to look at the trees. *Run.* All of my instincts were telling me to run. "Cate..."

But I was already off, casting off my human body like water and shifting to all fours. I ran, hurtling through the grove of pines from my dream. Larna was right on my heels, panting seconds behind me. She was too close, closer than she had been in the dream. I summoned my strength and dodged away, trying to throw her off by circling a pine tree. It worked, and she fell a few paces behind.

I listened for the river, my paws drumming over the forest floor. The sound of running water grew louder, but the pounding rush of my own blood in my ears almost drowned it out. Finally, I reached the bank. I bunched my muscles and launched myself into the stream. As soon as my body crashed past the surface, I swam furiously for the other side.

Larna jumped in behind me just as I scrambled onto the opposite shore. She was a strong swimmer, and it only took her a few powerful kicks to cross after me. I tried one last time to find cover in the trees, but I was not fast enough. Larna's teeth closed around my neck, and she pressed me gently to the ground. The bite was not painful, but it was unyielding.

I lifted my paws in the air, whimpering as Larna released my throat and nuzzled my exposed belly. She shifted back to her human form at the same moment I did, and her nuzzle turned into a light butterfly kiss. She looked up at me with familiar brown eyes, snaking up my body and brushing her breasts over mine. At last, she bent down to taste my lips. I sighed into her mouth, surrendering myself completely. Instead of kissing me again, Larna jumped back as if she had been burned. She thrashed and contorted on the hard earth. Her nails scoured the ground, too sharp to be human, and a howl tore from her throat. Sheets of muscle rippled along her stomach as she wavered on the edge of half-shape again. I did not understand. She had caught me, and I was hers. I could scent her need. She was supposed to have me.

"Larna, stop," I whispered, crawling over to her and cupping her face in my hands. Her eyes were wide and frantic, but clouded with desire. "Love me instead. Love me..." I took her mouth with mine, and her lips parted for me. My tongue traced the outline of her pointed teeth, but I did not kiss her too forcefully. Something deep and primal in me knew that I was not meant to be the aggressor in this dance. Not this time, at least.

"No," Larna moaned, pulling her head away from mine. My heart ached when she tried to scramble away from the warmth of my body, but I held her tight. "You did not...choose..."

"You are what I choose," I pleaded, not ashamed of begging. I needed her like sunlight and air. I locked my fingers behind her back, wanting to draw her in until she was a part of me. "I love you, I love you, I love you," I told her over and over again, kissing her cheeks, her eyebrows, her forehead.

"I...canna..." Larna tried to say, but she was already on top of me, caging me between her arms. My nails scoured down her back as her teeth grazed my shoulder. The slick warmth pressed just above my knee told me what she could not. Her lips covered every inch of me, sucking roughly at a vulnerable pulse point in my throat, pressing light kisses to the soft undersides of my wrists, biting the tips of my breasts. She devoured me, consumed me. I cried out into the open air, not caring what creature or person could hear.

"Larna." Her name was the only thing in my mind, the only word on my lips. Her trembling hands stroked my legs as her mouth tried to cover all of my skin at once. Everything was happening in a rush, but Larna was still holding back. I could feel her shaking. "Larna. Take me…"

"No," she whispered against my throat. She kissed a trail to my lips and tugged on the lower one with her teeth. "You are…not ready…"

But she was wrong. I was more than ready to be hers, and this time, it was all my decision. I dragged her hand between my legs. "I am ready. Take me now."

Larna gave up her fight and surrendered. "I'll be gentle," she whispered along my cheek. She did try to be careful as her fingers tested the ring of muscle at my entrance, but she quickly forgot. Her hand pushed forward, filling me with one quick stroke, stretching me until it burned. There was a little pain, but not the kind of pain I knew. This was a deep, steady ache that stretched out like a ribbon and made me forget my name.

Her fingers curled forward, dragging over a full place that made me pulse with want. I shivered as she put pressure against it, clinging tight to her broad shoulders. Luciana had never made me feel anything like this, but Larna's touch made my body blossom open and come alive with desire. My inner walls twitched, clinging tight to her fingers as she tried to withdraw them. I wanted her to stay inside of me forever.

I changed my mind when she finally began thrusting. Each smooth push of her hand made me cry out, and I became a mess of shudders. Before I could beg for more, she added another finger, and I gasped at the new fullness. The hard point just above my entrance throbbed, and I cried out when she scraped over it with her thumb. My hips began rocking instinctively, and the two of us moved as one, skin sliding together.

"Oh, Cate," Larna groaned against my neck, nipping just beneath my ear. "You're so soft. Warm. I've never felt anything so wonderful." Those words made me want to feel her, too. Somehow, I forced my hand between our sweat-slicked bodies. My fingers found her easily, and she sighed deep in her chest. The coating of wetness made her skin impossibly smooth. My stomach twisted as her thrusts halted, allowing me to adjust to what I was doing. She was right. I had never felt anything so wonderful.

"Cate, inside," she growled, and I obeyed. Her muscles trembled and pulsed around my fingers. I tried to move against her, but I was caught. After a few deep breaths, her grip relaxed. I could still feel Larna inside of me. Being inside of her at the same time was almost too much for my senses to handle.

Larna gave me quick, open-mouthed kisses with each thrust of her hand. I tried to hook my fingers forward, copying what she was doing, and when the rough pad of her thumb began to paint maddening circles over me, I searched for her as well. As soon as I found the right spot, her hips went rigid above mine. Her scent was in my hair, my skin, and all around me, driving me into a frenzy. Every touch, every sigh, every movement screamed of Larna. I could not forget who was loving me.

"Harder," I pleaded. I wanted her to fill me, to drive inside of me until I could not take any more of her.

"I'll hurt you," Larna mumbled, kissing a line of fire across my shoulder. Her left hand explored the strip of fur that still rested above my hips, where Mogra had sewn it into my flesh. I could feel her touch on the wolfskin belt as though it was a part of me.

"You won't." I knew that Larna could never really hurt me. Her Wyr blood made her stronger, but I was stronger, too, and I wanted all of her. And so Larna took me harder. Our arms and legs tangled together, and tears leaked from my eyes as she pumped into me. She had forgotten her promise to be gentle, but neither of us cared. My mate was finally claiming me as hers, and it was perfect.

Larna was tireless, her powerful muscles rolling under her warm skin as she moved against me. My head spun, my blood burned. My inner walls trembled around her, and I felt swollen almost to the point of pain. I could barely remember to keep moving my own fingers inside of her. Something terrifying and wonderful was happening to me, and I was afraid. "What...I can't...oh, please..."

She stopped my words with a brief, hard kiss before whispering in my ear and along my neck. "Shh, my little bird. Let go for me."

Our gazes locked, and I found paradise. I flung one of my knees around her hips, driving down onto her fingers until they were buried to the hilt inside of me. One more pass of her thumb shattered me, and I lifted my head and howled, pushing out a flood of warmth into her hand. She stayed inside of me, but each pull of her fingers drew out another hot, shuddering spill of pleasure. My first release. I had never been interested in achieving it on my own, and it was impossible with Luciana. Only Larna made me feel safe enough to let go.

Seconds later, I felt heated silk flutter wildly around my own hand. Larna clutched me tight against her, clinging to my hip and sinking her teeth into my throat as she jerked hard above me. Wetness covered my knuckles, and I did my best to keep moving within her even though I had no idea what I was doing.

Larna slowly stilled above me, and both of us collapsed in to each other. We were still pressed close. I could feel her heartbeat thundering against my arm. Gently, she withdrew her hand, and I did the same, whimpering a little at the loss. A sudden thought struck me, and I checked between my legs. No, Larna had not torn me, but I felt very tender. I hissed at the touch, even though it was my own.

"Do you be hurting, Cate?" Larna asked, watching me with nervous eyes as she stroked the side of my face.

"No," I said. The lingering soreness was a pleasant reminder of what Larna had given me. "You?"

A flush stole across Larna's cheeks beneath the moonlight. "Only a little." She took a deep breath before settling down beside me. "I have never been on a mating run before."

It took me several moments to realize what she was trying to tell me. When I finally understood, my eyes snapped open in surprise. "Larna, why didn't you tell me?"

Larna tucked her chin over my head and closed her eyes. "Wolves mate for life when they can."

My throat hardened, and my heart felt too big for my chest. A few more tears ran down my face and pooled on Larna's shoulder. "I didn't feel…I wasn't thinking…"

"I wasna thinking, either. But I am glad." There was a nervous, hopeful expression on Larna's sharp-planed face. Instead of a sleek, powerful hunter, she reminded me of a half-grown puppy, still unsteady on her long legs. "Did I…please you, Cate?"

She made such an adorable picture that I had to take her in my arms and hold her tight. "Larna, you were beautiful. It was the most amazing thing I have ever felt."

I could tell that Larna was embarrassed, but she squeezed me harder. My brave warrior was not used to being vulnerable, even around me. "Me too. Cate." The words coming out in a rush. "Stay with me. Be my mate. Please."

I closed my eyes and rested my head against her arm. "Forever? You promise?"

"Forever. I promise."

There was nothing I wanted more.

CHAPTER FIVE

THE NEXT MORNING WAS just as wonderful as the night before. I was alone when I opened my eyes, but Larna had left me a young deer for my breakfast. My lips pulled in a smile as I sat up and admired the young buck. I was flattered that Larna had given her kill to me. For any animal, especially Wyr, food meant survival. Placing someone else's survival above your own was the greatest token of affection in our world.

Still giddy with pleasure, I slipped effortlessly into my other form to eat. Once I was finished, I could change back without getting sick, but human teeth were useless for tearing through fur and crunching bones. I ate quickly, only pausing to look up when I heard the snapping of a twig or movement in the leaves, but Larna was nowhere to be found. Soon, the desire to find Larna outweighed my hunger. I lifted my nose, trying to scent which direction she had gone. Her trail led straight toward the river, and I hurried after her at an easy lope, leaving breakfast behind.

It took me less than a minute to find her. I stopped just beyond the tree line, freezing as soon as I spotted her in the middle of the river. Daylight flattered her form even more than moonlight, and I let my eyes wander along the smooth curve of her naked torso. They dipped into the shadows under her ribs, stopping just above her small breasts. Her broad shoulders and strong arms were covered in droplets of water. I wished I could look between her legs as well, but the river ran just above her waist.

After I had gazed my fill, Larna lifted her head and cast a glance into the trees. If she could not see me in the shadows of the forest, she could surely smell me. "You could probably be seeing better if you came closer," she teased, her lips pulling into a smile.

With no reasons left to hide, I pushed aside the branches of a sapling with my nose and padded out onto the grass beside the river. Larna smiled, her wet hair clinging to her cheeks and the side of her neck. It had grown a little longer since my arrival, but it was still well above her shoulders. I changed back into my human form and stood up. The desire in her eyes made me forget to breathe. I trembled as she stalked towards me through the water, and before I knew it, I was running to meet her. I splashed into the river and slid into her arms as if I had done it for a thousand lifetimes. We were a perfect fit.

Larna tucked her chin over my head and rocked me for a few moments. Our naked stomachs pressed together, and I could feel the thud of her heartbeat against my skin. She was wet, but not cool, and the heat from her body made me forget the river's chill. Her touch made my flesh burn. Impulsively, I stood up on my toes and pressed my lips against hers. We both stayed perfectly still for a long second, but finally, she opened her mouth to mine and wrapped an arm around my waist.

I kissed her until I had no more breath in my lungs. Even when we finally broke apart, Larna lips skimmed over my cheeks, my eyelids, my forehead. "Last night was too fast," she murmured next to my ear. "This time, we will be learning together."

My mouth wandered over her wet skin, exploring a warm shoulder. She tasted like salt and fresh, clean water, and I could not have enough. When she arched her back, allowing me to explore, I bent my head to kiss the outline of her breast. I cherished each low sigh, every encouraging stroke of her hand through my hair. Soon, I was lashing the hard point of her nipple with my tongue, refusing to give it up until she stroked the side of my cheek and moved me away.

Larna pulled us deeper into the river, walking backwards until the current tugged at our legs, forcing us to cling tighter to each other. Smooth river rocks slid beneath our feet, but she helped me keep my balance. I cupped water in my hands and poured it over her broad back, watching it roll down her spine and return to its source. A shudder rolled beneath her smooth, tanned skin, and I realized that I wanted to kiss every inch of her.

I pressed my face into Larna's neck and felt the throb of her heartbeat under my lips. Shyly, I pressed my mouth over her pulse point and sucked, smiling inwardly as the muscles along her back tensed beneath my hands. Before Larna, I had never understood how much trust a kiss like that could hold. For a Wyr to offer their throat, they needed to feel very safe. I was glad that I was the one who made Larna feel that way.

She turned, and I gave her my own throat. She latched on just above my shoulder, tugging lightly with her teeth. The bite was gentle, but clearly possessive, and I tightened my grip on her strong arms. Her palms stroked in circles over my stomach, and I let her and the water carry my weight.

"Do you trust me?" she asked, the words a low rumble against my neck. She smiled, shifting her weight and sliding her thigh between my legs.

"Yes. Please." I closed my eyes and made a satisfied sound in the back of my throat. "Harder," I breathed, pressing down above her knee.

"We are having time," she reminded me.

I rested my cheek against her warm shoulder, trying to calm my racing heart. I knew that she was right. The burning need of the night before smoldered just beneath the surface, but I wanted to experience everything she could give me, even if it required a little patience.

"I love you," Larna whispered, planting a soft kiss on my forehead.

"I love you, too." My hips jerked as Larna's fingers climbed higher. My legs started to shake, and I whimpered, trying to push myself against her hand. She skimmed kisses over my cheeks and face, teasing me with the tips of her fingers and brushing the pad of her thumb over the hard, swollen bud above.

"Relax," she whispered, kissing along my shoulder. "Open for me."

I went limp in her arms and let her have what already belonged to her. She eased inside of me slowly, pushing forward only to pull back moments later. Her thumb swept around the point of my clit in deliberate circles, pushing back its hood and teasing me to hardness. I had never felt so sensitive there before, and each pass made my inner walls shake. I trembled in her arms, hooking one of my legs around her calf and burying my face in her sweet-smelling neck. "Please, inside…"

Larna took pity on me. She eased two of her fingers forward. They sank into me effortlessly, even beneath the water. I shuddered, expecting her to begin moving immediately, but instead, she held perfectly still. Before I could start begging again, she gripped my waist with her other hand, urging me to hook my knees around her hips. "Hold on." I looped my hands behind her neck, and the muscles in her arms flexed. She lifted me up through the water, never faltering as she took my full weight. With her fingers buried deep inside of me and my legs wrapped tight around her waist, she carried me to a shallower spot.

"What are you doing?" I nipped the soft place beneath her jaw, pressing a soothing kiss there as soon as I let go. And since her lips were so close, I had to taste them, too.

"The water canna be stealing all of your wetness away," Larna said in between kisses.

She began moving within me again and I was grateful that we had found a shallower spot. Underwater, her quick, short strokes would have been dry and painful. But soon, I forgot all about water and the river, even though I was in the middle of it. The steady thrusts between my legs became uneven as both of us flew higher. The sounds that Larna was making drove me mad. Shallow panting, desperate whimpers, the occasional low growl. All of them sent a tingling rush of heat over my skin. It came from somewhere deep inside of me, near the base of my spine.

I angled my hips up, my hands opening and closing behind Larna's head. I was torn between clutching at her shoulders and tugging her hair as she kissed me. The feeling of Larna inside me sent heavy jolts of pleasure across my hips and along my stomach. It hurt wonderfully, and I wanted more. "I'm close," I murmured, not really aware of what I was saying. "Please. Let me come."

The soft words, half of them lost in our breathing, made Larna take me even harder, and the bliss I had known the night before washed over me again. The point of my clit jumped beneath her thumb, and I spasmed around her fingers with short, sharp pulses. My body arched violently into hers for several timeless seconds, and I was nearly carried away by the river. Larna clung to me, anchoring my weight as my muscles clenched with aftershocks.

Once it was over, I felt pleasantly sore and drained. I barely felt Larna's fingertips still stroking me, calming me down. As my misfiring senses started to sort themselves out, her gentle touches became painful. "Please, too much," I groaned.

Larna removed her hand and held it to her lips, sucking her wet fingers clean. Her other arm remained firmly anchored around my waist, and she held me tight until I found my balance.

***

"Larna, what happened last night?" We were stretched on the green grass, snug in each other's arms. Everything around us was still and peaceful. Even the river moved more slowly, and the voices of the birds were subdued. My eyes were closed, with my face resting on Larna's shoulder, but I could sense her thoughtful expression. She was choosing her words carefully.

"You came into your heat," she said at last. "All Wyr are needing to mate. Your instincts told you to run. I had to catch you to prove that I am strong enough to be giving you pups."

"Will we have children?" I asked, a little frightened. Larna smiled above me. Her hand caressed my stomach, and I imagined a tiny Larna growing inside. The fear receded, and I felt warm and safe. With her, the idea did not seem so overwhelming.

"Not yet, little bird. Two females canna have a litter without a bit of magic." I was relieved. The idea of children was appealing, but I wanted Larna to myself for a while longer. We were still getting to know each other, and I did not want to rush the process. All I knew was that I wanted to stay by her side for as long as possible.

"So, you want...with me?" My cheeks turned pink, and I was unexpectedly pleased.

Larna kissed my hair, and I opened my eyes, wanting to see her face. "Someday, maybe. But most of all, I want what you want."

"I want what you want, too." I sighed and closed my eyes again, cuddling closer to Larna's warm side. She was the perfect shape to rest against, and her arms fit just right around my waist. "Will you go into heat, too?"

"Eventually, in a few months. I did not know yours would be happening this soon, or I would have been telling you earlier." I felt Larna's frown, even though my eyes stayed shut. I was completely in-tune with her expressions, with every thought and emotion that flitted across her mind. "I am sorry, little bird. Everything happened so fast."

"I was with you. I wasn't afraid," I said in a tired whisper. The heat spreading from Larna's skin to mine was making me sleepy. I wanted to drift off beside her. "If a Wyr has no mate, what do they do when they go into heat?"

"They run. Some do mate with a lone wolf or temporary partner. Others go off on their own, frustrated, waiting. It is unpleasant." I realized that Larna was referring to her own experiences. "Some relieve the ache themselves, but it is not the same. It was you I was needing so horribly."

"You have me to take care of that now," I said, stroking her thigh. The muscles flexed against my palm. I suddenly realized that I had not really taken care of Larna. She had given me release over and over again, but I hardly paid attention to her. That needed to change. I kissed the pulse-point in Larna's throat, wandering down along her collarbone. Her skin was wonderfully warm. I took in a deep breath, enjoying her scent.

"Catie?" she asked, looking down at me with large brown eyes. I stroked the tips of her breasts to hardness with my thumbs. "Are you…"

But there was no stopping me. I wanted Larna to feel all of the pleasure that she had given me. I found every mark on her body, kissing each freckle, stroking every small scar. I wanted to learn which spots made her skin tingle and her breath quicken. Soon, she was breathing hard, and my head hovered just beneath her hips. I looked up at her. "Please? Let me?"

Larna let her legs fall open, her stomach rising and falling in short, sharp gasps. Feeling more confident than I expected, I gazed hungrily at the treasure before me. Her outer lips were full, swollen open for me, and her inner folds shimmered with wetness. They were red at the very edges, and so was the tip of her clitoris. The rest of her body was powerful, but here, she was completely soft.

I leaned closer, and Larna's fingers wove through my hair as I traced over her with my fingertips. A gasp caught in my throat as they glided through warm silk. I caught her between two fingers, tugging the base of the sensitive shaft. Her hips bucked, and wetness spilled out beneath my hand. I looked up into her eyes, seeing the strain in her face. She was beyond words, lost in pleasure. Her skin burned where it touched mine, and she looked so overwhelmed that I wondered if she would cry or scream. Secretly, I hoped for both. I wanted my Larna to shake apart and dissolve. I wanted her to find paradise.

As Larna shuddered above me, I scattered kisses across her thighs and outer lips. She blossomed open for me in a soft pink line. Her wetness made the skin impossibly soft. Part of me wanted to just stroke her and see what happened, but I found my face drawing closer and closer. Her hips jerked at the first swipe of my tongue, and she almost pulled away. I held still, waiting, until she settled back against my mouth.

Once she relaxed, I learned every inch of her with kisses. I covered her with broad, flat strokes of my tongue at first, teasing her until she pulled my hair a little too tight. I shifted down to explore the tight ring of muscle at her entrance. I tasted salt and sweetness, and I pushed inside, trying to coax more of her into my mouth. Her inner walls fluttered, and she pushed her hips down so hard that my jaw ached, but I did not care. I wanted everything she had to give me.

I spent countless minutes tormenting her, pressing inside and drawing back, savoring each reaction I pulled from her body. Her stomach muscles pulsed, and her thighs flexed in my hands as I held them open. Her voice wavered between loud and soft, sometimes screaming, sometimes whispering my name. They were the most beautiful sounds I had ever heard.

Finally, I pulled back, running my tongue over my lips as I stared at the slick, swollen flesh I had tasted. The point of her clit stood out from beneath its hood, begging for my attention. I dipped my head, tugging it into my mouth and lashing my tongue over the very tip. Larna's breathing became shallow and uneven. Her legs flexed, and her head tossed from left to right. I gripped her hips and pulled her down to me. She fit perfectly, swelling to match the shape of my mouth. My head swam, and my senses were flooded with Larna. Her warmth, her taste, her smell. And I wanted her.

I was so proud, so filled with love and joy, when Larna arched her back and screamed my name. She was beautiful. Her voice broke, and the clinging silk of her muscles trembled and fluttered in my hand. Glistening warmth spilled over my lips and into my mouth, and I drank all I could, savoring the salt and sweetness. My tongue kept gliding over her until I could not coax out any more wetness.

Reluctantly, I pulled my mouth away, but I continued stroking her with my hand even after her body went slack beneath me. I wanted to draw another peak out of her. I could not get enough of her tight, clinging heat, or the low, desperate noises that tore from her throat whenever I found just the right spot.

I kissed up along Larna's stomach, feeling the muscles twitch under my wet lips. Her strong arms wrapped around my neck, and she dug her nails into my shoulders before clutching at the back of my head. Her hands were gentle as they toyed with my hair, but her body was still pulled tight with tension. "Catie," she murmured, trying to push herself harder against my fingers. "Please, I need more."

I was too excited to hold her on the edge. One brush of my thumb, and Larna was lost again. I pressed a kiss to her handsome mouth, sharing her taste as she released a second time. Wetness ran over my fingers, and I pushed as deep as I could go, cherishing each twitch, each rippling pulse of muscle. The kiss did not break until I had drawn the last sharp contractions out of her, curling my fingers forward and moving my thumb in short sweeps.

"Ah, how I love you," Larna murmured weakly, pressing her damp cheek to mine as she finally floated back down to earth.

I kissed her again. "I'm glad."

"Proud of yourself?"

I blushed, but smiled at her. Our faces were touching, so she could not see it, but I knew she felt it. "Well, maybe a little."

CHAPTER SIX

RETURNING TO CAMP WAS awkward and embarrassing for both of us, and the fact that we had no clothes only made it worse. It was just a few hundred yards to Larna's house from the edge of the trees, but it seemed like a thousand miles. We walked the short distance in wolf form, but I still felt naked as several members of the pack watched us with knowing looks on their faces.

"I hoped no one would notice we were gone," I said when we changed back inside of Larna's cabin. Even without fur, my face still burned.

Larna kissed my hair, running a hand up and down my bare back. Reluctantly, she pulled away to find some clothes. "They would have smelled you coming into your heat anyway." I sniffed the air around me, trying to notice if my scent was different. Larna smiled and shook her head, watching me over one shoulder. She was bent down to look for a shirt, and I made a point of enjoying the view. "Your nose is used to your own smell. You wouldna be noticing it."

"That must be why the ladies at Prince Brendan's court never notice when they have on too much perfume."

"Perhaps," Larna said. "I have never been to any court."

"You're lucky, then."

Larna handed me one of her long shirts and a pair of my leggings to wear. I held the shirt to my nose and inhaled before putting it on. "Dinna be surprised if people are congratulating you," she warned me before we went back outside.

I realized that, in the eyes of the Farseer Pack, Larna and I were in something a little like a marriage. Perhaps it was not as official, but we were clearly coupled. That thought excited and frightened me at the same time, but mostly, I was happy. Maybe someday, once enough time had passed, Larna and I could have a ceremony so that Ellie could see my wedding. Thinking about Ellie reminded me of my journal. I wanted to write in it, but I wasn't sure what to say. Could I put something so personal on paper, even if the one reading it was my best friend?

I decided to save the letter for that evening and left the hut to meet the rest of the pack. I could not stay hidden inside forever. A small crowd was gathered on the front steps, with Seppea at their head. "You are glowing, little sister," she said when I stepped out of the door. "I thought I was seeing you creep back in here."

"I hoped no one saw," I mumbled over her shoulder as she pulled me into a warm hug. Once she let go, the others came forward to offer their congratulations. I was even more embarrassed than before, and wished that I had waited for Larna to accompany me.

Yerta gave me a teasing grin as he took his turn. "In my village, friends sang under the windows when a couple was joined. Should we sing under your window tonight, Cate?"

I shook my head. "No singing, please, at least not from you." Everyone laughed, and I felt better once the focus shifted away from me.

The next few minutes were a blur. There were hugs and handshakes and cheerful blessings. Before I knew it, people were preparing a large meal. Larna came out of hiding to join me, and I felt much better holding onto her arm.

"This will turn into a party," she warned me, whispering in my ear. "I was worried about this." I sighed. Part of me wanted to shut myself away with Larna for just a little while longer and forget the rest of the world, but the pack's happiness was infectious. Soon, I was talking and laughing with everyone else, unsure why I had ever been worried at all.

***

It started with a smell. One moment, everyone was eating, laughing, and telling jokes. The fire warmed my face, and my cheeks ached with smiling. Then, in less than a heartbeat, everyone around the fire pit went silent. As one, we turned and looked south, lifting our noses into the air. The scent was heavy and coppery, almost like blood, and it was thick with musk and fear. There was a twisted, humming energy in it, too, and I recognized the pulse of magic.

"What is it?" I whispered, but when I looked around the fire pit, no one met my eyes. They did not want to answer my question.

"Shadowkin," Larna said at last, setting her mug aside. She inhaled again. "Maybe kerak with them."

The names were unfamiliar to me. "Shadowkin? Kerak?"

"Demons made from bad magic. The Queen uses them."

"Canna be," Hosta protested from beside her. "They are only more of Mogra's twisted things. There have been no shadowkin or kerak here since we moved camp. And we dinna even know if the Queen is real..."

"She is real," Larna insisted. Her eyes locked with Hosta's in a silent challenge. The entire camp listened to them argue, gathering closer around the fire. "The witch was never making creatures like this before the old king died. And if she wasna real, there would be no army growing in the mountains beyond the Forest."

"There is no army, either." Hosta began to object, but Farseer silenced him with a look.

"Arguing will wait. Go and bring the torches, as many as you can carry." Reluctantly, Hosta turned his back and melted into the darkness, disappearing from sight without another word.

Farseer stood up from his seat and faced the rest of us. The fire cast eerie shadows in his hollowed face, and he looked older than I had ever seen him. "If the witch knows of our new camp, we must fight. We canna keep running every time she finds us." His word was final, and all of us accepted his judgment.

We stood up without being told. The few youngsters and the very old bolted themselves inside their huts, stacking chairs and tables in front of the doors. The rest of us started bringing firewood. A few gathered more kindling, leaves and twigs from the ground. We piled them in the fire pit, building it into a large blaze, and then an unsteady, stretching tower. Sparks leapt, licking the dry wood. It was the biggest fire I had ever seen.

The shadows beneath the trees lengthened, and still we worked. "Are they coming?" I whispered to Larna from the corner of my mouth. Her eyes were slits, and her jaw was a sharp, tense line. She looked wary.

"Their smell is heavy. They will be here."

"Why didn't we run?" I asked.

Larna was shocked. "Leave our territory? Never. Not again. We will defend it with our lives."

For the first time, I realized the danger we were in. I had never seen shadowkin or kerak, but if Mogra had created them, surely they were dangerous. Some of us might die. Even Larna. The thought left me cold. I was not afraid for myself, because I was sure that Larna would protect me. But who would protect her? I clung to her, drawing her close and soaking in her warmth, her heartbeat, the rising and falling of her chest. All the things that meant she was alive. "Be careful..."

There was no time for Larna to answer. A noise came from our left, and a rotting, sickly-sweet scent filled my nose. I gagged on air, spitting to rid my mouth of the taste. "Kerak," someone shouted, and I followed the sound with my eyes. A long, slender form stalked out from between the trees. Its body was vaguely human, but twisted and stretched like clay. Its arms and legs were too long, and its nails were curved hooks. The thing stalked forward on all fours like a prowling cat, and as it drew closer, I realized that it had no eyes. Instead, its entire face was taken up with a large, gaping mouth.

Larna was the first to react. She reached and grabbed a stick from the edge of the fire, setting its tip ablaze. As the kerak lifted its head, she charged. It raised its hooks to slash down, but Larna was faster. The second the flames touched its skin, a howl of agony erupted from its wide, gaping throat.

As if it had been a signal, the forest exploded with other shapes. Kerak prowled around the edges of the camp, lifting their heads as if to scent us. They were followed by big, blue-black shadows that looked like hulking dogs. I knew that they must be the shadowkin. Their mouths were filled with black teeth, and their muscles bulged under their tough hides. There were also changed Wyr among them, but not our kind. Their movements were jerky, like puppets on strings, and they did not smell like us. Mogra was controlling them, although I did not see her among the army of invading monsters.

"Cate, take this," Yerta said from somewhere beside me. I was surprised to see him, but he shoved a lit torch into my hand before I could say anything. "Fire hurts the demons the most. If you touch them with it, they will burn to nothing."

"What about the Wyr?"

"You are faster. Go!"

He pushed the middle of my back, forcing me forward. Around me, the rest of the pack tore out of their clothes, changing into their half-shapes. I did not have time to be embarrassed. I followed their example. Hair sprouted along my back, covering my skin, and my muscles lengthened. In this form, the scent of magic burned even more painfully in my throat, and my eyes watered. I held the torch closer to my face, trying to block some of the scent.

The demons did not give me a chance to prepare. They surged forward, trying to separate us into smaller groups, but we remained bunched near the fire pit, unwilling to split off from the rest of the pack. Larna retreated toward me, swinging her torch as one of the puppet-Wyr lunged for her face. With no idea what I was supposed to do, I ran at both of them and swung my torch.

By some stroke of blind luck, I managed to hit my target. The fire scoured its face, and it screamed, turning away from Larna and toward me. Instinct forced me to move. I dove at the monster's throat, clamping down with my teeth and shaking as hard as I could. Sharp claws scrabbled at my face, then my arm, but I locked my jaw, refusing to let go. Finally, we sank to the forest floor, and the body beneath mine went still.

After the first kill, fighting became a little easier. I knew that I was not powerless. My new form seemed to know where to strike, and I rarely missed. The puppet-Wyr were slower than we were, just as Yerta had said. It was easy to predict what they would do. Soon, the ground beneath my paws ran wet with blood. With the great fire at my back and the limp body of the Wyr in front of me, I felt a burst of confidence. I went after another, and this time, I was not surprised when my teeth met his neck.

The kerak were not so easy to destroy. Their reflexes were so quick that I could barely make them out, and it was only my own incompetence that saved me as one of them charged my side. I dropped my torch in surprise, fumbling it in my large, clawed hand and dropping it onto the ground. One of the kerak's thin, crooked legs brushed against the flame, and fire washed along its leathery brown skin. It barely had time to scream before pieces of its flesh crumbled away. Whatever Mogra had used to make them was defenseless against fire.

The shadowkin did not like fire, either, but they did not burn instantly like the kerak. It took more than one Wyr to kill them. They were slow, but their crushing blows were deadly. As I lingered by the fire pit, three or four others tried to bring down one of the huge beasts. I recognized Hosta's sleek black form as he came bursting out from the group. He darted under the shadowkin's belly so fast that I almost missed him. I could not make out what he was doing, but he reemerged seconds later from between its back legs. It stopped, staggered sideways, and let out a low bay of pain. Hosta had sliced its soft underbelly during his dangerous run.

In its weakened state, the rest of the pack brought the shadowkin to the forest floor in a matter of seconds. When the same group went after another beast, I joined them. I did not dare to fight alone, but I felt confident with the others. We formed a circle around its legs, just like we had done on our hunt. It lunged, trying to break free, but we closed in. I dropped to all fours and clipped its leg when it stepped close enough, remembering how I had met the giant stag with my teeth. But the shadowkin did not jump back in fear. It bellowed in surprise and kicked me with its giant foot, sending me sprawling across the ground.

As my head swam with lights, I saw a lean brown kerak above me. Its endless, gaping mouth opened, as if it was trying to devour me from the inside out. I tried to curl into a ball to protect my belly, waiting for the hooks to rip into my flesh. Before it could touch me, its skin erupted with fire. It screamed and fell, thrashing on the ground beside me. Oily black smoke consumed its body. Farseer was standing over me, holding a torch in his left hand. The skinning knife in his right was covered with blood, and his giant paw nearly swallowed the handle. As I watched, he turned to use the torch on another demon, barely dodging a swipe of its claws.

I scrambled back to my feet as quickly as I could, scanning the battlefield for Larna. It was dark and hard to see, but she was unmistakable. She was wild, tearing through everything in her path, swinging her torch in one hand and slicing with the other. A shadowkin tried to crush her in its jaws and she stood her ground, shoving her torch down its throat. It made a choking sound and collapsed hard enough to make the forest floor shake, twitching as it rolled onto its side. Smoke poured from between its teeth until the torch died out.

We were only forty, but when I looked around the battlefield again, there were more of us than them. Mogra's puppet-Wyr had been taken down quickly. They were not very good fighters. Most of the kerak had been burned. A few baked corpses had fallen into the fire pit. All that remained were a few the slow, lumbering shadowkin. I rejoined another of the small groups struggling to bring them down. I practiced dodging their giant legs, darting in to slit their bellies from underneath as I had seen Hosta do. They were strong, but I was fast, and soon, my fur was covered with foul, slippery black meat. The smell burned my nose and eyes.

When I came up for air, I saw Farseer fighting one of the giant dogs near the trees. He dodged its teeth while Hosta fought beside him, trying to burn it with a torch. Suddenly, the shadowkin lurched forward, swiping at Hosta with its massive paw. Farseer saw the hit coming and tried to block it with his body. The blow connected, throwing him off his feet. Larna saw Farseer fall from across the camp. She started sprinting, but there was no way she could get to him in time. The shadowkin picked Farseer up in its huge jaws and shook him like a doll, tossing him carelessly to the ground. He did not get up again.

Larna launched herself through the air, landing on the beast's shaggy spine and digging her teeth into its throat. Its neck was as thick as a tree trunk, but she held her grip anyway, refusing to let go as it thrashed beneath her. Hosta raised his torch again, and this time, he had a clear opening. He seared the shadowkin's eyes as it roared in agony. Finally, it dropped to its knees and went still. I realized with an aching heart that it was the last one to die.

After the fighting ended, we counted our dead and tended to our injured. Six members of the pack had lost their lives. It had seemed like more while we were fighting, but perhaps that was because the corpses of Mogra's puppet-Wyr littered the ground. The kerak were no more than piles of ash.

Bleeding from several places and breathing hard, Larna found me with my back propped up against a tree. Aside from a few bruises and cuts, I had no injuries. I had been very lucky. "Here, use this," she said, handing me a small pouch. I opened it, and fine white powder spilled into my palm. "Put it on your open wounds. It will be stinging."

"Ouch," I shouted as I shook some of the loose powder onto my torn arm, wishing I had heeded her warning first. It bubbled and hissed like boiling water, and the sting made my eyes tear up. Thankfully, the pain faded quickly. I loosened my tight throat and unclenched my teeth, but blood had stopped running from the gashes.

"Dinna use it all," Larna cautioned. "I am needing some."

Carefully, we dusted each other with the powder. I ran my hands over every inch of Larna's body, reassuring myself that she was safe and whole. I did not care that we were naked this time. "I am fine," she insisted as I cleaned three claw marks on her thigh, but she could not hide a sharp breath of pain when I used the powder. "Do you know if Farseer is all right?"

"I don't know. The last thing I saw was Seppea walking over to him after he fell." But I wondered, too. I remembered the way his torn, limp body had spilled from the jaws of the shadowkin. Neither of us knew what to say. After I was sure that Larna was all right, we went to Farseer's hut. The rest of the pack was already gathered there, sitting outside the door. We waited silently through most of the night, pressing close together for warmth through the long, black hours.

CHAPTER SEVEN

JANA FARSEER WAS DEAD. We did not need to be told. The expression on Seppea's face as she came out of his hut said everything she could not. Her gaze was bleak, resigned. The entire pack had taken turns waiting outside, as if our presence would guard his soul, but our vigil had been useless. "Go in," she told us from the top of the steps, standing aside so that we could pass. "Say goodbye."

Larna put her arm around me, and together, we stepped through the door into the darkness of Farseer's hut. We were the first two inside, but the others quickly followed. With Farseer's corpse, we numbered thirteen. His tough brown face had not been damaged, and it seemed as if he might open his eyes and greet us, but the smell of death lingered around him. My vision blurred, and perhaps it was my imagination, but I thought I saw the familiar sparks of white magic crawling along his skin.

"Travel safe in the next world." Yerta's voice shook as he broke the silence that blanketed us. It seemed like I should bow my head, so I did, lowering my eyes to my feet. Others around me did the same. Kera opened her mouth to speak, but no sound came out. There was nothing to say. The pain was still too fresh, too new.

In the stillness, Larna's hand found mine. We laced our fingers tightly, sharing our sadness and strength. The warmth made a small part of my heart feel still and safe, even while my mind was spinning. When I glanced over at her, I could see the grief plainly on her face. Her lips were pressed together and her neck was stiff. But instead of looking at Farseer, she was watching Hosta. I had not noticed him in our group of twelve, but he had come into the hut with the rest of us. An unpleasant shiver ran down the middle of my back.

"He will be missed," Hosta said at last, but even though his face was sad and his eyes were dark, I doubted he meant it. I still did not trust him, despite what Larna said about the pack being family.

"He is not gone," Larna said. "Farseer has not vanished completely." In the light of day, faced with life's painful realities, it might have been a silly thing to say. In the dark hut, it did not seem silly at all.

Hosta was quick to correct himself. "No, of course not."

We all stood in silence for another minute. The longer I waited, the more restless I became. My bones ached. I wanted to move, to run, to go as far away from this place as I could. Something was very wrong. A deep sense of foreboding seeped into me, and I Knew that we were not meant to stay in Farseer's hut. Instincts even more powerful than my Wyr-blood were screaming at me, and I felt the familiar surge of warmth that often accompanied...

...the spill of blood. Flashing white teeth sink into Larna's throat, piercing fur and flesh, dragging her toward the ground. The circle around them howls, pressing in on all sides...

Scorched earth. The scent of rotting magic. More kerak, an entire army of them, weaving between the giant legs of the shadowkin as the air erupts with screams and fire...

Hosta watches, his eyes rolling wildly in his dark head, his lips pulled back in a furious snarl. Larna is still. Like Farseer, she does not move.

When I returned to my body, no one was looking at me. The warm circle of the deadeye hummed beneath the dip of my collarbone. This was like, but unlike, any vision that had taken me before. I Knew what I had seen, but I did not feel weak, and my muscles did not shake with exhaustion. Some of Kalwyn's teachings must have taken hold already. I had slipped into the spirit world without anyone else noticing my absence.

Larna was still beside me, staring forlornly at Farseer just like the others. "Larna," I whispered beside her ear, trying to keep my voice as low as possible, "we need to leave."

"Leave? Now?" she whispered back, as if she could not believe what I was saying.

"Yes. Come outside."

Something in my voice must have convinced her, because she followed me as I walked out into the light. Dawn had broken, and weak, pale beams of sunlight filtered down through the trees. Even though the sky was grey, it would have been a beautiful morning if the light had not revealed the large bodies of the shadowkin. We had been too concerned with our own dead the night before to bother moving them.

"All right," Larna said once we were a fair distance away from Farseer's hut, "what were you needing to tell me? We were not finished saying our goodbyes, and it was rude to leave."

I felt guilty for dragging Larna away from Farseer so quickly, but I could not stay silent. The more I thought about my vision, the clearer its form became. Hosta's face flashed behind my eyes. This would not be one of the visions that slipped away from me as soon as it was over. "Something dangerous is about to happen, Larna. We have to get away from here."

Larna glanced over at one of the corpses near the fire. "I would say something dangerous has already happened."

After everything the pack had been through, I forgave her for the comment. Instead, I pleaded with her to listen to me. "Larna, this is serious."

"Have you had a vision?"

I hesitated. I wanted to tell Larna what I had Seen, but I knew she would not take it well. The pack was everything to her, and hearing that a member of her chosen family wanted to hurt her would shake the foundation of everything she believed in. But there was no use lying to her. I would not let my vision come to pass. "I think Hosta is going to try and kill you."

Larna's eyes widened in disbelief. "Kill me? No. Hosta doesna always like me, but he respects me, and he respected Farseer."

My heart sank. Larna's stubborn streak had flared up again, and I doubted that even my vision would be enough to convince her. Still, I tried my best. If I was supposed to be her mate, she would need to start listening to me. "I Know what I Saw. He is going to try and fight you. Maybe he wants to take over the pack, or maybe it's something worse."

"Something worse?" Larna repeated doubtfully. Her jaw stiffened, and she folded her arms over her chest. "Like what?"

"Think about it. How did Mogra know where we were camped? Farseer said himself that her Wyr could never track us. Why did the kerak and the shadowkin come now?"

Larna studied me for a long moment before glancing back toward the hut. She spoke without turning back. "When my family turned me away, Farseer took me in. He rescued me. He fed me. He gave me a purpose. He put his trust in me, and now he is dead. And now you ask me to...what? Leave the rest of my family because of a feeling you are having about Hosta? Because you think he led the witch here? Not all visions come true, Cate. I canna...I willna believe this one."

I almost wavered then. Almost submitted to her stubbornness and resigned myself to staying behind. But Kalwyn had taught me to trust in myself, and I could not ignore what I had Seen. "I saw him with your throat in his jaws, Larna. He isn't your family. We need to leave, and quickly."

Larna whirled around to meet my eyes again. There was anger there, and a coldness that bit through my skin. "I am staying here. The pack needs me."

"If you care so much about the pack, you'll listen to me," I shouted. I did not care if anyone else overheard me. Larna's stubborn, blind loyalty to someone who was so obviously trying to harm us simply because he was a member of the pack had pushed me past the breaking point.

Larna balled her fists so tightly that the blood drained from her knuckles. The grey sky peeking through the treetops sucked the color from her face. "There are no traitors in the Farseer pack."

"Are you sure?"

Her face was stone. "Yes."

I turned away, wiping the back of my hand across my stinging eyes. "If you won't believe me..." My voice wavered, and I had to pause and swallow down a lump in my throat. "I'll just have to bring someone else to convince you. I'm going to Kalwyn's. Maybe then you'll listen." I hurried off into the forest, not even bothering to look back and see if Larna was reaching after me.

CHAPTER EIGHT

I MADE MY WAY to Kalwyn's hut as fast as I could. After last night's attack, I did not know what I would find there, but I hoped that Mogra had only discovered the location of our camp. Kalwyn was powerful, but she was also old. She would not be able to fight off the witch's creatures on her own. I wished Larna was with me, but forced myself not to think about her. I was still too angry to forgive her, but I could not let my vision come to pass. Despite her hard-headed resistance and her lack of faith in me, I loved her.

Finally, the trees opened up into a small clearing. From the outside, Kalwyn's house looked unchanged. I let a little of my breath spill out in a sigh of relief. Maybe I had been right after all, and the demons had missed Kalwyn on their way to slaughter us. Still, I was careful as I approached the door, just in case any unpleasant surprises were waiting for me.

I knew that something was wrong as soon as I entered the house. Kalwyn's hut was always untidy, but it looked like a hurricane had torn through the front room. Papers were scattered over the floor, a cracked wooden bowl had fallen from the table, and the chairs were overturned. "Kalwyn?" I called out, picking my way over the rubbish and heading toward the kitchen. I peered up at the mask above the door. Its open mouth was twisted in surprise, and its eyes were wide with fear. Perhaps its warning had been enough? Kalwyn had told me that it was good at announcing unexpected guests.

Carefully, I pushed open the kitchen door. It was no better than the front room. Pots were tossed every which way, and there were five deep gouges in the table. Claw marks. Next to them was a knife. I reached to grasp the handle and lifted it. A thick black sludge dripped from the blade. It smelled of fear, death, and tainted magic. Demon blood. I had learned its taste the night before.

This time, I did not bother calling Kalwyn's name. Whatever had destroyed her house might still be lurking around. Instead, I gripped the knife's handle in my shaking fingers and headed for a door that I had never ventured through on my other visits. I suspected it was Kalwyn's bedroom, but she had never invited me in. I hesitated just outside the door, listening at its crack. There was no noise from inside.

Suddenly, the door swung open on its own, inviting me to step through. All of the lights in the room had been put out, but I thought I saw a figure move in the darkness. It sat up in the four-poster bed, and something about its shape looked familiar. "Kalwyn!" I rushed into the bedroom.

The figure on the bed did not say anything.

"Kalwyn?" I said again, lowering my voice to a whisper.

At last, the shadowy form spoke. "Come closer, so I can see you." Twin points of light flashed from the headboard, piercing the dim and dark. Were those her eyes? They were so large...

I stepped forward.

"Come closer," murmured the voice, "so I can hear you." For the first time, I saw Kalwyn's face. It was her, but it was not her. Her eyes were too bright. The angles of her face were too sharp. Her thin lips peeled back, showing pointed, gleaming teeth, and her mouth became a gaping, endless hole of black. I was frozen. The jaw stretched wide, wider than I imagined a mouth could open. It took up half of her face.

"COME CLOSER, SO I CAN EAT YOU."

I acted without thinking. There was a tearing sound as I shifted into half shape, ripping through my clothes. My muscles bunched, and I leapt at her. There was a thud, and a high screech as my jaws latched onto the creature's neck. It rolled out of the bed, flinging its arms and shrieking. Its hooked claws raked at my fur, and my body swung wildly through the air, flung from side to side as it writhed.

But I did not let go. I clamped my teeth down harder, and the thing howled. The sharp, coppery taste of blood on my tongue made my gut burn. I sliced at muscles, crushed bone, tore into its flesh with my claws. Its abdomen split, and I was drenched with slimy, dying pieces of the thing. It reeked of foul magic. Finally, with a violent shudder and another high wail, the monster fell. It was a shredded mess, and my fur was matted and stained black.

Heart still pounding, I pressed my nose to what was left of the creature's—Kalwyn's—flank, nudging gently. She did not respond. I did not want to change back to my other form. My human heart would not be able to handle the deed I had just done. My linked wolf-heart could barely comprehend it. Kalwyn? I asked with my body, pressing against her, sniffing, whimpering.

The thing did not respond. It did not even smell like her. I staggered to my feet, putting my nose to the ground. My ears lifted, listening intently. Soon, I heard a soft sound coming from underneath the bed. Small scratches, and a barely audible groan. I limped over and peered beneath the frame, trying to ignore the places where the creature's claws had torn through my hide. I saw a small, huddled form, and this time, the scent was familiar—Kalwyn!

Kalwyn's body was shriveled and small, but she was still breathing as I dragged her out from her hiding place. "It bit me," she said in a weak, shaking voice. Her arm was torn, and there was more blood than I had expected. Not knowing why, I lowered my nose to the wound. The blood smelled wrong. Poisoned. I knew that Kalwyn was going to die, but the knowledge did not come as a surprise. I could only rest my head on her belly and curl up beside her. She was my teacher and friend. She still had so much to share with me.

"A...cha...eat..." Kalwyn said haltingly. Her light was fading, but she had the strength to reach for me with one hand. I bent my head closer to hear her whisper. "Eat...my heart...willna be a kerak..."

I shook my head, hoping I could convey my horror without words. *Eat your heart? Are you insane?*

"Mogra. She will burn it...take the ashes, and make a kerak. Please, acha..." They were her last words. She passed while I stayed pressed against her side. Her death was not a huge shock. I was still reeling from what she had asked me to do. I looked down at her still form with brimming eyes. Could I really eat her heart, even to keep her safe?

I lifted my head from Kalwyn's lifeless chest. There was no reassuring thump from inside. I closed my eyes, held my breath, and met her flesh with my mouth. I tried not to taste as I stripped away the thin layer of fat, searching for the bone underneath, but I should not have been worried. My stomach lurched, and I had to turn my head away and spit to keep from vomiting. I might have been in half-shape, but I knew exactly what I was doing, and I was horrified. No part of me actually wanted to eat her.

Trying not to completely destroy Kalwyn's body, I used my claws to go under the yellow ribcage and find her heart. It was slick and purple-red, and I thought I saw it shiver in the cavity of her chest. I could not look. I could not think. I pretended it was not happening as I snapped her heart into my jaws and forced it down my throat.

My nausea came back immediately. I gritted my teeth, smiling grotesquely to keep from throwing up what I had just eaten. I howled, ignoring the blood matted around my lips as I collapsed onto the ground beside what was left of Kalwyn's body. The horrible smell of magic was still everywhere, and white spots danced before my eyes. I was not sure if they were magic or visions of the pounding ache in my skull. My skin prickled with the chill of death, and I could not stop shaking. Tears ran from my eyes, and my last thought before I surrendered to blackness was that I had not known wolves could cry.

CHAPTER NINE

SLOWLY, WARMTH RETURNED TO my muscles. They tingled as I tried to move, but I could not summon the strength. My eyes remained shut, but slowly, my other senses returned. I heard. Voices, familiar ones, spoke from nearby. I felt. There was a deep, slicing pain somewhere along my back. I smelled. A familiar scent surrounded me. Larna. I breathed deeply, trying to take in as much as I could.

It took me several moments to realize that I was lying on a cot, with a pillow pressed against my face. That explained the smell. I was relieved that I had woken up here instead of on the cold, wooden floor, still covered in blood. Perhaps fighting the monster and eating Kalwyn's heart had only been a nightmare. But why did the flesh behind my shoulder blade still sting? Why couldn't I remember how I had gotten here? And where was Larna? My heart battered against the walls of my chest, and my stomach lurched as I remembered what I had done. I clutched the sheets in my hands, the only small movement I could manage, and swallowed down the bile that stung my throat. It was all real. Kalwyn was dead. So was Farseer. The camp was torn apart, and Larna was still in danger.

At last, I opened my eyes. I was not alone in the room. Two dark figures moved beside me. "We need to get rid of her," I heard Hosta say. I snapped my eyes shut again, hoping he had not noticed. "She will be going mad soon. She must be taken far away so that she willna be a danger."

"It is a stupid law," Larna argued from somewhere above me. I wanted to look at her, but I continued feigning sleep. I was not supposed to be listening to this conversation, even if hearing Larna defend me did soothe some of my hurt feelings. "It is kept so that no Wyr kills a human. But Cate didna kill a human. She was trying to save Kalwyn. She fought well for the pack. She is my mate. Farseer would keep her."

"Farseer is dead, Larna." The venom in Hosta's words surprised me. With my eyes shut, I could not see his face. I could imagine it, though, twisted with anger. He was trying to give his first order as the new Alpha, and Larna was clearly challenging him.

"And that means we shouldna follow his example anymore? Cate will be in danger on her own."

"Will you disobey me?" Hosta growled. "Jana Farseer is gone. I am the Alpha. The law says that any Wyr eating human flesh must be banished."

"If she is banished, so am I."

I was astonished. Banishment? The pack was Larna's life. It was her family, the thing she cared about most in the entire world. And yet, here she was, standing at my bedside, defying orders and willingly volunteering to leave if they forced me out. Even Hosta seemed surprised. He took several moments to gather himself. "You dinna have to leave. You were not eating human flesh."

"Her crimes are mine. Her fate is mine."

Hosta brought his fist down on the table with a loud crash, and I felt it shake from the bed. There was a brief, tense moment of silence before he stomped heavily to the door, slamming it shut behind him.

When he left, some of the tiredness and worry in my chest dissolved. I tried to lift my head, and Larna noticed that I was awake. "Little bird. You are feeling all right?"

I nodded. "Larna...what just happened?"

"Nothing," she murmured, sitting at the edge of my cot. She leaned down to stroke my hair, pressing kisses to the side of my face. "Nothing you are needing to worry about yet. Wen you ran, I gathered some of the others and came after you. You're safe now."

I did not believe her. I could not unhear what I had heard and the grief in her eyes was unmistakable, even in the dark. I sat up against my pillow, pulling away from her hand. "I know Hosta wants to banish me. I wasn't sleeping."

Larna's face fell. "Then you heard what I told him."

"Yes, I heard."

We stared at each other, unsure what to say. Larna's heavy hand settled on my shoulder, squeezing as she stared down at me. "I...I am sorry. About Kalwyn. And for not listening to you. I am not knowing if Hosta is a traitor to the witch as you said, but I will find out. And I willna let you go into the Forest alone. I meant what I said. You are my mate. Your fate is mine."

I lowered my eyes. I could not look at Larna as I forced out the words I had to say next. "You don't have to go with me, Larna. I can take care of myself." And for the first time in my life, I believed it. I had left Seria and all my friends behind and returned to Amendyr. I had learned to run with wolves. I had accepted my place as a shaman. I had killed monsters. And I had fallen in love. I was not the same frightened, quiet girl who had crept like a ghost in Baxstresse's halls. I had a purpose here, and newly-awakened strength.

Larna's fingers reached beneath my chin, and she tilted my face up, forcing me to meet her eyes again. This time, they were not quite so sad. "I let you leave once. I willna let you leave again. I have learned my lesson about stubbornness."

I blinked rapidly to hold back tears, but I suspected that Larna could see them shimmering in my eyes anyway. "What about the pack? Your family?"

"You are my family, Cate. And if Hosta canna treat both of us like family should, he is no brother of mine. I will go with you." She gave me a sad smile. "It is not the first time I have been cast out by those who should be knowing better."

Even as my heart healed with forgiveness, it broke again for Larna. She had proven that I was important to her, but at what cost? "Maybe Hosta will change his mind," I said, even though I did not really believe it. I wanted to keep Larna as far away from him as possible, but I could not bring myself to crush all of her hopes. "Perhaps after a while, he might let you come back."

"Let us come back, not just me," Larna insisted. "And he would have to be doing a lot of apologizing first. Dinna cry, little bird. It isn't all bad. We will find somewhere else."

That was another problem, one I had not even considered. "Where? You told me that most humans don't trust Wyr. Maybe we could move among them without being noticed for a few days, but we couldn't settle anywhere permanently. I would suggest going back across the border to Seria so that my friends could help us, but..."

Larna shook her head. "No. Too dangerous, especially for Wyr. The patrols would never be letting us pass. Even if we made it across, it would only take one frightened peasant to send a mob after us. Amendyr is better. At least here, there are some who are not afraid of magic."

"Well, do you have any ideas?"

She thought about it for a moment. "Perhaps we should be heading for the Rengast. The rebels have camps there. They might take us in. We can both hunt and fight, and you are a shaman. They have other *Ariada* with them. And best of all, it is far away from Mogra and her demons."

I shuddered as I remembered the empty, gaping black gullet of the creature in Kalwyn's bed. Whatever it was, I did not want to encounter anything like it again. The kerak and the shadowkin had been terrifying enough on their own. "All right. We'll head for the mountains." I made as if to push myself out of the bed, but Larna stopped me with a firm hand on my chest.

"Not yet, little bird. Hosta will be letting you stay one more night. Rest. You will be needing all of your strength."

Larna's words reminded me of my exhaustion. I slumped back down onto the mattress. Suddenly, it was difficult to keep my eyes open. Still confused and afraid, but glad that Larna was with me, I scooted to the far side of the cot to make space for her. "Sleep next to me. Please? Just until morning."

She seemed hesitant at first, but eventually, she slid beneath the covers and tangled her legs with mine. One of her hands settled over my hip, and her forehead touched mine. Our lips met softly, and the last of my resentment melted away. She was prepared to give up everything she cared about for me. The least I could do in return was forgive her.

CHAPTER TEN

I WOKE THE NEXT morning to find Yerta standing beside the cot, peering down at me with warm grey eyes. I gave him a weak smile, careful not to disturb Larna. She had fallen asleep beside me, and her breathing was still even and deep. I could not bring myself to wake her yet.

"I came to see you," Yerta explained quickly. He looked nervous, but I did not know why. Maybe Hosta had forbidden him from visiting us, and he was worried about getting caught.

"Yerta..." I tried to speak, to tell him to leave, but my throat was dry. I still felt weak after what I had endured the past two days. My entire body ached, but the memories of what I had seen and done in Kalwyn's hut were even worse.

"Here, wait." Yerta stood and went to get me a glass of water. While he did, I studied Larna's face, brushing the dark hair that clung to her forehead. Her cheeks and forehead were smooth, and I could feel her heartbeat thumping slowly against my chest. In sleep, she finally seemed at peace. I removed my hand when Yerta came back and offered me the cup. "There you are. Have this."

The water was cool and sweet as it slid down my throat. My strength began to return, and when I spoke, my voice was much clearer. "Thank you."

"I tried to talk to Hosta, but he will not change his mind. He is Alpha now, and I am fearing what will happen to Larna if she is challenging him. You must both leave quickly, at least for now."

"What? I thought he was angry with me, not her. I was the one who..." I could not bring myself to finish the sentence. Surely the entire camp already knew what I had done anyway. "Never mind. When do we need to leave?"

"As quickly as you can. I brought you a few things." Yerta nudged something beside the cot with his foot, and I peered over the edge. Two brown travelling packs were sitting on the floor, and they looked full. "Food, water, knives, and tinder. It isn't much..." He looked at me guilty, as if he wanted to do something more to help us.

"You've done more than enough, Yerta. It's best for us to leave anyway." I considered telling him about my vision, but decided that it no longer mattered. If we were leaving, it would not come true, and despite how much I hated him, I did not want to speak badly of Hosta in front of Yerta.

"I canna help feeling responsible. He is my brother."

"This isn't your fault."

"Nor is it yours." He shifted his weight awkwardly from foot to foot, occasionally glancing at the door. "Are you knowing where you will go?"

I thought about it. Larna had been right the night before. I could not go back to Baxstresse. That place was so far away, so completely alien to me now. My life was different. I was different. Too different to exist in that world anymore. Larna had no home to go to, either. We would be on our own. "Larna wanted to join the Rebellion. She says they're looking for people who can fight. If they're enemies of the witch, they're allies of ours."

Yerta bit down on his lower lip. "And what if you are not finding them? Some say there are no rebels at all..." When he saw that I would not be convinced, he heaved a sigh. "Will you ever come back?"

I wanted to say no, but then I looked over at Larna. She was still sleeping peacefully beside me. The Farseer pack has been her family for a long time. It would be a shame for her to lose that connection simply because of Hosta. "Maybe in a few months, we can come back. By then, it will be clear I'm not mad because of...you know. And Hosta's temper might cool once he sees that Larna isn't trying to take control of the pack."

Yerta sighed. "Hosta does not forget disobedience. Your problems will not disappear."

"We will be fine."

A scratching noise outside the door startled both of us. Yerta's head jerked sharply as he looked over his shoulder. The door opened, and Hosta came in. He did not shout or grow angry. He only stared at the three of us with eyes that looked almost fearful. "Yerta. Come here," he snapped.

Reluctantly, Yerta trudged toward him, holding his shoulders low. Even though he was in human form, I could picture him with his tail tucked between his legs. I was not angry with him for leaving without a goodbye. He was *Pekah*, and Hosta was his brother and his Alpha. Both of them left the room without speaking to me, but when the door to Larna's hut closed, the shouting started. "What were you thinking? You will never be visiting those two again."

"But—"

"Dinna think that because you are my brother, I will not punish you. I have been forgiving so far, but one more mistake, and..." The voices grew fainter as Hosta and Yerta moved away from the door. I was left alone. Well, not alone, I corrected myself. Larna was still with me, and her eyes were open.

"What was that about?" she asked, pushing into a sitting position beside me and staring at the door.

"Yerta came to say goodbye. Hosta wasn't pleased."

Larna's mouth twitched into a frown, and her forehead creased with worry. "We should be leaving as quickly as we can. I dinna want any of that anger turned on you."

"Actually, I'm more concerned about you. Yerta told me that Hosta is worried you might challenge his new position. He thinks you want to be Alpha."

"Me? No. He has been here longer. I willna challenge him." She hesitated for a moment. "Are you thinking that is why he has banished you? Because of me? You only broke the letter of our law, not its spirit."

"Yes. I do think so."

I tried not to remember the vision, but images of Hosta's teeth sinking into Larna's throat forced their way to the front of my mind. I blinked, trying to clear the bloody picture away. It was impossible for me to know whether leaving would change the vision or not, but the further away we went from the Farseer pack, the better.

***

We left an hour later, just before first light. Larna and I did not say goodbye to anyone in camp. We knew that it would only be awkward and painful. Seppea, Yerta, and the rest of our friends did not want to see us go, but they were not brave enough to defy Hosta's orders. Larna and I held no grudge against them. We did not want them to feel guilty.

The two of us headed for the river first, planning to fill the empty waterskins that Yerta had provided for us. "What should we do when we get there?" I asked, shifting the weight of my traveling pack on my shoulder. It was heavier than before, since I had taken the time to add a few changes of clothes, Kalwyn's hourglass, and my magical journal. I wore Sarah's red cloak around my shoulders, glad for its protection against the cold. Even deep in the forest, with the trees to protect us from the worst of the wind's bite, the temperature was lowering as winter approached.

Larna glanced over her shoulder at me. I tried to read her expression, but only saw emptiness in her eyes. Leaving the Farseer pack had hurt her deeply, but I would not push her to talk about it before she was ready. "We follow the river. It flows down from the Rengast mountains. That is where the rebel camps are."

"Well, since we're going there, don't you think it's about time you told me why there are rebels in the first place?"

We reached the river and Larna took the opportunity to delay her answer, pulling out one of her two waterskins and unplugging the top. As she bent over and dipped it into the water, I could not help admiring the movement of muscle beneath her shirt. I felt a little guilty for staring at her when we had so many other things to worry about, but I did not look away, either. After a while, she stood back up and tucked the dripping waterskin back into her pack. "I suppose I should, little bird. You have not been here for many years. Things have...changed."

"Changed how?"

"For the worse. It was starting six years ago, before I joined the pack. When the king's first wife died, he took a new bride. My village was nowhere near Kalmarin, but the entire kingdom was celebrating." She gave me a soft smile, and I could tell that she was remembering something happy. Then, her face fell. "It was not lasting long. He died a few months later. His little daughter was far too young to be taking the throne, so his bride became regent. New laws were passed. Higher taxes, fewer imports. She named herself Queen and shut off the kingdom from the outside world. Then, strange things started happening..."

"The kerak?"

"Aye, and worse. Villages disappeared. People died. Creatures that had not been seen in the kingdom for centuries returned. They came from the Forest, but even the farms on the plains and the cities in the southern sweep were targeted. When I was joining the Farseer pack, I learned Mogra was behind some of it. She is building an army, but we know she isna working alone. This is too great even for her power. The Queen is never leaving her palace, but we know she is part of it. Anyone who questions her is silenced." She sighed. "Farseer did what he could. We were protecting the Forest, killing the creatures Mogra stitched together and freeing the travelers she captured from the road."

"And now, she's found the camp," I said in a whisper. "That mob of creatures was just a scouting party, wasn't it?"

Larna nodded. She turned toward me, and I saw red rings in her dark eyes. She had not just given up her family for me. She had left them in a very dangerous position. If my guess was right and Hosta was acting as a traitor to the pack, they would not stand a chance.

I opened my arms and let Larna fall into them. We knelt on the ground beside the river, and she curled into my embrace, weeping against my shoulder. Hot tears spilled onto my neck, but I did not care. I clung to her shirt, holding her tight and letting her cry. "It's all right," I whispered, not even sure if she could hear me.

Tears began running down my cheeks, too, but they were tears of anger. Anger at what I had lost, at what Mogra had taken from me. Farseer and Kalwyn were dead. Larna had been driven away from her family. I would not let the witch or Hosta, ruin anything else. I would turn our banishment into something worthwhile. "We'll go back for them, Larna. We'll bring the rebels with us. They can help us fight her."

Larna raised her head. She was still crying, but her eyes were hard with determination. She felt just as I did. "Aye. I lost my family once. I will not be losing them again, even if Hosta is too blind to see the danger."

I feared that Hosta was worse than blind, but did not say anything. It didn't matter. Our banishment had become a quest instead, and Larna's family was now mine. If he was a traitor, we would deal with him when we returned—hopefully with an army at our back.

Rae D. Magdon

Part Three:

As told by Cathelin Raybrook, recorded by Lady Eleanor of Baxstresse

CHAPTER ONE:

THAT NIGHT, LARNA AND I took shelter beneath the trees by the river. We could have kept travelling in the dark, since our eyes could pierce the blackness, but both of us were exhausted. I suspected it had little to do with how far we had walked and everything to do with what we had left behind.

Once we selected a spot that looked safe enough, Larna stretched out on the grass beneath a large oak and rested her head on her travelling pack. The color of her face was paler than usual, even in the weak starlight that managed to filter down through the last remaining leaves. I lowered myself onto the ground and rested beside her. Her body curled around mine, and both of us sighed.

"What are you thinking about?" I asked, shifting so that her cheek rested on my chest and I was lying against the pack.

Larna pressed her face into the crook of my neck. With her head tucked against my shoulder, she surrendered her secrets. "I grew up on the edge of the Forest, in a small village. But it was big enough to have a name. Katar." I knew the village, but did not say so, afraid that if I spoke, it would break the spell. "My father was an apothecary there. I remember, in the afternoon, the sun would strike the colored bottles...blue and green, amber and brown."

"It sounds beautiful," I whispered.

Larna smiled against the skin of my throat. The shift of her lips made my heart beat faster. "They were only bits of glass. You are beautiful...I had a younger brother, and a mother. I was closer to my father, though. Sometimes, I wondered if she resented me. Maybe she was wanting more of his attention. Or mine." Larna tried to hide it, but I could hear the strain in her voice. She held me tighter. "One day, I went into the forest to check the traps. That was when Mogra was catching me. She took me to her cave."

I remembered my own fearful awakening in Mogra's lair, but tried to suppress the thoughts. Whatever evil she had done to me, it could not touch me here. "Did Farseer rescue you like you rescued me?"

"Aye. He took me back to camp and taught me to run as a Wyr. But still, I was missing my family. After a while, I went home and...you know how that went already." She let out a slow exhale through her nose, and it pushed the strands of hair along my neck. Wetness brushed my skin, and I knew that she was crying. "My father turned me away. I was changed, and he would not see me." I could only kiss Larna's hair and wait for her to calm. Her tears ran hot against the naked skin of my shoulder. "Farseer was becoming like a new father to me. He offered me a place. He cared for me."

I thought of my own mother, dead for over ten years, of my grandmother, and of Kalwyn. It was hard to believe that she had only died yesterday. That I had watched her pass on to whatever came after. That I had defiled her body, even if she had asked me to do it. This time, I cried with Larna. Our tears mixed together and left our cheeks damp and slick.

"I miss him," Larna whispered, swiping the back of her hand across her eyes. "And I miss the pack. They were there when I was needing them, but now..."

I blinked back my own tears and swallowed down the lump that had grown in my sore throat. The deadeye hummed below my collarbone, warming my skin, and I stopped crying. I was sad, but not helpless. I had enough strength to share. "And now, I'm here."

Larna looked up at me, and I thought I saw the first traces of a smile soften the hard lines around her mouth. She sighed and lifted her head, pulling away from the damp patch on my shirt. "You are here, aren't you, little bird?"

"I am. And I'm not going anywhere." I laced my fingers through hers and lifted her hand to my lips, kissing each knuckle, tracing my thumb over the small white scars. I found that I already knew where they were. Larna had been right when she said that we would learn each other. Even in a short time, both her body and her heart had become familiar to me. "You're my *Tuathe*. No matter what happens, I'll always be your family."

This time, Larna's smile was brilliant. I caught a gleaming flash of white teeth before she pushed herself up onto her powerful arms, hovering above me. Her face blocked out the pale moonlight filtering down from above, but with her body pressed over mine, I was too distracted to mind the darkness. "I love you, Cate," she whispered. "I feel as if I have been waiting a very long time to hear you call me *Tuathe*."

I started to tell Larna that I would say the word over and over again if it would make her happy, but she silenced me with a kiss. Her lips were soft, but they were insistent, and when her tongue pressed forward, I opened my mouth to hers. She tasted warm and sweet, and a shudder ran the entire length of my body. Somehow, my hands found themselves wrapped around her neck, threading through her hair, pulling her closer.

It was like we had never left the forest after making love for the first time. Our bodies awakened to each other. A deep ache started in my lower belly, coiling down between my legs and pulsing there as Larna's mouth teased mine. My clothes felt constricting, and the fabric rasped over my burning skin. "Please," I whispered in between deep, searching kisses, barely drawing in enough breath to speak. "I need to feel more."

Larna stared at me with a dazed expression. The dark pupils of her eyes nearly eclipsed the brown irises, but when I raised my arms over my head, she understood. She helped me pull off my shirt, and her own followed a few moments later. I stared at her breasts, admiring the stiff points and subtle curve. Dark dips of shadow were painted above her collarbone, and the light of the moon ran along her strong jaw. She was breathtaking, and I could hardly believe that this woman, this perfect blend of strength and softness, wanted me.

This time, when our bodies pressed together again, she was not quite so gentle. I knew the moment when she became lost in her own need. She trailed a hot thread of kisses down the column of my throat, working over my skin in a frantic line until her teeth sank into the soft place where my neck became my shoulder. The slight pain brought heavy throbs of pleasure with it. I sucked in a quick breath and threw my head back, offering myself to her. "Larna..."

She let go with a soft pop, murmuring my name as the warmth of her mouth grazed down the slope of my chest. "Cate..."

When her tongue circled the peak of my breast, I threaded my fingers back through her hair, clutching her to me as best I could. My limbs shook, and I twisted beneath her, trying to press more of myself into the heat of her mouth. The light pressure of her teeth made my hips leave the ground. She pushed her knee between my legs, offering me some purchase, but it was not enough. The ache within me had doubled, and I was desperate for relief.

"Please." I tore one of my hands away from the back of her head and groped for her fingers in the darkness, dragging them between us. "I need..." My words faltered when Larna tugged at the hem of my leggings. She pulled them down past my hips, and I did my best to help her. We left them bunched at my knees, too eager to waste any more time. A sob broke in my throat as her nails raked up along my inner thigh, urging me to spread my legs wider and cradle her lean hips.

At last, Larna's fingers found me. A powerful jolt rippled through the muscles in my stomach, and I melted into her hand. She grazed over the hard point above my entrance, circling lightly at first, but pressing harder when she heard my gasp of approval. "Oh, *Tuathe*," she murmured against my shoulder, "I feel what you need."

The rough pads of her fingers dipped down to gather more of my wetness. They circled there for a while, teasing and pulling back whenever my hips rocked down to take her, but at last, they dragged back up. This time when she touched me, the movement was smooth, almost like silk. She began circling again, coaxing the swollen bud of my clit from beneath its hood. Fire filled my cheeks, and my eyes fluttered shut. Surely Larna could feel how swollen I was. How wet. How close. The last threads of my control were unravelling under her hands, and I could do nothing to stop it.

Her lips took mine again, and I whimpered into them, rocking desperately against her hand. She slipped inside of me effortlessly, filling me with her fingers. When they scraped against a full, heavy place, my muscles squeezed hard around her. She shuddered in my arms and repeated the motion, and I gasped as a flood of heat poured out around her knuckles.

I kicked my leggings the rest of the way off, doing my best to ignore the new trick Larna had discovered. Once my legs were free, I threw one of my knees around her hip, pushing up to give her an even better angle. I couldn't tell how many of her fingers were inside of me, but she was deeper than she had ever been before, and the curling, stroking motion of her thrusts nearly made it impossible to breathe.

Just when I thought I could not bear anymore, Larna broke our kiss and stared down at me. "Tell me you're mine for always," she said, her voice trembling. "Tell me I'll always have you."

The haze of my desire faded enough for me to realize that Larna felt as vulnerable as I did. This was about more than simply giving me pleasure. She wanted reassurance. She wanted to know that she was not alone. It was hard for me to speak, but I managed to summon a few words, the words she needed to hear. "I'm yours. You'll always have me."

I felt Larna's emotional release seconds before my physical one consumed me. The tension along her back relaxed, and her face shone with love. Her grip tightened on my thigh, and she pulled my knee higher around her hip as she drove into me one more time. The moment her fingers hooked against the full place inside of me, I poured everything I had into her palm, shuddering beneath her as a gush of wetness ran between us.

"More," she whispered against my cheek, pressing a few light kisses there. "Give me more..." I stiffened and dug my nails into her back. This time, she timed a swipe of her thumb over my sensitive tip with her curling fingers. I screamed. My entire world became endless ripples as I shivered and spilled around her hand. I lost track of how many times her thrusts pushed me over the edge. My pleasure rose and fell, cresting and breaking over me. I went limp beneath her, letting my hands drop away from her back and my legs fall apart as she forced out one last, weak round of pulses.

As I floated back into myself, I saw that Larna was still staring intently at my face. Her gaze was searching, and I summoned enough strength lift one of my hands and cup the side of her cheek. "I meant what I said," I told her, trying to heal all of her pain, all the old scars. "I'm yours. You'll always have me."

We rested together for several heartbeats, breathing each other in. Larna's weight was comforting, and when she finally pulled out of me, I sighed at the loss even though the stretch was beginning to grow painful. I realized with some surprise that I had not even thought about giving her pleasure in return, and I was a little ashamed at my selfishness. "Larna, do you need...?"

Larna shook her head, rolling onto her side and wrapping one of her arms around my waist. This time, she was the one who smiled first. "No, little bird. You were already giving me exactly what I needed."

***

No matter how hard I tried, I could not fall asleep. Nighttime sounds drifted through the trees, and although my body was tired, my mind was wide awake. Lying still wore on my nerves, even with Larna's soft, steady breathing by my ear. I could not see much of the moon through the tree branches, but I could feel its pull. When I closed my eyes, silvery light danced behind them.

I decided to go through our supplies, desperate for something to occupy my mind. Larna's arms and legs were tangled with mine, and it took me several minutes to ease away from her. Finally, I freed myself and rolled over on the grass, opening the flap of my traveling pack. As I looked down at it, I realized that I could see everything clearly. I had forgotten my new eyes. Sometimes, my heightened senses still surprised me.

I noticed Ellie's journal laying half in and half out of the pouch. My stomach tugged with guilt. It had been several days since the last time I had written to my friend. She would be wondering where I was, what I was doing. Maybe she was worried.

When I flipped open the cover, there were three letters waiting for me to read. The first one was mostly about current events. Rumors about the turmoil in Amendyr had grown in Seria. Prince Brendan's council of advisors was calling for a trade embargo, even though Amendyr had shut off trade from their end already. The second letter was probing. What was I doing? How was Larna? Had I kissed her yet? I smiled softly at the questions. Ellie probably wanted to know if we had made love, but was too polite to ask.

The third message was short and frantic, only one sentence long. *Where are you?* My mouth tightened to a thin line. There was no way to tell Ellie what I had been up to without worrying her. I should have written to her before this, but as I turned the journal to an empty page, I realized that there had been no time.

I spent several long, silent minutes deciding what to write. My life was much more dangerous than it had been a few months ago. I had fought and killed demons. I had tasted blood. I had seen death. My life had also become unbelievably wonderful. I had found the other half of my soul. I knew what it felt like to make love with my *Tuathe*. I was not the same meek girl that Ellie had rescued from Luciana's torture. I was a woman instead. But how could I explain so much in a letter? I decided to try anyway. I owed Ellie a recounting of events, especially after my long silence.

Once I started writing, the words came easily. I told Ellie about

Kalwyn and how she had died, and I did not omit my own complicity. A sour taste rose in my mouth, and I had to stop and swallow it down. I told her about the kerak and the shadowkin, Farseer's death, and how Hosta had forced Larna to leave the only home still open to her. I told her we were going into the mountains to find the rebels And I told her about how wonderful it was to make love under the moon by the river, and how Larna's kisses left me drunk with happiness even as the rest of the world seemed to be unraveling at its seams.

By the time I sketched out everything that happened, I was exhausted. Perhaps, I thought, there was a reason Ellie and Belladonna both kept journals. It was strangely soothing to put my thoughts down on paper, and it left my head blissfully empty. That was how Larna found me the next morning, one hand cradled protectively over the front of my journal and the other still holding my quill.

CHAPTER TWO

LARNA AND I WATCHED the sun rise above the mountain peaks during the last hour of the early morning. It was absolutely breathtaking. Streams of scarlet and orange light streaked out from behind the giant, purple-blue shadows of the Rengast and fell on the last of the autumn leaves. The air was crisp and cool, and traveling birds called out high above us, gliding through the sky on their way to the coast.

"I have never been near the Rengast before. It's beautiful," I said, gazing up at the slope.

"It is," Larna agreed. "I am thinking so every time I see it."

I blushed when I realized that instead of staring at the mountains, she was gazing at my face. The grief she had worn so heavily the night before had lifted, and she seemed cheerful as she smiled at me. I hoped that my reassurances had helped her. Instinctively, I reached out and touched Larna's hand. She paused before tightening her fingers around mine. We kept walking, our hands still clasped together. "You've been here before?"

"A few times. It is the way Farseer was using to reach the mountains."

"How long until we reach the top?"

"Three days. We would be going faster if we changed."

"But we couldn't carry clothes or food. I don't think the rebels would appreciate us arriving without clothes."

Larna bumped her hip playfully against mine. "They might. Two young, attractive women wandering naked into camp...They should be so lucky."

I snorted. "Somehow, I have a feeling you would be jealous instead of amused if that happened." I turned to the side, studying Larna's profile. The lines of her face were strong, but gentle. She was so young, I realized, startled by the thought. She was probably the same age as me, certainly no more than a year or two older. It did explain her shy, fumbling moments in our relationship.

"I didna think about nakedness much when I was joining the Farseer pack," Larna said, breaking my concentration. "But when you came to stay with us, I noticed."

"Noticed?" I repeated, dragging the word out. Since Larna seemed receptive, I decided to be a little flirtatious with her. Moments of happiness had been few and far between for her since Farseer's death. "Noticed what?

Larna was completely unapologetic. "Well, I was curious. I was wanting to know if those pretty red curls of yours were the same further down. And I dinna think I was the only one."

My face burned. Many Amendyrri had red hair and freckles just like mine. I never considered them unique or attractive traits, but the way Larna viewed me made me feel special. Still, I could not help pretending to be a little scandalized. "Larna!" I slipped my hand out of hers and nudged her shoulder. She held her hands up to offer a truce.

"I was only teasing. You always turn around in front of the others, anyway."

"And you always stand in front of me." Now, it was Larna's turn to blush. "It's all right. It's sweet of you to defend my virtue...even though you already compromised it."

Larna rolled her eyes. "Virtue is found through good deeds, little bird. It isna something that can be stolen or compromised with sex. That be the Serian in you speaking."

"Well, if you think I'm Serian now just because I grew up there, then you've had plenty of Serian in you as well these last few nights, *Tuathe.*"

Larna looked startled for a moment, but her face relaxed into a warm smile. "You called me *Tuathe* again," she said dreamily, reaching for my hand again.

I gave her fingers a gentle squeeze. "Yes. I did."

As we wove our way through the trees, picking over the rocks and dirt, we came to a cluster of dry, tangled branches. I pressed my hand against the wrinkled bark of a tree to rest. Larna walked just ahead, pushing past the branches and making her way steadily through the thick undergrowth.

"How much longer are we going to have to do this?" I asked, scrambling after her to regain the ground I had lost. I did not mind the walking, but fighting our way through the shrubs at the base of the mountain was tiring.

"Not too much longer," Larna said in a cheerful voice. She did not seem to be bothered by the uneven ground or the branches and leaves closing in all around us. "Soon, we will be finding the path."

"There's a path?" I asked hopefully. For the past day, I had thought we were lost, with only the tops of the mountains to keep us going in the right direction. "Why are we wandering around in the thickest part of the forest, then?"

"I knew we would be finding it eventually."

"You should have told me," I grumbled, crunching behind her. The ground was too full of rolls and bumps to walk on properly. Still, we traipsed onward, pushing our way through the dry undergrowth, clearing space to pass through. I brushed away some loose strands of hair that were clinging to my forehead.

Larna let out a cry of excitement. "Ah! Here we are."

I hurried forward. In front of us was a narrow, flat path stretching off into the trees. I stepped onto it, kicking at the dirt with the toe of my boot. "Shall we go, then?" Larna's excited smile softened my heart, and some of my exhaustion faded. I nodded as we stepped forward onto the path.

***

The path led us in a straight line, and it was not until the next day that anything interesting happened at all. The land started to slope upwards, and the trees thinned out. Soon, we were in the mountains. It happened more gradually than I expected. The forest seemed to stretch up along the sides of the lower slopes, blending the two landscapes together. The trees around us became shorter, and a few were tilted at odd angles, as if floodwater or wind or the rocky soil around their roots had warped their growth.

We had already been walking for a good part of the morning when we reached a fork in the road. One path led to the left, winding off into the trees until it was buried under scattered piles of dead leaves. The other path led up and to the right, and despite its steepness, it looked well-traveled. "Which path should we take?" I asked, looking to Larna for a decision.

She did not answer. Instead, she lifted her nose and sniffed the air, her wide brown eyes reflecting the light and taking in every small movement around us. "There are humans behind those trees up ahead," she whispered.

I looked hard, but could not see anything. "How do you know?"

"Smell." I sniffed the air, sifting through the usual scents of wood, leaves, and cold air. Beneath them was something else. Larna was right. There were humans in the forest. Not just one, but a group of them. They had animals with them as well, although I did not recognize the scent. They smelled a little like horses or livestock.

"Bicorns," Larna explained, answering my unspoken question. Bicorns were the horses of the mountains. With two horns on their heads, one in front of the other, and cloven hooves, they were as surefooted as rams. They were excellent at carrying humans and their supplies up and down the mountains.

"Do they see us?"

"I dinna think so."

"What should we do?"

Larna smiled, showing her teeth. "We should go and say arim dei." Moving quickly and quietly, she left the path and melted into the trees. I copied her, but not without one last backward glance over my shoulder at the path.

"Strip," she ordered when we were far enough away. "It seems that two young, attractive women will be after wandering into a rebel camp sooner than we thought."

"But why are we changing?"

Larna gave me a surprised look. "Surely those humans are having weapons. All we have are our packs. If they be enemies instead of rebels, how else can we defend ourselves? I feel safer with my fangs, thank you all the same."

I remained unconvinced. "Those fangs might be a problem. How do you think they're going to react when two wolves come out of the forest toward them?"

"Better to meet friends as wolves than enemies as humans," she said. "There is no scent of kerak or shadowkin, but demons are not the only servants the witch has."

Larna began undressing beside me. I gave in and followed along, loosening ties and pulling at buttons. Soon, we were naked and changing into our other bodies. It was easier now, I reflected, scratching at my chin with a hind paw. I felt comfortable wearing my fur and muscle, and the change did not frighten me anymore. Larna moved her large head to say, *Come*, and I padded softly behind her, rolling the pads of my feet the way she had taught me. Silently, we stalked back up the road, staying behind the trees this time. The scent of humans grew stronger, and I wondered why I had not noticed it sooner.

Larna's tail stiffened, and her nose pointed toward a large pine with several small, craggy rocks around it. *There*, her eyes said. Without looking at each other, we split in two different directions to approach the circle of humans hiding behind the tree. There were ten of them, eight swordsmen and two archers. All of them wore simple leather armor and carried supplies. The land dipped down briefly behind the pine tree, leaving a wall of dirt and leaves just high enough for a person to rest their back against – which was what most of the group had decided to do. There were ten bicorns as well, but they were not as oblivious as their handlers. They scented us and began tossing their heads in fear.

I saw Larna's dark form crouched on the other side of the group, only thirty feet away from me. Her muscles were not tensed, and her tail hung low. She did not consider this group to be a threat. She broke from the shelter of the trees and walked out at a slow, deliberate trot, I copied her. Immediately, the ten humans scrambled to attention, grabbing for their weapons. The archers nocked arrows to their bows. The bicorns reared, panicking. Fortunately, their reins were tied, and none of them broke free.

For a moment, I thought Larna had made a mistake and the humans were going to shoot us on sight, but before they could attack, one man stepped out of the line and raised his hand. "Stand down. These be not wolves." The archers lowered their bows reluctantly, and the others re-sheathed their swords. The bicorns were still distressed, and one member of the group hurried to calm them. "What do you want?" the man asked, addressing us. Even in my wolf form, I thought that he looked intimidating. He had a huge barrel chest, and his legs were like thick tree trunks. Streaks of silver ran through his grizzled hair, and a scar slashed down his left cheek.

Without embarrassment, Larna changed back into her human form so that she could speak. Truthfully, the humans were in such awe that they hardly noticed her nakedness. It was clear from their shocked faces that none of them had seen a Wyr shift before. "You are Jett Bahari's men," she said, gesturing at them. It was a statement, not a question.

"Why are you wanting to know?" the man asked.

"They are spies," another voice shouted. A second man came forward, clunking in a pair of large metal boots that were far too big for him and totally impractical for walking around in the forest. He was better groomed than some of the others, but had a twitchy nature about him, almost like a small rodent. My hunting instincts told me that he was behaving like prey, despite his pompous nature.

Larna almost laughed at him, but managed to bite her lip in time. "We are not spies. We are here to be joining you."

"How do we know you are telling the truth?" the foolish man asked. His tone was accusatory, and Larna frowned.

"Who else would come here?"

"Spies," he said again, looking at his companions for support. Instead of agreeing with him, they all remained silent, averting their eyes. They seemed almost resentful of him, and I could not blame them. He certainly did not act like a proper soldier.

"We are not spies," Larna repeated calmly.

"Wyr are dangerous. You should have shot them on sight!" the man in the boots cried, flailing his hands.

Finally, the silver-haired giant lost his patience. "They are not puppets of the witch. They would have been attacking us instead of showing themselves." He gestured at Larna. "She changed to speak to us."

The man with the boots glared at him. "Get back in line," he spluttered, his purple cheeks shaking with rage. "I am supposed to lead this division!"

One of the others spoke up, a slender woman who had gone to calm the bicorns when we first arrived. "This is no division, Teb. It be a scouting party, and you are only leader because you were drawing the short straw."

Teb still seemed uneasy, throwing suspicious glances at us before turning to address the rest of the group. "We will question them further..."

"Jett Bahari will question them," said the silver-haired man. "He will know what to ask. We will take them to him."

"They could be friends of the witch or the Queen," Teb insisted, his flushed face turning an even deeper shade of purple. "You want to lead them right to our camp."

The woman laughed. "And how many spies have we been seeing in all these months, Teb?"

"None," another man called out from the line before Teb could speak. "Let's just take them to camp so we can eat."

"Fine, we will take them," Teb agreed sourly, grunting and clanking in a circle until he was facing up the road. "All right, everyone, get moving." Reluctant to follow Teb's impolite orders, but eager to get to the camp, the scouting party started up the path.

"We canna come with you," Larna called out after them.

The procession stopped. "You will follow us," Teb said. The quivering purple flush on his face began to crawl down his neck.

Larna raised one eyebrow, a trick that I envied. "You are wanting us to follow you naked? Without our supplies?"

Teb swallowed nervously, apparently noticing that Larna was not wearing clothes for the first time. He sputtered, his mouth opening and closing like a fish as he struggled to find a response. "Where did you leave your things?" the giant man asked when it became clear that the self-appointed leader had lost his words.

"A few yards that way." Larna pointed into the trees. He headed off in that direction, and the rest of the group followed. Teb was last, muttering about spies and suspicious behavior and traps the whole way, the sound of his metal boots clanking raucously behind him.

***

After we put on our clothes and traveling packs, which seemed to make the suspicious Teb a little more comfortable, we followed the rebels higher into the mountains. The forest thinned out, and the trees were quickly replaced with crags and uneven outcroppings of rock. My thighs and back burned with the effort of trudging uphill, but it was not entirely unpleasant. My new gifts made me stronger, and I enjoyed the physical challenge.

Larna did not seem bothered either. She could move even more swiftly than me, but I quickly realized that there was one advantage to walking behind my lover. Thanks to the steep slope, I had ample opportunity to admire her backside if I remained a few paces lower. I noticed the way the small of her back curved, revealing a strip of tanned skin just beneath her shirt. Still leading their bicorns, the men hurried to keep up with us. Teb in particular seemed annoyed that we were walking in front, and he tried several times to pass us, even though he always fell back again a few minutes later.

"The humans shouldna turn this into a competition," Larna said, sounding amused as she watched the rebels take the lead once again. Only the large, silver-haired man kept at a steady pace behind us. "They will tire themselves with their foolishness."

"I don't know," I said, giving her a sidelong look. "Some Wyr I know can be foolish sometimes, too." Larna just rolled her eyes and pretended not to hear me.

We walked through the hottest part of the day, which was still very cold now that we were in the mountains, but stopped before the sun had finished setting. "We must be posting a guard on them tonight," Teb said to the others as he glared in our direction. "Someone needs to be making sure they dinna try to run away."

"If they are spies, and they run away, how will they find our camp?" the thin woman asked. "They have to come with us if they want to see Jett Bahari."

"Posting guards on them willna do any good," the giant pointed out. "They are Wyr. They can overpower us."

Teb complained and tried to bully the others into seeing things his way, but eventually, he gave up and sat down while the rest of the party began building a fire and laying out rough sleeping pallets. We found a place beside the large man with the silver hair. "How much food do you have left?" Larna asked him, knowing the small packs that we all carried could not hold much.

"Enough to last until we reach the top of the mountain, if we are being careful."

"My mate and I can find meat," she told him, phrasing it as a polite offer.

"Your mate?" Teb, who had been eavesdropping, looked surprised and a little too interested in our conversation. His attention made my face wrinkle with displeasure. Larna sensed my annoyance even from several yards away, because she glared at Teb, warning him to stop talking. One threatening look convinced the bumbling, would-be leader to stay silent.

"It would be good to have fresh meat," the large man said, pointedly ignoring Teb. He held out his hand to Larna, then to me. His large fingers swallowed mine as we shook. "I was never telling you my name. I am Jerico."

"My name is Cate. This is Larna."

We talked for a few more moments before Larna and I went off into the forest to look for food. Now that we were higher in the mountains, there was less game to be found. There were no large herds of deer, only a few scruffy goats and some wild rabbits. We did manage to bring down a tough old ram, although he almost knocked my skull with his horns.

The fire was blazing bright and the sky was dark when we brought the ram back to the rebels,. We cooked it over the fire and salted it, even though Larna and I wished that our portions had stayed raw. We did not want to remind the men of our differences. We sat next to Jerico and his friends while Teb sulked on the other side of the fire, his back partially turned to us.

"I do not like that little man," Larna said, gesturing at him with her head, "but he is right to be suspicious. The Queen is gathering allies. That is why we are wanting to see Jett Bahari. The witch's dogs and the shadowkin attacked our pack. Kerak were with them. Mogra and the Queen are building an army."

"We have heard rumors," Jerico admitted. "This is very bad news."

"Then why do you trust us?" I asked

He shrugged his great shoulders. "If we were turning away everyone who wanted to join the rebels, we wouldna have an army. You will be questioned by the truth-seekers when we reach camp. Until then, you share our fire as friends."

CHAPTER THREE

WE WERE UP AND moving before first light broke over the mountains, but it did not take us long to find the rebel camp. The trail leveled out quickly, and we arrived on a large stone plateau. My sensitive nose caught the scent of cook fires before the edge of the camp came into view. I fiddled with the piece of twine around my neck that held the deadeye. It was warm against my collarbone. Perhaps there were other magic-workers here.

"They will not be welcoming at first," Larna warned me, adjusting the weight of the pack on her shoulder.

"Why?"

"That little man was not entirely wrong to be distrustful. As far as they know, we might be working for the Queen. I have not been to my village for years, and you are from Seria. We have no one to speak for us."

Although I saw the sense in her words, I could not help being a little offended. "We came here to help, and they're going to treat us like prisoners? That seems like an impractical way to build an army."

"But the safest way. Dinna worry, *Tuathe*. They will only question us, not torture us." I was still wary as the sounds of talking and movement drifted toward me. I tensed the tiny muscles behind my ears, but they would not rotate in my human form.

Finally, we reached the center of the rebel camp. Tents were scattered about in a lopsided ring, and a few semi-permanent buildings had been erected from wooden planks. In the middle was another large bonfire, and it was lit even though the sun was climbing swiftly into the sky. I shuddered, remembering the kerak and the shadowkin. Keeping the blaze fed throughout the day was certainly worthwhile.

The weather was cold, but several people were outside when we arrived. All of them turned to watch as Teb and Jerico's party led us toward the second-largest of the plank buildings. "Wait here," Teb ordered, leaving us to wait outside with Jerico and the others.

"Someone go with him," Jerico muttered. "We canna let him be the only one to give a report. He'll be getting it all wrong." Another of the young rebels nodded respectfully and followed Teb inside of the building. The rest of us lingered by the door, waiting for them to emerge again. "You must be talking to the truth-seekers," Jerico explained. "If you pass their tests, you may ask Jett Bahari to join the camp."

"That is how you weed out spies?"

Jerico nodded. "We do not let our group grow too quickly, and everyone is tested. So far, we have not been betrayed." My heart sank. It embarrassed me that I could not say the same for our pack, and I knew that the thought of a traitor living among us hurt Larna even more.

"If you are so afraid of spies," Larna asked, "why are you trusting us?"

"You are Wyr. You have more reason than most to be hating the magic-stealer and the witch. Wyr only fight for her if they are puppets, and you are not."

Cold fear twisted in my belly. "I almost was," I whispered, allowing myself to feel grateful that Mogra had not put me under her control.

"Then you were lucky," Jerico said.

"How are you knowing so much about us?" Larna asked. She did not sound suspicious, only curious and perhaps a little surprised. "Humans hate the Wyr. My village turned me out."

"I am a woodsman. I lived in the Forest long before the rebellion. It has no secrets from me." I wanted to ask if Jerico had met other free-willed Wyr like us, but Teb and the young soldier came out of the meeting house, and voice called to us from inside. "Go in," Jerico said, pushing gently at the middle of my back.

Larna's fingers linked with mine, and she did not let go when we stepped through the door. It was dark inside, even though candles flickered on the simple table. The room was not decorative, only practical. There were some chairs, two tables, papers, quills, and a barrel of drinking water.

A large man was sitting at one of the tables. He was enormous, like

Jerico, and without looking at them side-by-side, I could not tell which was taller. His skin was black, darker than I had ever seen before, and his chin was cut in a firm square. There was an old woman beside him, but she wore a black cloak, and it was hard to make out her face. Behind the leader and the woman were two guards. They seemed unnecessary, since the large man could probably defeat anyone that tried to attack him without any difficulty.

"Some of my men," he said slowly, examining us, "seem to think that you are both spies." His voice was very deep, and he had a strange accent that I could not place. "I do not think so. But if you bring a weapon inside of this room and do not give it up, the penalty is death." Immediately, Larna took the knife from her belt and dropped it onto the ground. "Do you agree to be searched, or will you leave?"

"We agree," Larna said, looking at me to make sure.

Jett Bahari waved at the two men. "Search them."

The men were quick and professional, without any wandering hands. We were not asked to remove our clothes, but we did have to take off our boots and turn them upside-down. It did not take very long. I had braced myself for something much more intrusive and time-consuming.

"You may step forward," Jett Bahari said when he determined that we had no weapons. "My men have also told me that you are Wyr. If you change in here without warning, my guards will attack you. Do you understand?" Jett Bahari did not seem to think that we would try and kill him, but he wanted us to understand the rules. Since my other-skin was a weapon to him, I was not offended.

"We understand," I said. Larna did not look happy, but she did not object, either. "Stop pouting," I whispered. "You told me that they were strict until the truth-seekers approve of us." Larna gave me a look, but did not say anything.

"I will be testing you," said the old woman, speaking for the first time. She pulled back her hood, and I realized that she was even more ancient than I thought. Her face was a network of deep, craggy lines, especially around her eyes, and her skin was a tough, leathery brown. In a small way, she reminded me of Kalwyn. Instinctively, I touched the deadeye as it rested over the dip of my collarbone. I felt the humming aura that came from the old woman and was comforted by the familiar sensation of magical energy. The woman looked surprised. I wondered if she could feel it when I sensed her, like an invisible touch.

"This one is a shaman," she told Jett Bahari. "That is Kalwyn's totem."

Jett Bahari's face softened. "You know Kalwyn?" he asked, sounding much friendlier.

"I was her student."

"Was?"

"An evil creature took her shape. I killed it, but I couldn't save her."

Jett Bahari looked very upset, but the old woman did not seem surprised, although a sad, thoughtful look crossed her face. "It is a great loss," she said. "Did Kalwyn give you the deadeye, or did you take it from her when she died?"

"She gave it to me, along with two other things. They're in my bag."

"What were the other things?"

"An hourglass with a golden dragon, and a sketch from her library." Since I was not prompted, I did not tell them what the sketch depicted. Some deep-rooted instinct warned me not to talk about Umbra and the stolen dragon magic.

The old woman nodded. "I would like to see the hourglass, but Kalwyn gave it to you, and I will not take it. Maybe another day, you will allow me to examine it." I nodded, not making any promises. I felt very protective of Kalwyn's gifts, since they were all I had left of her. "We will not test you, young shaman. I will trust any student of Kalwyn's with my life."

I was touched by her faith in me, a complete stranger. "Thank you," I said, surprised that I did not need to prove myself. I remembered Larna and reached down to touch her hand with mine. She squeezed my fingers lightly. "What about my mate?"

If Jett Bahari was surprised by my declaration, he did not show it. His face remained blank. "We will test her, but it will be quick. I do not think that she will betray us."

Part of me wanted to insist that if they trusted me enough to skip my tests, they should trust Larna, too, but I stayed silent. I did not want to cause any more trouble for her. She was not a traitor, and she had nothing to lose. Larna took it in stride, as though she had expected that response. "I am ready," she said. Her chin was held at a steady angle, neither proud nor afraid.

Light flared before us, and I saw that the old woman had lit a red candle. The flame jumped and danced even though there was no wind. In the flickering light, she held up something that had been sitting in her lap. It was an unlit stick of incense. She touched its tip to the candle flame, causing the end of the stick to smoke.

Soon, the scent of burning thyme filled the tent. Kalwyn had not taught me much about herbs, and the few that I knew how to use were for healing. Herbs were a much greater part of an oracle's work. As the smell grew stronger, I could sense magic mixed with the smoke. Perhaps the woman had prepared them in a special way beforehand.

The old woman's voice rose above the incense. "What is your name?" she asked. I did not know what I had expected—maybe a mysterious couplet or spell—but this procedure seemed too simple.

"Larna."

"What is your last name?"

"My family rejected me. I am not using my last name anymore."

She did not object to that answer. "Where were you born?"

"Katar."

She moved on to the more serious questions. "Why have you come here?"

"We were banished from our pack. We want to help the rebellion."

"Why do you want to help the rebellion?"

The flame of the candle danced in both of Larna's shining, dark eyes. "The witch threatens my pack. She must be stopped."

She nodded, approving of her answers. "Have you ever been in contact with the Queen, or other enemies of the rebellion?"

"No."

"Are you loyal to the Queen, or other enemies of the rebellion?"

"No."

"Do you plan to communicate with the Queen, or other enemies of the rebellion?"

"No."

"If you join the rebellion, do you swear to be loyal to Jett Bahari and help him restore order and peace to the Kingdom of Amendyr?"

Larna answered without hesitation. "Yes."

The old woman put out the candle and incense, the dark sleeves of her cloak pooling on the surface of the table as she set them down. "Step forward, Larna." Larna obeyed, curious about what would happen next. "Closer. Hold out your hand." Carefully, the old woman took clippings from Larna's nails with a small pair of silver scissors. Then, she snipped a piece of Larna's hair.

"What is that for?" Larna asked.

"I can use them to trace you if you ever do betray us, or if you are captured. I can also use them for spells." She smiled, and once again, I was reminded of Kalwyn. "Congratulations, you have passed your test. Welcome to the Rebellion."

Larna looked surprised. "That is all?"

"You want more tests? I can give them to you. I do not think you are a spy. My incense should have made you tell the truth."

Larna shook her head. "No. I just expected...I am not sure what I was expecting."

"Now that you are finished your tests, I will tell you my name. I am Auriye."

Larna brushed her palm on her leggings and held out a hand for Auriye to shake. I stepped forward, taking my rightful place beside my lover again. Auriye took my hand, too, and her grip was surprisingly strong.

Jett Bahari offered his hand. "Let me be the second to welcome you. You are the first Wyr to join us, but we hope that others will follow, maybe even some Liarre."

"There are Liarre here?" I asked, unable to conceal my excitement. I had always wanted to see a Liarre for myself. Many people on the eastern side of the kingdom went their entire lives without meeting one. Although they had been created by magic like the Wyr centuries ago, the Liarre survived on their own. They lived in a small territory to the northwest of Amendyr. Half human and half beast, they came in many strange combinations. The Feliarre had the lower bodies of giant cats. The Dracarre had human torsos on top of scaly lizard legs. Most frightening of all, the Arachniarre's lower halves were shaped like the round, bulbous bodies of spiders. In the pictures I had seen, they even had all eight legs.

"Not yet," Jett Bahari said. "We have sent delegates to them, hoping for an alliance." He examined us thoughtfully. "Perhaps they will be more receptive to other magical creatures."

"Oh no, more traveling," Larna muttered.

"There are no plans yet," he assured us. "It was just an idea. My men will show both of you to a tent for the night. Usually, our fighters train together for the first part of the day, unless they have other duties. In your case, I doubt that weapons training would be of much use to you."

"Thank you for offering us a place to sleep," Larna said, lowering her shoulders and placing her feet close together to take up less space. Her body language with Jett Bahari surprised me. Normally, Larna was a confident Wyr. She held her head and tail high, not afraid to show her dominant disposition. The only time I remembered seeing her take a submissive stance was while talking to Farseer. For the moment, she had accepted Jett Bahari as her commanding officer.

"Thank you," I echoed.

"Elaran, come here," Jett Bahari said, and a familiar person stepped forward. It was the young soldier that had come to fetch us earlier while we were waiting with Jerico. "You will show our guests to an empty tent for the night."

Elaran, who was little more than a boy, looked only too pleased to accompany us. He almost seemed ready to thank Jett Bahari for the honor. "Aye. I'll be taking them with me right away, Sir." His light eyes glanced shyly toward me, and then he quickly looked away. I almost blushed. I could smell his interest, and wondered if that was the reason he wanted to show us to our tent.

We said goodnight to Jett Bahari and Auriye and followed Elaran out of the building. He had a long-limbed step for such a young man, and he might have been even younger than Larna and me. We passed through camp quickly, and it did not take us long to arrive in front of a small, empty tent. Elaran stopped and turned to face us. "Here you are," he said, giving me a wide smile. "Is there anything else you're needing?"

Larna, who had finally noticed Elaran's interest in me, stepped closer to my side. She did not seem upset. In fact, she was almost smug as she reached behind me, patting the swell of my backside through the fabric of my leggings. "No, but thank you for the warm welcome."

Elaran's face fell a little, and a flush spread across his cheeks. "Aye. Well…we dinna have much here, but we share what we can. If you like, I could show you around tomorrow. Give you a tour of the camp," he offered, rubbing at the back of his neck with his hand.

"Perhaps," I said, not wanting to commit to anything. Elaran seemed nice enough, but I did not want to encourage him further.

There was a short, awkward pause until Elaran realized that there was no reason for him to stay. Reluctantly, he left us in front of the tent, taking one last look over his shoulder. As soon as he was out of earshot, Larna laughed softly and gave my behind another squeeze. "Proud of yourself, are you?" she teased. "Only here a few hours, and already breaking hearts."

I pulled away from her. "I don't want to encourage him," I said, flushing with embarrassment. "He's just a boy…"

"Exactly. I may not be a boy, but I notice pretty girls often enough. I know some of how they are thinking. Just be careful, little bird."

169

I smiled and reached up to stroke Larna's cheek with my hand. "If you want me to tell him no tomorrow, I will."

Larna shook her head. "Let him show us around. It willna do him any lasting harm. Now, come inside," she said, kissing my hair. Together, we took our traveling packs into the tent and got ready to sleep.

CHAPTER FOUR

MY NEW ADMIRER FOUND us again the next morning at breakfast. Larna and I were sitting by the fire pit when Elaran approached us, finishing up an early breakfast of dry bread and salted meat. "Your new friend is here," she murmured when she saw him peek around one of the tents. "Let the poor boy down easy." She gave my side a playful nudge before returning her attention to her meal, leaving me to fend for myself.

"Armi dei," Elaran said cheerfully, taking a seat opposite us. Larna took a large bite from her hunk of bread, probably so that she would not have her mouth free to tease me. Elaran's obvious interest in me amused her, but I knew that she did not want to embarrass me or hurt his feelings.

"Arim dei," I said, since Larna could not respond.

An obvious blush crawled across Elaran's cheeks. "Did you sleep well?"

"Mostly." I gave Larna a sidelong glance that could have been interpreted several ways, hoping that Elaran would take the hint. "Anyway, we've decided to take you up on your generous offer to show us around the camp. That is, if you don't mind..."

"I don't mind at all," Elaran said, either ignoring or not noticing my use of the word 'we'. "In fact, I know the first place we should go. We'll visit Jett Markku's tent. He's Jett Bahari's son, and he's in charge of registering all the new arrivals. You'll need to see him today anyway."

Larna swallowed down her mouthful of bread and joined the conversation. "It seems a little dangerous, aye? Keeping a list of traitors to the Queen, even if it's in our hands?"

Elaran could not suppress the shudder that ran through him when Larna said the Queen's name. "I, er...well..."

"I suppose it doesna really matter," Larna added, unable to resist riling him up a little more. "If the Queen made her way into camp and took the list, we would all be dead anyway."

Elaran's eyes widened even further. I hurried to reassure him. "Surely the list is guarded by something more reliable than humans. What about Auriye? If she can create incense that makes people tell the truth, I'm positive she could think of a way to protect it with magic."

Elaran looked visibly relieved. "Well then, we'd best be getting the two of you registered." He stood up from the log across from us and brushed off his pants. "Jett Markku's tent is that way." He gestured past the small wooden building where we had met with Jett Bahari the day before.

We hurried after Elaran, trying not to lose him in the busy, bustling center of the camp. Men and women were clustered around fires, eating, talking, and working together. There were one or two small children, but not many. I stared at a tiny, smudge-faced boy with scruffy hair, and Larna caught me looking. "Sometimes, the children are having nowhere else to go," she said in answer to my silent question.

Larna and I received a few strange looks from the other humans going about their business. Some offered us smiles, but most of them seemed wary. "Gossip must travel fast in a place like this," I said when I noticed a small group of soldiers staring at us. "They know we're Wyr instead of human. They're probably afraid."

"They'll get used to you," Elaran said. He waved at another group passing by on our left. "Where do you come from, anyway? Outside of the Forest, I mean." He glanced over at me. "Your accent is Serian, isn't it?"

I nodded. "It is, but I'm not. I was born just outside the Forest. My parents brought me to Seria when I was small."

"I'm from Katar," Larna volunteered. "Havena been there in years, though. No more ties."

Elaran stopped before a large tent, but made no move to go inside. Instead, he gave Larna a hesitant look. "Katar?" he repeated, twisting his hands nervously in front of him.

"Yes. Why?"

A shadow darkened Elaran's face. "So, you haven't heard?" When Larna did not say anything, he continued. "Katar is gone. The village burned a few months ago."

Larna remained silent, unsure how to react to the news. She held Elaran's gaze, but the smile dropped from her face. I reached out and took her hand, lacing her fingers through mine. "Larna? Are you all right?"

She closed her eyes and shook her head, as if trying to banish a memory. "Aye. I'm all right. My family was making their choice years ago. I have a new family now." She gave my hand a soft squeeze before letting it fall. After a moment, she looked up at the tent and let out a long, unsteady breath. "Inside, then," she said, squaring her shoulders. "Time to become an official part of the rebellion."

Elaran seemed relieved that Larna had not burst into tears or snapped at him. His pleasant disposition returned as he held open the tent's flap, allowing us to step inside first. The interior was larger than I expected it to be, with a high, tapered ceiling, some basic furniture, two sleeping cots, and a small square table in the middle of it all. Sitting at the table was a pleasant-faced young man with dark skin and even darker eyes. The resemblance to Jett Bahari was unmistakable. He smiled at us and stood up, holding out his hand. Larna took it first, and shook. I followed her example.

"Arim Dei. My name is Jett Markku, just in case Elaran was so busy staring that he forgot to tell you." He gave Elaran a friendly nudge. Elaran grinned and nudged him back. "Stop," he laughed, "I'm supposed to be in charge here."

"Which is good for me," Elaran said. "Markku and I grew up together. When his father is busy, I get to do whatever I want."

"Not true," Jett Markku objected, poking Elaran playfully in the chest. I smiled. Both of them were still young boys, and even though they were part of the rebellion, I wondered just how much combat they had seen. Something about them was still innocent, untouched by the cold fingers of death. "Right now, you are going to follow my orders and get the registry."

"And not even a please for my trouble," Elaran muttered. He wandered over to one side of the tent, digging through a pile of papers. Finally, he came up with a half-used sheet and handed it to Jett Markku, who smoothed it out on his thigh and set it on the table. He reached into his tunic and fumbled about for a moment before producing a quill. "Now, if you two ladies would please give me your full names?"

"Cathelin Raybrook," I said, saying it slowly and clearly so that he could copy it down.

"Larna."

Jett Markku looked up at Larna for a moment, but he wrote it down. "No last name?"

"I am not using my last name," Larna said. Her voice made it clear that she would not say anything more on the subject.

Jett Markku continued to stare at her for a moment, but decided not to press her. "Where are you from?" he asked, turning back to me.

"I was born in the Forest, but I lived in Seria for several years."

"That explains the accent. I understand...I was born here, but my father grew up across the sea, in Shezad."

I had never been to the Kingdom of the East, all the way across the sea from Seria, but I had heard stories of it growing up. The people there were magical, just like in Amendyr, and just as ancient, even though their appearance was often very different. I wanted to ask Jett Markku how two men from Shezad had come to make their home all the way in Amendyr and fight for its freedom.

"And you? Where are you from?"

"Katar," she said. "Elaran was just telling me what happened there."

Jett Markku dutifully wrote it down. "I'm sorry for your loss. If any refugees turn up from that city, I'll be sure to let you know, but to be honest, my hopes aren't high. It's been too long. Now, do either of you have any particular skills or specialties?" He suddenly seemed to remember what we were. "Oh, sorry. I suppose magical shape-shifting covers that question." He finished scribbling on the piece of paper, and stuffed the quill back into the folds of his tunic when he was finished. "Good. Is there anything else you need?"

"I would like to check the registry," Larna said, and I caught a note of uncertainty in her voice. "I havena spoken to my family in many years, but I am hoping that..."

Jett Markku shook his head slowly, standing up and pressing his hands into the small wooden table. "No one has arrived from Katar since the village burned," he said softly. "No one but you."

***

The moment that I opened my eyes, I knew that Larna was gone. My senses told me that it was still nighttime. There were no loud voices, and the dirt and stone outside smelled wet with rain. I stretched and ran my fingers through my hair, noticing for the first time how unruly it was. I would have to trim it soon, or it would grow wild.

Larna had not seemed too upset in the hours before we fell asleep. Even though she had not seen her parents and brother for several years, I knew that a secret part of her hoped that they would be here. She could not completely let go of the idea that, if they saw her again, they might apologize and accept her back into the family. I felt a wave of sympathy for her. She had been rejected by both of the families that should have loved her.

As quietly as I could, I pulled on a fresh pair of clothes and crept out of the tent. It was not difficult to find traces of Larna's scent, and I walked the perimeter of the campsite, picking my way over rocks and patches of gravel. I saw a small group of night guards chatting over their dinners, but they hardly noticed me as I slipped away from them, keeping to the shadows.

The stars were high in the sky and cool wind started to blow when I finally found Larna. She was sitting on a flat rock, looking down the mountainside even though it was too dark to see the forest or the plains below. The sight of her curled up into a ball, with her shoulders hunched up and her arms wrapped around her knees, made my chest tighten. I came up behind Larna and put my hand on her strong back. I could feel her body shaking.

"Do they believe in life after death in Seria?" Larna asked in a small voice.

"Yes," I said. "The Serians believe in an afterlife, just like we do. They call The Maker 'God,' and he takes your soul to paradise after you die."

"God?" Larna repeated, not turning around. "But how do they know? Where is the proof?"

"You seem like you are having trouble believing in The Maker right now," I said softly. I liked to think he existed myself, but I often slipped into doubts of my own. Larna nodded, but remained silent, not trusting her voice. We sat in silence for a long time. I climbed up on the rock next to Larna and folded her into my arms, letting her rest her cheek against my shoulder. We stayed absolutely still, afraid that if we moved, the moment would break.

"Do you believe in this God? The Maker?" Larna asked after a long time, her voice muffled by my hair.

"I'm not sure. I like to think the Maker is real, but sometimes I wonder." Larna stopped crying, but I still held her tight in my arms. "But I do think there is something after death. I don't think people just disappear." I pressed a kiss to the back of her dark hair. "And I don't think love disappears. Our love won't disappear. My love for Kalwyn and your love for Farseer won't disappear. And even though they hurt you, I know you loved your family."

Larna swallowed several times before she spoke, but when she did, her voice was still hoarse. "I am hardly better than them. I left the pack when they were needing me. I didna believe your vision. I let you run into the forest without me. I should have fought harder to keep you...to help them..."

"It's all right. You're here now. You left the pack to follow me. And soon, we'll go back and save them from themselves. You haven't abandoned anyone. Not them, and definitely not me."

"I am trying to tell myself that." Larna sighed and leaned further back into my embrace. "How were you knowing to come after me now, Catie?"

I gave the top of her head another kiss. "I'm your *Tuathe*, remember? I knew something was wrong when I woke up without you. Besides, it always hurts worse at night."

"I wasna expecting my parents and brother to be here, but I was hoping..." She sniffed and brushed the last of her tears away with her thumb. "We should be going back to our tent."

"We can stay here, if you want."

I could feel Larna's smile at me through the dark as she pulled away. "No, it's cold out here." I knew that she was not cold, but did not argue with her. Our Wyr blood kept us warm on cold nights.

I held her hand, letting her fingers wrap around mine. "Come with me, *Tuathe*. Let's go back to bed."

***

Larna and I slowly began to gain the camp's trust. Despite his embarrassing attraction to me, Elaran was a great help. He made sure we knew all of the goings-on, introduced us to his friends, and spoke warmly of us whenever anyone asked. Thanks to his efforts, most of the suspicious looks we had received during the first few days transitioned into friendly greetings. It probably also had something to do with the fact that Larna and I were able to provide the cooks with a steady supply of small game. There was not much to hunt in the mountains, but rabbits and other small animals lived in the crags and crevices.

Once they were no longer afraid of us, the rebels became curious instead. Several of them asked us questions about shifting. They wanted to know whether it hurt, and what part of our minds remained the same. Although the two of us were hesitant to provide a demonstration, a few had caught glimpses of Larna prowling the edge of camp.

Jerico was the only one who did not seem interested in the fact that we were Wyr. I asked him why one afternoon, while he was busy chopping up a small, gnarled tree into fuel for the fire pit. As I had suspected, the fire remained lit throughout the day just in case kerak or shadowkin decided to leave the forest and venture into the mountains.

"Everyone else always asks so many questions," I said, standing a fair distance away so that none of the chips would strike my face. "Even Elaran wants to know how it feels to change into our other-skins. But not you. You don't care."

Jerico grunted, but he did not pause in his chopping. His muscles pulled and shifted beneath his shirt as he swung his giant axe above his head, and his movements were as strong and smooth as a river. He used the axe like an extension of his arms, and I was almost fooled into believing it was a part of his body. I had not known that chopping wood could look so effortless. It had always seemed like a brutal affair to me, even when Larna had done it.

"Wyr and people be no different," he said at last. "Same thoughts. Same feelings. Same fears. One just hunts better...unless they are pets of the witch."

I was surprised, but also pleased by his simple explanation. The others insisted on pointing out our differences, even when they liked us. But Jerico understood. He knew that sometimes, I forgot I was Wyr at all. It had not changed who I was. "How did you learn so much about Wyr?" I asked, curious how he had come to understand us so well.

Jerico finally split the last piece of wood. He brought the axe down one more time and left it buried in the stump of the tree he had felled. Then, he turned towards me. "Dinna think you're the first Wyr I've met, Cate. I've known your kind before. Wyr are older than your pack, older even than the witch. She was not the first to be making creatures like yourself. Your history is going all the way back to Lyr the Shaper."

Again, Jerico had surprised me. I had not expected him to know so much about magical history. I blushed and reminded myself not to judge people by their appearances. "When did you meet other Wyr? The only ones I've known were from my old pack. Are there many others?"

Jerico shook his head. "No, girl, not many, and fewer still thanks to me."

My eyes widened, and it took me a moment to realize what Jerico was saying. "You mean you've killed us?"

"That depends on who you think of as 'us'." He dropped to his knees, stacking the neat pieces of wood that he had chopped into a pile. Normally, I would have helped him, but I hesitated until he offered the rest of his explanation. "Some Wyr think the witch's pets are their brothers. Some think they are monsters. Perhaps both opinions have some truth."

I remembered back to when I had first joined the pack. Farseer had reprimanded Goran for calling Mogra's Wyr 'dogs'. The taste of blood rose in my mouth, and I thought of the Wyr I had killed by the fire pit. Both memories seemed old, even though Larna and I had only left the Farseer pack two weeks ago. "So, you're a killer of monsters?"

"Aye. But you would be knowing about that, wouldn't you, Cate?"

"I'm not sure how you know...but, yes. I've killed before."

Jerico stopped what he was doing and studied me for a long moment. "Aye. It leaves a look about you, facing creatures of evil. I've killed kerak, shadowkin, and more Wyr than I can count. Hunting Mogra's servants was the only way I could think of to find peace within myself before I was coming here."

"You don't just hate Mogra because she's evil, do you? There's something personal about it."

"Aye, it's personal. She took someone I loved. I will keep killing the witch's creatures until she has no more army, and she is dead. Anyone, human or Wyr, that helps me can call themselves my friend. Anyone that tries to stop me will become acquainted with my axe." He stood and gripped the giant handle, pulling it from the stump and propping it over his shoulder. "Come now, and be helping me with the wood. The fire's almost out."

CHAPTER FIVE

EARLY MORNING FOUND ME lingering near the rocky outcropping where I had comforted Larna, journal in my lap and quill in hand. I felt welcome in camp now, but it was difficult to write with too many other people around me. Although the tent I shared with Larna offered us some privacy, something about it felt stifling. Since leaving Baxstresse, I had learned to enjoy solitude, especially out of doors.

I paused in my writing and looked out over the mountains. The sun cast streaks of red and gold over the forest below. Most of the trees had shed their leaves, and the few that still clung stubbornly to their branches were the same color. In the daylight, and from this high up, I could see farther than I ever had before. "It's beautiful," I murmured, even though there was no one around to hear me.

"Beautiful, and also wise."

I looked up with a start and snapped my journal shut. Apparently, I had not been speaking to myself after all. I let out a relieved sigh when I saw that it was only Auriye. Even my Wyr senses had not told me that she was there. She stood a few paces behind me, looking out over the forest just as I had done. I could not be sure, but part of me wondered if she could see even farther than me, even with my enhanced sight.

"What do you mean, wise?"

Auriye continued gazing out beyond the mountains. "The earth speaks to those who know how to listen, young shaman. It speaks to me just as the spirits speak to you." She turned toward me, and her eyes settled heavily on the deadeye hanging beneath my throat. "How much was Kalwyn able to teach you before she passed? What did you learn?"

Thinking about Kalwyn made my heart sink. "Not nearly enough," I said, unable to hide my regret. "She showed me how to see the magical energy around me, and how to remember more of my visions, but the more I learned, the less I seemed to know."

The lines around Auriye's face grew deeper as she smiled at me. I wondered exactly how old she was. "Then you have learned something valuable. You might be surprised how many young *Ariada* cannot grasp the vast amounts of knowledge that exist in the world."

I gave her a hopeful look. "I don't suppose there's anything you could teach me? I feel..." I paused, searching for a word. "Unfinished."

"Another gift. The fact that you know how much you do not know will keep you hungry. You will never tire of learning. But I fear there is only a little I can teach you, young shaman. Our powers are different. I will help you, but you must rely on what Kalwyn has already taught you, and we must hope that it will be enough." I frowned, not understanding why anyone's hope rested on me at all. "When you arrived at camp, you told me that Kalwyn had given you three things. I have already seen one. I must ask you to show me the other two now."

I only hesitated for a moment. Although I was protective of Kalwyn's gifts, I did not think that Auriye would take them from me. "I have them here," I said, putting the journal next to me on the rock so that I could pull my pack onto my lap. I almost always carried it with me unless I wore my other-skin. Kalwyn's gifts were too valuable to lose.

I took out the hourglass first. The sunlight made the scales of the coiled dragon glisten with gold. All of the sand was still stuck in the top half. I handed it to Auriye, and she smiled again. "Yes, I know this hourglass, although I've never seen it like this before. It has been in Kalwyn's possession for years. Did she ever tell you what its enchantment does?"

"She told me that it's supposed to tell us when the dragons are coming back." A few months ago, I would not have believed it. Dragons were practically considered mythical beings in Seria, even though the Amendyrri knew that they were very real. None had been sighted in either kingdom for centuries.

Auriye passed the hourglass back to me. It could have been my imagination, but I thought that the glass and metal felt warm in my palms. "Aye. It is very old, and very powerful. Be careful with it. My signs say that you will be needing it before the end."

"The end of what?" I asked, but Auriye ignored my question.

"There was another gift Kalwyn gave you. A drawing? Please, show it to me."

Carefully, I put the hourglass back inside my pack and took out the drawing. I had not opened it since copying the picture for Ellie in my journal. Looking at it again made me feel uneasy, and the morning air around me was suddenly colder. Auriye did not take the picture from me. Instead, she peered over my shoulder, as if she did not want to get too close. "I am not sure why Kalwyn gave you this, but I know what it is. Who it is."

"Kalwyn gave it to me because I asked her. Before this, I lived in Seria. Cieran, the King's magical advisor, told me to ask any *Ariada* I met about Umbra. This is all that Kalwyn could find."

Auriye nodded. "Most of the history books have forgotten him, maybe through dark magic. His name is rarely written. It is only kept alive through stories now." But something in her voice was doubtful. I was surprised at how much fear Umbra could inspire despite being dead for hundreds of years. He had been gone since the time of the dragons, although since Ellie had discovered his sorcerer's chain, perhaps something of his memory still lingered.

"We think we've discovered his sorcerer's chain," I said, deciding to tell Auriye the whole story. "When I lived in Seria, someone I knew had a necklace. It looked like an eye of silver and gold." I pointed to the circles on the drawing. "And even though I never held it, my friend Ellie told me that it burned to the touch. She's *Ariada*, too." Thinking about the sorcerer's chain made me remember Luciana as well. I wondered, as I often did, whether Luciana had been able to use Umbra's focus object because she was already evil, or whether it had made her that way. It was a question that had no satisfactory answer, and it could do nothing to erase the pain she had caused me.

If Auriye was surprised, she did not show it. Perhaps she simply believed me because I was Kalwyn's student, or maybe she had seen something in her own visions, because she did not question my statement. "If you truly did find Umbra's focus object, you also must have destroyed it. Otherwise, the shadow over Amendyr would be even larger."

My eyes widened. "You think the Queen has something to do with Umbra?"

"I think that it is not a coincidence you came here with these things, young shaman," she said, gesturing at the drawing and the hourglass. "Now, put them away. Keep them safe. When the time comes, you will know how to use them."

***

The circle again, pressing in on all sides as two sleek shadows lunge for each other. Fire blazes around them, and sparks shower down on their rippling bodies. They fall to the ground, snarling and barking as they struggle to find holds...

Blood runs out around Hosta's teeth, a thick, pulsing river of red matting the fur around his jaws. They are still locked around Larna's neck, and no matter how hard she thrashes, he will not let go.

I try to run to her, but my legs will not move. She looks at me with cloudy eyes, and I can see the life seeping out of them...

"Larna!" I woke with a start, bolting upright on my sleeping pallet and clutching my throat with my hands. The dark bodies were not there. There was no circle, no teeth, no blood. It was only another vision. I slumped my shoulders and swiped a hand over my burning face, trying to stop myself from shaking. Even though I knew it was the Sight, Larna's death had seemed real. It had felt real. And I knew that if something did not change, it would become real.

Larna stirred beside me, reaching out a sleepy hand to stroke along my leg. She blinked her eyes open, staring up at me through the dark. "Nightmare, Catie?"

I felt guilty for waking her, but I clung to her anyway, desperate to feel her heartbeat and the steady rhythm of her breathing. "You were dying. You were..."

"I am right here." She pulled me back down onto our sleeping pallets, shifting over and holding her arms open so that I could rest my head against her broad chest. I tucked my face into the safety of her shoulder, breathing in and out, hoping that her scent would calm my racing heart. Larna wrapped one of her arms around my shoulder and pulled me close. "Now, are you wanting to tell me what happened?"

"It was the vision again," I told her. My voice shook, but I forced myself to continue. "Hosta killed you. I watched him tear out your throat."

"Hosta is with the Farseer pack. He canna kill me if he is still in the Forest," Larna said, but I could tell that she was worried. She believed in my vision. She just did not want to say so. At last, she sighed and tucked her chin over my head. "How will we be stopping this from happening? There must be a way."

"I...I don't know. Usually, seeing the vision and telling someone is enough, but this one feels different. Like a warning. Unless something changes, it's still going to happen." I pulled my face away from Larna's neck and stared at her through the darkness. "I wish Kalwyn was here. She would know what to do."

"We will be finding a way. I am not going to die." Larna's face leaned closer through the darkness, and before I could answer, her mouth took mine. Her hand cupped my shoulders, slid up, pushing my hair aside and cradling the back of my neck. I stiffened, torn between fear and relief. She pulled back just far enough to whisper against my lips. "Let me prove it. Let me show you that I'm alive. That I'm here."

I realized what Larna was doing. When we first left the Farseer camp, she had needed the reassurance of my touch and the strength of my love. Now, I was the one who needed her. I answered her with a kiss, putting all of my fear and need behind it, pressing forward with my tongue until she bit down on my lower lip to stop me.

"Not so fast," she murmured. "Let me help you..."

But I did not want her to help me. I wanted her to hurt me. To put her marks on me so that they would not fade. To leave me so raw and open that I could not bear to think of the world without her in it.

My hand curled around Larna's hip, and I pulled her closer, wanting to feel her body tight against mine. I pressed hard, broken kisses to her lips as she dragged my shirt over my head, freeing my breasts and ruining my hair. I was past caring. All I wanted was her, against me and inside of me and alive.

She kissed her way across my chest, hardly giving me time to think or breathe. She had sensed what I wanted. Not slow, and not gentle. Her teeth bit down hard above the peak of my breast, and I arched my spine, raking my nails down her back as she shifted on top of me. The feel of fabric under my hands was unacceptable. I hungered for her skin instead. I tugged at her clothes, demanding that she take them off without words.

Stripping Larna was difficult. She did not want to leave my breasts, and she held tight to my waist whenever I tried to pull off her shirt. Finally, I gave up and moved lower, shoving her leggings down over her narrow hips instead. Soon, they were tossed in a corner of the tent. I lifted her shirt up under her arms, but I could not get it over her head. "Off," I whispered, and to my surprise, it came out as an order instead of a plea.

Larna did pull away long enough to tear off her shirt, but when her lips touched me again, she would not be rushed. Slowly, torturously, the warmth of her mouth slid down along my stomach. She stopped to pay attention to each freckle as she tugged at my remaining clothes. Pressure pounded between my legs, and I felt myself swell open as I lifted my hips to help her. My inner muscles shivered, releasing a pulse of wetness as I parted my thighs. She had not even touched me yet, and I was already trembling.

I fisted the short, dark tangle of her hair with my fingers, trying to push her head between my legs, but nothing I did could move her. She trailed kisses between my hipbones, stopping to bite down just beneath the dip in my navel. Suddenly, I realized what I was doing. I looked down at her with wide eyes, taking in shallow sips of air. We had never done this before. I had tasted her, but Larna had only used her fingers. She felt my quick heartbeat and soothed the place she had bitten with soft swipes of her tongue, stroking my side with a large, calloused palm. "Relax. Open for me."

It only took a few moments for my desire to outpace my fear. I still needed her. My inner muscles clenched as I imagined her fingers sliding inside of me, and the hard bud of my clitoris jumped at the thought of her lips drawing it in. I let her ease my thighs open.

At first, Larna only used her hand. Wetness greeted her as soon as she touched me, and the pads of her fingers moved over me like silk. My skin was sensitive, sparking, and the lightest contact made my stomach muscles tighten. But it was not what I wanted, and I tightened my grip on her head, letting my nails bite into her scalp. "More. I need…"

I went stiff as she slid inside of me. My muscles caught her fingers, clutching down. She did not move her hand at first, but I pushed forward, driving myself onto it and taking her as deep as I could. I was so ready that the stretch barely stung. It wasn't until she began curling forward, hooking against the full place deep within me that I finally let go of her hair and clawed at the sleeping pallet beneath me. "Yes. Harder. Just like…"

The rest of my words broke off as warmth sealed around me. I looked down past my heaving stomach, and what I saw nearly brought the end crashing down before we had even started. Larna's brown eyes shone in the darkness. I couldn't see her lips, but I could feel them pulling at me, folding around the base and lashing the tip. The first scrape of her tongue caused another pulse of wetness to run over her fingers. I was torn between heat and pressure. It was almost too much to feel at once, so overwhelming that there was no more room in my world for thoughts of death. It was just what I had needed.

Larna understood. Her fingers curled forward sharply, and she grazed me with her teeth, tugging until I screamed and bucked against her. She started a harsh, rocking rhythm with one hand as the other jerked my thighs further apart, forcing me open. It hurt wonderfully. The swollen, tight spot inside of me throbbed with fullness as she drove against it over and over again, and I pulsed with each flick of her tongue. With Larna possessing me, I could allow myself to forget.

Each thrust was bliss. Every stroke was shattering. My mind went blank, and all I could do was let my desire consume us both. I had not known that making love could hold such power along with pleasure. My hands shot down to Larna's shoulders, and I clutched them as tight as I could, rocking forward to meet the warm velvet of her tongue. Somehow, she managed to follow the uneven, jerking motion of my hips. She drew the point of my clit further past her lips, circling until I was sure the pressure inside of me and along the hooded shaft would burst. I clutched desperately at the back of her head, unable to decide whether it was too much, or not enough.

Larna held me on the edge for what seemed like ages, but was probably only seconds. She wanted my release almost as much as I did. Perhaps more, if that was possible. She drove into me with powerful strokes of her wrist, catching at the perfect angle as her lips folded around me and pulled. Our eyes locked, and I forgot everything except for her.

Her fingers and tongue unleashed a flood. My body seized up, and then everything loosened as I spilled around her hand. Sharp pulses tore through my lower belly, and each one forced out a heavy stream of wetness from deep within me. I twitched wildly between her lips, but she did not let go. Rippling waves of heat ran between us as tears streamed over my cheeks. I could not decide whether it hurt or felt indescribably wonderful.

When the stars stopped flashing behind my eyes and my tears started to dry in salty streaks on my face, I floated back to earth. Larna's head was still tucked between my legs, gently cleaning me and tasting her reward. For a brief moment, I was embarrassed. There had never been so much wetness before. But when Larna looked up and smiled at me with glistening lips, I knew that what we shared had been beautiful.

"That was wonderful," Larna murmured, scattering kisses across my belly and working her way up to my breasts. "I love your taste, little bird."

Before she could work me into another frenzy, I locked one knee around her hip and flipped her onto her back. It was not as difficult as I had expected, mostly because my forcefulness took her by surprise. I was glad that she had enjoyed pleasing me, but our last encounter had been far too one-sided for my liking. I also had my own selfish reasons for wanting to touch her. It was yet another reminder that my vision had not come true.

Larna did not protest as I slid one of my hands down along the hard surface of her stomach. She opened her legs for me, and a groan caught in her throat as my lips found her shoulder. I did not waste time. My patience was gone, and she was already close after giving me release. I kissed up along the line of her neck, stopping at the place where her pulse hammered just beneath the skin. My fingers found her, and she pressed against them eagerly, shifting until they slipped over the right spot. Once I discovered the motion she liked best, I repeated it, biting down when I felt her swell beneath the pad of my thumb.

"Cate, yes, don't stop," she gasped out in a breathless stream beside my ear. Hearing Larna, my brave, unshakable warrior, fall to pieces as I touched her made me feel dizzy. I craved the moments when she took control of me, but the knowledge that she trusted me enough to give herself over as well only made me love her more.

Once I thought the words, I had to say them aloud. "I love you." My fingers slid lower, lower, until they were teasing the tight circle of her entrance. I pushed inside, trying not to cry all over again as her warmth clutched down around me. "I need you." I searched for the same place she always seemed to find so effortlessly within me, and her entire body tensed when I found it. My thumb swiped over the tight bud of her clit, pressing into it until she began to shudder. "I'm not going to lose you."

She came with a sharp howl. The sound vibrated through her throat and against my lips as she squeezed hard around my fingers, drawing them even deeper. She was all shudders and sighs, pulsing endlessly into my hand. Fierce pride swelled in my chest as her warmth ran along my wrist, and I did my best to keep thrusting through her release. Larna was my *Tuathe*, and I wanted to take all of her, just as she had taken me.

Finally, her body stilled. She went limp beneath me, and a wide, sleepy smile spread across her face. The afterglow was infectious, and I felt my own heartbeat start to slow down as I rested on top of her. It was different, lying on top of Larna instead of the other way around. I was coming to realize that I preferred the way her weight felt when she was pressing down over me, but our bodies were a perfect fit, and the smoothness of her skin was far more comfortable than the sleeping pallets.

"I'm surprised at how fast the two of us were learning how to do this," Larna said, still grinning as she stared up at the ceiling. "I thought it might be taking a while, but that was…"

"Incredible," I finished for her. I returned her smile. "Who knows? Maybe we're still terrible at it, and we just don't know because it feels so good."

"If that was terrible, I dinna think I can bear wonderful. I am thinking your vision was wrong. A few more months of this might be killing me."

The joke should have upset me, but instead, I laughed against her neck with relief. While Larna's love surrounded me, I was no longer afraid. I could feel the steady rise and fall of her chest beneath me, the warmth of her body, and even the fluttering aftershocks of her inner muscles around my fingers. I pulled them out and rested them on her thigh instead. "You're not going to die," I said, pressing a kiss to her flushed cheek.

"Aye? And why is that?"

"Because I've decided I'm not going to let you." During the vision, I had been frozen and Larna had been helpless, but in reality, we had more control. Hosta was not some invulnerable monster. He was Wyr, the same as us. He could be stopped, or even killed. If he did try to hurt Larna, I would not hesitate.

Before I could translate my thoughts into words, we were disturbed by a noise outside our tent. Larna lifted her head. If she had been in wolf form, her ears would have perked up. "Who is there?" she called out, clutching the crumpled blanket beside us and throwing it open to cover our nakedness.

"Elaran," came a familiar voice from outside. "Jett Bahari wants to see you."

CHAPTER SIX

DRESSED IN FRESH CLOTHES, I stumbled after Larna and Elaran, combing my fingers through my mussed hair. I could see clearly in the darkness, but Larna's touch had left my legs unsteady, and it was difficult to coordinate my movements. "What do you think Jett Bahari wants?" I asked, jogging quickly to catch up with her.

Larna slowed down until I reached her side. She did not seem upset, but she was wary. "I am thinking it is something serious, or he wouldna be calling us in the middle of the night." She looked curiously at the back of Elaran's head, hoping that he would explain the summons, but he just shrugged his shoulders.

"Dinna be looking at me. I'm having no idea what he wants. I was just waking up myself."

The rest of the short walk through camp continued in silence. We waited outside as Elaran ducked into the wooden building to announce our arrival. He was only gone for a few moments. "Come inside," he said, holding the door open so that we could enter.

The interior of the building was dimly lit, and most of the light vanished when Elaran shut the door behind us. Jet Bahari sat at a large table in the center of the room, and candles flickered in front of him. He was alone this time, and I wondered whether Auriye was asleep. "More of your kind have come to camp," he said, getting straight to the point. "They claim to be your pack. My men are with them now."

The news was not what I had expected. I hadn't dreamed that the Farseer pack would follow us into the mountains. The Forest was their home, and if they had left it behind, something must have driven them out. That, or Hosta had changed his mind and come after us...*Red-streaked fangs piercing the fur of Larna's throat, bubbling over with blood*...I shook myself, pushing down the memory and squeezing my hands into tight fists. My nails bit into the skin of my palms, but I did not care. I would not let fear control me any longer. Still, it was several moments before my breathing evened out again.

Larna was even more surprised than I was, and just as suspicious. She did not seem to notice that I had retreated into my own head. "Were they saying why they came?" I could hear the distrust in her voice.

"They want to join us. Their leader, Hosta, told me that the witch had driven them out." His gaze moved between us. "Apparently, they trailed you here. If we are this easy to find, perhaps I need to reconsider our location."

I tugged at my lip. It was bad enough that Hosta's shadow had followed us into the Rengast, and even worse if my suspicions were right. If he was working with the witch, he could betray us again, and my vision would come true. I felt Larna tense beside me, and I relaxed my hands enough to pat one of her shoulders. "Maybe they want to apologize," I suggested, trying to comfort her even though I did not truly believe it.

"Not likely," she muttered. "Hosta would rather die fighting me than admit he was wrong. He wants something else. We need to be finding out what it is."

Jett Bahari cleared his throat, recapturing my attention. "So, does that mean you think the pack is a threat?" The rest of his thoughts might as well have been spoken aloud. A pack of Wyr wanting to join the rebellion could be very useful, very dangerous, or both. He did not want to make any rash decisions, but he saw the benefits of a potential alliance.

"They know where camp is now. You canna just order them to leave," Larna said. I could tell she wanted Jett Bahari to do exactly that, but she also knew that it was not a practical solution. She might have missed the Farseer pack, but she had not forgiven them yet, either. My own feelings were less rational. I wanted Hosta as far away from us as possible.

Jett Bahari stood, bracing himself with his hands on the surface of the table. "I do not want to kill them, but if they react violently, I will have no choice."

Larna nodded. "Fair enough. Where are they?"

"On the edge of camp. Most of the guards are there as a precaution." He gave Larna a searching look. "I know you are not eager to forgive your old pack, but they could be useful allies. If you think they are dangerous, we will do whatever is necessary to keep the rebellion safe. But if they can help us, I hope you will put your own feelings aside. The more people that join us in the fight against the Queen, the better."

I could tell that Larna was torn. So was I, but for different reasons. I did not want her anywhere near Hosta. I trusted the rest of the pack, and I could see why Jett Bahari wanted them to join us, but I could not banish the visions from my mind. Simply thinking about them made cold sweat run down the middle of my back and pool at the base of my spine.

"Aye, I will speak to them," Larna said at last. "If the pack truly wants to join, it be not my place to stop them. But be careful. Have Auriye and your other truth-seekers question Hosta. I dinna have any proof, but Cate and I are thinking he may be helping the witch."

Jett Bahari looked surprised, and then thoughtful. "We might be able to use that to our advantage. Does he know you suspect him?"

I shook my head. "No. We were banished after Farseer and Kalwyn died," I said, trying to explain the story as gracefully as I could. I did not want to talk about forcing myself to eat Kalwyn's heart. "Hosta thought that Larna was a threat to his power, and he used something I did as an excuse to make her leave. He might have been afraid we would find out his secret, but we never accused him of anything."

"Good. We should keep it that way. The two of you will invite him to join us, and we will have our truth-seekers question him. If Auriye suspects him to be a traitor, perhaps we can feed him false information. It would be good to meet the witch on our own terms instead of hiding from her. And if you are wrong, and he truly does want to help us, a pack of thirty strong Wyr could make all the difference in our next battle. Either way, we win."

Larna and I nodded our heads in understanding. I did not like this plan at all, but I had no authority to question it. All that I could do was trust in my visions and do everything in my power to keep Larna safe.

**

The Farseer pack was waiting for us just beyond the furthest tents, surrounded by guards. At least half the camp had been dragged out of bed to keep an eye on the new arrivals. The two groups—rebels and

Wyr—eyed each other nervously, whispering among themselves. Everyone turned to look as we approached through the darkness, and the weight of so many eyes made me shiver.

My breathing grew shallow as Hosta stepped forward from the crowd of familiar faces. Larna had not been this close to him in a long time, and I was more certain than ever that he wanted to kill her. As I studied him, I realized that he had a new scar across one cheek. He was not the only one. Several members of the pack were missing, and a few others sported injuries.

I watched as Larna and Hosta stared each other down in a silent battle for dominance. Their eyes locked, and if they had been in their other-skins, their fur would have been bristling. In the end, neither of them won. They relaxed the lines of their shoulders, circling each other warily. "Why are you here?" Larna asked, breaking the silence first.

"We were attacked twice," Hosta said. His tone was gruff and clipped. "Somehow, the witch keeps finding our camps."

"I thought that her puppets had trouble tracking us?" I doubted that anyone else caught the slight hesitation before the word 'us', but I knew Larna well enough to hear it. Her feelings for the pack and her place in it were still conflicted.

"That was before. It is too dangerous to be staying in the Forest. We must kill her."

Larna's eyes narrowed. "And you have come to ask me for help?"

"Not your help. The rebellion's help," Hosta said. "They are wanting her dead, too. We have similar goals." As he spoke, I could not help staring at his teeth. In his human body, there were no fangs behind his lips, but I could still see the wolf in him.

"Jett Bahari has asked me to decide whether you should join the rebellion," Larna told him, standing a little taller. It was not entirely the truth, but it would not do any harm to let Hosta think she had more power here than he did. Hosta squirmed uncomfortably under her harsh gaze, and I could tell that she was enjoying her brief moment of control over him. After a long, tense wait, she pretended to come to a decision. "Even though you exiled my mate, I am thinking that the pack can be trusted. I will tell Jett Bahari that you will be joining us. But first, you all must be tested by the truth seekers."

Hosta clenched his teeth. "Truth seekers? We are coming here to form an alliance, and you accuse us of being traitors?"

"Not all of you," Larna said. "It only take one." She and Hosta continued staring at each other for several long moments. Neither of them wanted to back down.

"Just me, then," Hosta said. He swallowed his pride and let the angle of his chin drop ever so slightly. "That is what you're wanting isn't it? The rest of the pack will follow me. I am their Alpha."

Larna looked as as though she wanted to object, but I put my hand on her arm. As much as I hated the idea of Hosta joining the rebellion, he would be an even more dangerous and unpredictable enemy outside of camp. She knew it. too.

"Fine," she conceded. " If you submit to the truth seekers in the morning. I will speak to Jett Bahari on the pack's behalf and arrange a meeting. The rest of your business is with him, not me."

"That is well enough. You are still not welcome in the pack."

Larna bristled, her teeth and fists clenching. "If you refuse us, we will stay away, but Cate is not mad from eating human flesh, and I am not wanting to take control of the pack." She stared at the rest of the group, making sure that they were all listening to her. "You are weaker for having lost us, and it be your fault. Not ours."

"She was banished. You were choosing to go with her," Hosta said, as if that explained everything. "I was not making you leave." But behind him, many members of the pack had disappointed looks on their faces. They wanted us to return. Sadly, I was not surprised when none of them stepped forward to protest his decision. He was their Alpha. Despite his poor choices, Hosta was a strong leader, and their instinct was to follow him.

"I will tell Jett Bahari that you should join the rebellion. You are good fighters, and I think they can trust you. Dinna prove me wrong." Larna stormed off, unwilling to let Hosta have the last word. Not wanting to be left in an awkward position, I followed her, breathing a sigh of relief as soon as we had stepped back past the line of armed guards.

"Do you think it worked?" I whispered once we were a safe distance away.

"Aye, it worked," she said. "He would be more suspicious if I was welcoming. But are you sure we did the right thing? Jett Bahari willna be happy when I tell him the truth-seekers will only be testing Hosta."

"Hosta is the only one they need to test. He's the one I saw in my visions."

"Aye. I suppose that's the most damning evidence of all. At least we're prepared."

Her words did nothing to comfort me. Fear still gnawed at my stomach, climbing up to coil around my heart. "Larna, my visions don't always come true, but they don't lie. Hosta wants to kill you. Stay as far away from him as possible. Do you promise?"

Larna hesitated, but at last, she took my hands in hers and cupped them in the warmth of her palms. "I promise. I didna trust you once before. I will never be making the same mistake again. I will leave Hosta to Jett Bahari, and if he comes for me, I will be ready." I did not say it, but I would be ready, too. Hosta was not the only one with a set of teeth.

CHAPTER SEVEN

MORNING FOUND ME LINGERING near Jett Bahari's cabin, waiting to
see whether Hosta would meet with Auriye's approval. I hoped that she
would uncover his treachery and advise Jett Bahari to banish him from
camp, but I knew that would not solve all of our problems. The Farseer
pack was still under Hosta's control, and he would remain a threat to
Larna whether they joined the rebels or not. She had wanted to wait
outside with me until Jett Bahari made his decision, but I had begged
her to stay as far away from Hosta as possible. The fear in my eyes must
have convinced her that I was serious, because she only protested for a
little while before returning to our tent.

And so I waited alone, drawing close to the glowing embers of last
night's fire and holding my hands over the edge of the pit to keep them
warm. Winter came early in the mountains, and the morning sky was
already a dim, cloudy grey, hardly any different from night. My eyes
flicked over to the building every few seconds, watching and waiting for
someone to emerge. The only people inside were Jett Bahari, Auriye,
Hosta, and two guards. No one had come out during the past hour.

I was debating whether to stand up and find myself some breakfast
when someone called out to me in a loud, hoarse whisper. "Cate!
Here!" Startled, I whirled around to see who was calling my name. The
voice sounded familiar, but I could not quite place it. Yerta peeked out
from behind a tent, motioning me closer with a wave of his hand. I cast
one final, nervous look at the entrance to Jett Bahari's cabin before
standing up and leaving the fire.

Yerta glanced nervously over his shoulder as I approached, making sure that no one was watching. Once I drew closer and ducked behind the tent with him, I caught his scent. He smelled uneasy, worried. "What are you doing here?" I asked. Yerta's scent, along with his secretive body language, had me feeling almost as nervous as he looked.

"I came to see you," he whispered.

"Hosta just banished us," I reminded him. "He never officially ordered you not to talk to us."

That did nothing to calm Yerta's fear. "He wouldna like it," he said, twisting his hands and shifting from foot to foot. He continued peering over my shoulder, watching to make sure that we were still alone. "My brother, he has...changed."

"If you're so worried about Hosta's reaction, why are you here?"

Yerta gripped my wrist lightly, pulling me with him behind the tent and crouching down. Even though I was sure that no one had seen us, I crouched beside him, tucking my loose hair behind my ears so that it would not hang in my face. "Because I need to warn you. Before we were coming here, he went missing for three days."

I was shocked. Alphas never left their packs behind. Without a leader, Wyr had no direction. Their instincts would urge them to find a new Alpha as quickly as possible. "He left? You mean he just disappeared?"

Yerta nodded. "He told us before he went. He was leaving Seppea in charge." Seppea was a clever choice. She was too old to challenge Hosta when he returned, but wise enough to lead the pack while he was gone.

"Do you know where Hosta went?"

The muscles in Yerta's cheeks twitched, as though he wanted to lower his ears and pull a submissive face. "You canna guess?" He let his voice trail off, not wanting to speak his thoughts aloud.

I finished for him. "You think he went to see the witch."

"How else is she always finding our camps? Someone is telling her. We were raided twice after you left."

I put a steadying hand on Yerta's shoulder. He looked very pale, and his pulse hammered hard in his throat. If his tail had been there, it would have tucked between his legs. "I'm sorry," I said, pushing aside my own feelings. "I mean, your own brother..."

He brushed the comment aside. "Doesna matter. You must be telling Larna to challenge him. If Hosta belongs to the witch, we are needing a new Alpha. She has to kill him."

My blood froze. Challenge Hosta? Part of me had always known, always feared that this moment would come, but I did not want to accept it. I remembered the teeth, the blood, the light leaving Larna's eyes. Even looking at Yerta was difficult. I could see Hosta's face in his. I shook my head, clenching my jaw tight in denial. "No. Larna doesn't need to challenge him. Jett Bahari already suspects Hosta. He can help us..."

"Jett Bahari canna lead the pack," Yerta said, still pushing. "He isna one of us. Larna is next in line. Besides, Hosta banished you. She must be upset and angry about that. Larna has every right to challenge him."

I opened my mouth to protest and tell Yerta that it was too dangerous, but he shot a panicked look over my shoulder and ducked further out of sight. "He is coming," he panted, drawing further back. "He canna see me talking to you."

I gave his arm a light shove. "Go. Leave before he notices that you're missing."

"Talk to Larna," he called back to me, keeping his voice soft. "Tell her to challenge him." With one last look, he slipped away, leaving me alone behind the tent. I stepped out toward the fire pit just in time to see Hosta, Jett Bahari, and the two guards emerge from the cabin. I let out a sigh of relief when I saw that one of them was Jerico. His large axe was strapped to his back, and although he did not smile, he acknowledged me with a small nod. I felt much safer knowing that he was nearby.

Hosta noticed me a moment later. His narrow face twisted, and the scar along his cheek looked even worse in the weak daylight. His lips curled back in what would have been a snarl, but he kept his words to himself when Jerico folded his giant arms over her chest in disapproval.

"We've made a decision," Jett Bahari told me. If he noticed the tension between us, he did not show it. "The Farseer pack will join with us for now. We stand a better chance against the witch as allies than as enemies." I looked into his dark eyes, trying to guess whether he had allowed Hosta to join us because he was innocent, or because he was a traitor. Regardless of what Auriye had found, my mind was already made up. He was dangerous. Not just to Larna, but to all of us.

"Very well," I said, since Hosta still did not seem inclined to speak. "I'll inform Larna. Our part in this is done."

Jett Bahari nodded in dismissal, and I left as quickly as I could. I was sure that Jett Bahari would summon us to speak with him later in the day, perhaps while the pack was busy settling in with the other rebels, but I was unwilling to remain around Hosta any longer than necessary. Whenever I looked at him, all I could see was the angry, snarling face of my visions, its muzzle dripping with blood.

***

When I returned to our tent, I found Larna lying flat on her back, tossing and catching one of her skinning knives. She threw it just as I pushed aside the flap, and the blade glinted as it spun through the air. At the last moment, her hand shot out and caught the handle, fingers curling loosely around the polished wood. When she looked up at me, she seemed to know what had happened before I spoke. "He's staying, aye?"

I nodded. "For now. I'm not sure whether that means he passed Auriye's tests, or whether he failed."

"It doesna matter." Larna stared down at the blade of her knife, turning it in her palm. "Hosta is dangerous. Too dangerous to be staying near us."

"Yerta told me that he disappeared from camp for several days after we left. When he came back, the witch's creatures attacked them. You saw how the pack looked when they came here."

Larna's face darkened. I had not needed to remind her of the injuries we had seen, or the faces that were missing from the crowd. She was silent for a long time, but when she spoke at last, I knew what she was going to say. "This is too much, little bird. Banishing you to make me leave was one thing, but working with the witch...I canna let him live." She stood, and her fingers tightened around the handle of the knife until her knuckles shone white. Small twitches ran along the muscles of her upper arm.

I lowered my eyes to the ground. The determination in Larna's voice was unwavering. Nothing I said would convince her to change her mind, but I had to try anyway. "You told me you wouldn't die," I whispered, refusing to look at her. If I did, I would see the flash of teeth again. The dark red stain of blood matting the fur around her throat, the dull glaze of pain swallowing up her clear brown eyes...

"Cate." Larna's hands cupped around mine, and I bit down hard on my lower lip, staring at our joined fingers. Her thumb ran over my knuckles, but instead of soothing me, the tender gesture only sent a sharp pain through my chest. "How could I be dying now, when I have so much to live for? Nothing could make me leave you."

I wanted so badly to believe her. Perhaps if I hadn't already watched her die twice in my mind, I would have. But I knew what I had seen, and Larna knew it, too. Tears ran over my cheeks as I pulled my hands away from hers. I turned and folded my arms in front of my chest. "You believe me, don't you? You think my vision is going to come true, but you want to challenge him anyway."

Larna did not say anything. She stepped forward to stand behind me, and I trembled as her large hands cupped my shoulders. I couldn't bear to pull away from her again. I let her hold me, tipping my chin down so that my hair would fall around my face. After my first vision, I had wanted nothing more than for Larna to believe me. This time, her faith in my powers was no comfort at all. I just wanted her to live.

"If you..." My voice cracked, and I had to try again. "If you believe me, tell me. Tell me why you have to do this. Is your pride really worth dying for? Worth leaving me alone for?" Larna stiffened behind me, and I could tell that my words had hurt her. I did not care. I would say anything, even lies, if it would keep her from challenging Hosta.

"You know why, little bird. Pride is having nothing to do with it." Larna used her grip on my arms to turn me around. The mix of gentleness and force surprised me enough to stop my tears. Before I could say anything, her mouth covered mine.

I stiffened, then melted into her arms. Larna had not needed to answer my question with words at all. Her kiss said everything she couldn't. She did not want to fight Hosta because of her pride. She was doing it for love. Because she loved me. Because she loved Farseer. Because, despite how they had rejected her, she loved the pack. Hosta wanted to destroy everything she cared for. Love gave her the strength to try and stop him.

But I would not let her fight alone, no matter what my visions said. Heat flared from the core of my chest, spreading out to the very tips of my fingers even as tears streamed from my eyes. I threw my arms around her neck, raking my fingers through her hair and parting my lips beneath hers. She took the invitation and pressed forward with her tongue. Her taste made me so dizzy that I had to clutch her shoulders for balance. I needed to show her how much I loved her back.

I broke away from her, ignoring the ache of regret as I left the circle of her arms. She gave me a hurt look until she noticed my hands reaching for the hem of my shirt. When she realized what I was doing, her breathing sped up. She held perfectly still as I pulled my shirt over my head and shoved my leggings down past my hips, but I saw her fingers twitch. Her eyes grew darker with each strip of skin I revealed. "Cate, please. I willna..."

I already knew what she was going to say. She was remembering what had happened the last time we had made love. I stood naked before her, but I did not feel vulnerable as I brushed aside my tears. "I don't need you to make me forget that you're going to die someday, Larna. This time, I just want to show you that I love you."

A smile lit up Larna's face, and all of the tension melted from the stiff line of her shoulders. She opened her arms and I stepped into them. She ran her hands down along my back, tracing my spine, and I shuddered. Her palms were a little rough at the heel, but they were warm and achingly familiar. My body had learned her touch so well. She dipped her head to kiss me again, and I cradled her face in my hands, stroking the warm curve of her cheeks.

We fell to the sleeping pallet together, only parting our lips long enough to breathe. I let my mouth wander along the graceful slope of Larna's shoulder as she pulled off her clothes, stripping them away as quickly as she could. I helped her with her undershirt, desperate to feel the heat of her skin on mine. I could not bear to let anything remain between us. My heart pounded in my throat as the last piece of fabric fell away, and I had to swallow it back down. There were only three words that I could say.

"I love you..."

As I ran my hands up along the powerful muscles of her arms and laced them around the back of her neck.

"I love you..."

As I pulled her on top of me, sliding one of my thighs around her lean hip.

"I love you..."

As I took one of her hands in mine, brushing a soft kiss across her knuckles and guiding it between my legs. I would have said it over and over, but she took my lips again, groaning into my mouth as her fingers found me. They knew just where to go. Larna had learned all of my secrets. I blossomed open under her touch, shuddering as the pads of her fingers grazed over me in soft circles. Every part of my body opened to her, and so did every part of my heart.

She found a stroke I liked, rough and a little demanding, but tempered just enough to let me know that she was trying to be careful. Her fingers tested my entrance, making sure I was wet enough before pushing inside. She did not need to worry. Her kisses had caused a flood, and even more warmth ran over her hand as she filled me. The stretch made me hiss, but my body offered no resistance. Her thumb settled over the aching point of my desire, teasing me until I was swollen and heavy with want, but it was not enough. I needed more.

I worked one of my own hands between us, stroking up along her thigh until my fingertips skimmed through heated silk. She shuddered above me and let out a soft sigh against my cheek. I wanted us to share everything. Pleasure, love, and even death. We were *Tuathe*, and nothing could separate us.

We moved as one. Our hands and lips knew secret places. Our bodies gave and took, and our hearts fell into a shared rhythm. Each time the smooth velvet of her inner walls clutched at my fingers, I pulsed and rippled around her. Whenever the slick spirals of my thumb over her clit made her cry out, I throbbed harder against her. Both of us pushed deeper, drew closer, opened further until it was difficult to tell where my body ended and hers began.

Pressure began swelling within me, pushing out against each curling stroke of Larna's fingers. It was so sharp, so intense that I was nearly too overwhelmed to control my movements. Only instinct helped me to keep touching her. Larna's muscles tightened above me, around me, and I knew that she could feel everything I felt. Her thrusts faltered, and she shook with each ragged breath. "Cate?"

"Together," I whispered against her lips. And we were together as we shattered, as we split apart and emptied into each other. She was within me, and I was within her, and each breathless wave only pulled us closer. Larna's hips bucked, and I drove down onto her hand, taking her as deep as I could.

Somewhere between heartbeats, the two of us tipped over the edge. The pressure burst, and the tension within us unraveled as twin cries tore from our throats. I arched beneath her, releasing everything I had to give. Larna's body bowed with mine, and her wetness ran over my fingers. I curled them harder, determined to coax out every hard pulse that I could. Her thumb never stopped circling, and each pass over my sensitive tip forced shuddering spills of heat into her hand.

It seemed to go on forever. Feeling Larna flutter around me was enough to send me crashing down all over again. We were locked in an endless loop, and we could not find it within ourselves to stop. The fullness inside of me grew and grew, almost to the point of pain, but each thrust brought heavy throbs of relief. I did my best to carry her with me, and I kept up the movement of my hand despite the burn in my wrist. Larna and I were as close as we could be, but I still wanted her closer. The craving was beautiful.

At last, our bodies gave out. Larna collapsed on top of me, panting hard beside my ear. My knee fell away from her hip. Neither of us bothered to reclaim our hands. We were not ready to sever the connection yet. Slowly, we drifted back into ourselves and into the present. Fear, the same black ghost that had haunted me from the beginning, began to settle into its old home. But before it could take root, Larna spoke. "I love you, too," she whispered in the darkness, her warm breath grazing the shell of my ear.

My lips pulled into a smile. One of my arms settled around her waist, and my free hand traced patterns over the dip at the base of her spine. "I know."

CHAPTER EIGHT

WE WOKE TO THE blaring of a horn in the night. The noise filled my ears and jerked me from sleep. I sat up on my pallet and pushed my hair away from my face, trying to ignore the pounding of my heart in my throat. Larna stiffened beside me, shifting in the dark. "What's happening?" I asked, but I already knew. A sound like that could only mean one thing.

The two of us scrambled to our feet and staggered to the edge of the tent, not even bothering to pull on our clothes. We pushed back the flap and stared outside. The darkness of the night had been driven back with fire. Torches were everywhere, lighting the sky until it looked almost like daybreak. The entire camp was up and moving, but none of them noticed us. Instead, they clustered into groups, reaching for their weapons. I turned back and tried to find my shirt, but Larna put a hand on my shoulder. "No," she said. The clang of metal and several shouts nearly drowned out her voice. "Just change."

I obeyed, but the shift to half-shape was slower and more painful than usual. My mind was still fuzzy, and my body did not want to bend. I trembled and gritted my teeth, forcing myself to push forward into my other-skin. Sweat broke out along my forehead as my new flesh finally began to knit around me, burning over my bones and muscles. I could not even take comfort in the familiar hum of magic. I was too afraid.

Beside me, Larna had almost finished changing. She stood a head taller than me, her shoulders rippling with muscle as coal-black fur spread down along her back. Our eyes met, and together, we returned to the front of the tent. When we charged outside together, teeth bared and claws gripping the hard earth, we found more than just the rebels waiting for us. My nose stung with the scent of corrupted magic and rotting flesh. Dark shapes moved between the tents, just beyond the light's reach. They avoided the fire pits, but I knew what they were. The witch's kerak and shadowkin had found us again. All around us, the rebels frantically tried to organize themselves. They stayed close to the light, swinging torches and striking out with whatever weapons they could find

The sound of the horn blasted above us, and a startled look crossed Larna's face. Pain and anger flashed in her eyes, and she turned away from me, dropping to all fours and bolting toward the center of camp. I knew exactly where she was going, exactly who she was looking for. Hosta had betrayed our location again, and this time, Larna would not let him go. I tried to run after her, but she disappeared into the patches of shadow alongside the tents before I could summon the strength to follow.

I hurried to the last place that I had seen her, away from the torchlight and into the darkness. The smell of blood and death hung so thick in the air that I could barely breathe. My eyes stung, but I saw well enough to dart out of the way when a heavy shadowkin corpse fell beside me, making the earth shake. Its muscles quivered, then fell slack. Blackness oozed from its sliced belly.

A lanky brown kerak heaved itself over the mountain of the shadowkin's body with hooked hands. It peeled its lips back over its fangs, whining in its long throat. I showed my own teeth, hackles raised, muscles corded and tight. When it slashed with its claws, I was ready. I ducked under most of the blow and ripped its torso open from shoulder to hip. Its hooks pierced the middle of my back, tearing into the flesh on either side of my spine. I felt skin split, mine and the monster's, as its blood pumped into my mouth. It went still, finally letting go of me as its false life ebbed away.

With the kerak's wet blood matting my fur and my fangs stained black, I looked for Larna again. Moving was agony, but I loped forward, heading back toward the middle of camp. As I passed through another circle of light, I caught a glimpse of Jett Bahari fighting alongside his men. His twin swords were curved blurs as they sliced through the air, and I realized what had cut down the shadowkin.

He was not the only one I recognized. Several members of the Farseer pack were trying to take down another shadowkin nearby, using the same strategy I had seen before. They took turns darting beneath its vulnerable stomach, dodging the powerful kicks of its feet. Standing beyond them was Jerico, impossible to miss even among so many others. He swung his giant axe, scattering monsters left and right. None even dared to go near him.

The battlefield was clearer as I made my way closer to the fire pit. Many of the kerak were already dead or dying. Suddenly, I felt a sharp pain in my head. I pawed behind my ear, but there was no blood. The pain came again, almost toppling me over as it throbbed through my skull. I jerked…

…to shake the teeth from my neck, but they dig further into my throat, cutting off my air. My head is filled with a loud, piercing scream, but I can make no sound. The circle presses in around me, blocking out the flickering light of the fire as I am dragged to the ground. But before my vision fades, I see the limp, sprawled form of a wolf stretched out across the dirt beside me.

"Hosta!" I fell back into myself screaming his name. I could not make sense of what I had seen. There had been teeth at my…at Larna's…throat. I had felt them press in as my pulse jerked beneath the curved points. But the body I had seen next to me looked just like Hosta's. The fur along his sides was the same color as his hair. The silvery scars were in the right places. His eyes had been closed, but his appearance was unmistakable.

Before I could wonder further, I heard a sharp howl coming from my right. I whirled around, shaking off my vision and ignoring the twin lines of fire that raced along my back. The sound came again, and this time, I followed it, dropping to all fours so that I could run faster. A few of the rebels gave me terrified looks, but they all parted for me, too afraid of my teeth and claws to come closer.

At last, I reached the source of the noise. Two dark shadows were circling the large fire pit. Flames lashed up toward the sky, bright enough to blind me, and it took me several moments to see past their silhouettes. I recognized Larna first. She was still in half-shape, standing at her full height before the blazing fire. Her eyes were narrowed to slits, and the white gleam of her teeth shone in the middle of her dark face. Hosta stood a few yards away. His fur bristled, and his paws were clenched into bulky fists.

My heart stopped. This was it. The moment I had dreaded since leaving the Farseer pack. The others knew it, too. Several lean shadows emerged from the darkness, forming a circle just where the light of the fire faded. I did not know whether they heard us or sensed us, but the pack had come to witness Larna's anger. I remembered the crowd, the glowing eyes looking on as Larna's life faded away in ribbons of red.

I tried to dart forward, but before I could come between them, Larna raised her head and called out to Hosta in a rough, scraping growl. It was all she could manage in half-shape. "I challenge you, Hosta. I call for you to step down, or fight me."

Hosta dropped into a protective crouch, and Larna followed moments later. They formed a twisting circle before the fire, their sleek bodies lowered beneath the peaks of their shoulders. The way they moved was almost hypnotic. Both refused to show their backs, knowing that it would mean a killing blow before the fight had even started. "Why are you doing this?" Hosta asked. The fear in his voice surprised me. My visions had made me think that he would be eager to fight Larna and solidify his place as Alpha, but he looked almost hesitant. "Neither of us has to die…"

"I should be asking you why," Larna snarled. "You were Alpha! I wasna going to challenge you. Why would you betray us?"

Hosta stopped in his tracks, breaking off the motion of the circle. "Betray you?" he asked, abandoning his aggressive posture. "You are thinking I betrayed you?"

Larna narrowed her eyes. She did not move, although she kept her back to the fire. "How else was the witch finding us? Yerta told Cate everything."

Yerta told me everything…

I gasped. Memories and visions mixed together in a confused blur.

Hosta, lying still on the ground, but also tearing at Larna's throat. His voice, rough with fear instead of anger, "Dinna think that because you are my brother, I will not punish you. I have been forgiving so far, but one more mistake…" And another voice, one I recognized. "You must be telling Larna to challenge him. If Hosta belongs to the witch, we are needing a new Alpha. She has to kill him."

Hosta was not a traitor. It had all been a lie. As the new Alpha, he had nothing to gain by allying with Mogra. But someone else did. I only had Yerta's word that Hosta had left the pack at all. Larna and I had been gone…gone, because Hosta had deliberately sent us away. Not because he was afraid that Larna would challenge him, but because he knew who the real traitor was.

"Larna, don't! It's—"

But I was already too late. Larna exploded forward, claws outstretched and teeth bared. Hosta caught the blow with his shoulder. As soon her teeth met his flesh, both of them shifted, changing into their wolf-skins. They rolled across the ground, kicking out with their legs as they searched for a hold and nearly crashing into the fire. Sparks rained down on them, but they were too focused on each other to notice.

"Stop," I shouted, trying to fight my way past the other Wyr. They barely looked at me. This was something primal, an ancient blood-rite, and their instincts would not let them interrupt it. Larna and Hosta came together again, surging up into the air and meeting teeth with teeth. It was almost like a dance, leaping forward and back, rushing and dodging. Larna pulled back to duck beneath a swipe of Hosta's paw, and her neck was exposed for a single heartbeat. I was sure that his jaws would close around it, and red swam before my eyes.

I tensed my muscles, preparing to rush forward, but instead, Hosta ducked his head down at the last possible moment. His powerful jaws clipped Larna's foreleg, and I flinched as I heard something snap. She screamed as only a wolf could scream, tucking her leg to her chest. White splinters of bone stuck out through her skin like tiny spears. Her eyes glazed over with pain, and she flattened her ears to her head as she limped backward, still snarling and prepared to fight.

Before Larna and Hosta charged at each other again, another creature burst out of the darkness. It was large, larger than either of them, and it charged at Hosta with such force that he was thrown off his balance. He fell to the ground, kicking up dirt and sparks from the embers of the fire as he struggled to find his footing.

The attacker did not wait. It dove for his throat, and Hosta let out a high-pitched yelp of terror, lashing out with his back paws. He was not fast enough. The creature's teeth sank into his throat, and blood gushed around its black lips. Its mighty head shook until Hosta trembled and went limp. It stared up at me with glowing yellow eyes, and suddenly, I realized what it was. Who he had once been.

"Yerta!"

It was Yerta, and it was not Yerta. He was bigger and stronger, just like the Wyr that I had seen in my visions. His hair was thicker, and his muscles bulged beneath his hide. He was no longer the small, timid wolf that I knew. His resemblance to Hosta was striking, and I could barely tell them apart. He released his grip on Hosta and let him collapse into a heap on the ground, raising his head to the sky as a howl vibrated out from his great chest.

Larna surged forward, digging her back paws into the ground and launching herself through the air. She ignored Hosta completely and dove for Yerta instead, crashing into his side. He whirled on her, snarling deep in his throat. He was stronger, but Larna was faster. Before he could find a hold, she tore into the scruff of his neck, biting down as hard as she could.

Her hold did not last. Yerta shook her off as if she was nothing, pushing against her with the full weight of his body. She staggered back, but summoned her strength for another lunge, pulling down into a crouch and making herself as small as possible. When she leapt again, Yerta found her throat. His teeth sank into her neck...

...and blood spilled out in a surge, flooding down her chest and over his mouth in a river of red. She writhed and thrashed beneath him, trying to break his hold, but it was useless. Her strength slipped away, and so did the light behind her soft brown eyes...

This time, I did not hesitate. Warmth flooded through me, crawling beneath my skin. My heart pumped wildly in my chest, and I regained control of my body. I finally managed to break through the rest of the pack, dashing out into the open and ramming into Yerta's side. He reared up on his back paws, releasing Larna's throat in surprise. She fell to the ground at his feet, as limp and lifeless as Hosta. Yerta turned on me.

I reacted on instinct. When he lunged, I darted back, barely dodging the snap of his teeth. They clipped my shoulder instead, and fire exploded through me. I twisted to pull free, and the injuries on my back burst open again, burning as they ripped apart. The pain made my vision swim, and I snarled and lashed out with my claws. I pulled free of his teeth, but not before he had left several deep gouges in my shoulder.

I fell onto the dirt, shuddering as pain rippled through my body. I could see Hosta's blurry form lying before me, his chest rising and falling with faint breaths. A dark shadow passed over me, and I tried to lift my head, but even that was too much of an effort. Yerta was staring down at me, his maw streaked with dripping strands of black blood. He opened his mouth, and I prepared for another flash of agony.

But it never came. Instead, Larna's bulk flew between us. She took the strike for me, barely dodging Yerta's teeth. Despite her broken foreleg, she pushed forward, forcing him to stagger back with sheer desperation. Her movements were so quick and powerful that even Yerta was surprised. He began to back up, taking a defensive crouch as Larna's claws slashed down the side of his face.

Summoning the last of my strength, I pushed myself back up onto my paws just in time to see Yerta take another reluctant step backward. The white heat of the fire blazed behind him, and with a jolt of clarity, I knew what Larna was doing. Yerta was strong, but she was clever. She only needed to push him back a little more...

One last, desperate lunge was enough. Yerta shifted his paws even further back to brace himself, and the flames caught. Yerta bawled in surprise and pain, staggering off to the side. Sparks licked at his fur, and he dove down into the dirt, rolling to try and put them out. Larna took her chance. She seized his throat, latching on with her teeth. Yerta tossed his large head and tried to shake her off. Larna's paws scrabbled over the ground, and her muscles quivered with effort, but she did not let go. Her jaws were locked in a death-bite that she would not release.

The fight was over in seconds. White froth poured from Yerta's mouth, and his thrashing became uneven twitches. I could not see his eyes, but I knew that the life was leaving him. He went limp, and his breathing shuddered to a stop. Larna finally released his throat, standing over him for several seconds to make sure that he was dead. Then, she shifted back. Even as a naked woman, she looked powerful and strong. Her right arm was torn open to the bone, and there were still marks along her throat, but she was able to move. She left Yerta where he had fallen and hurried over to me. "Catie? Are you all right?"

I shifted as well, shivering as my fur melted back into my skin. I did not want to change while I was in so much pain, but I needed my voice, and I did not think I could find it in half-shape. "I'm fine," I gasped, hoping that it was true. "Hosta...see Hosta." He was sprawled on his stomach, but he lifted his head to look at Larna when he heard me speak. The light in his eyes was already fading.

"I did it–to...to save...you..."

"What?" Larna asked in disbelief.

Hosta's voice was weak, but both of us could hear him. We listened closely. "Yerta...betrayed me. Betrayed us...all. He...he told the witch where our camp was."

"Why?" I looked at Yerta, but his corpse held no answers. Tears of pain and betrayal stung my eyes. How wrong I had been.

"And you protected him," Larna murmured.

"He was my brother. I knew he would hurt you next...the strongest left...So I banished you...to save you. I thought, maybe...I could change his mind. Stupid..." There was silence for a long moment. We could hear nothing but Hosta's raspy breathing.

"Cate, I didna want to frighten you. For-give me..." Despite the pain in my shoulder, I put one of my hand on Hosta's chest, in a place where the skin was not torn. A shudder passed through him, and his eyes closed forever.

Larna lowered her head, giving him one last sign of respect. "Sleep, brother. And I should be the one asking forgiveness." She stood, her legs shaking slightly beneath her, and turned to face the rest of the pack. Her tanned skin was paler than usual, and still streaked with blood. She pulled back her shoulders and lifted her chin, but I could see that she was shaking. "I am Larna, Alpha of the Farseer pack. Will anyone challenge me?"

The other wolves did not move. I knew she would find no challenge here.

She spoke again. "I am Larna, Alpha of the Farseer pack. Will anyone challenge me?"

Nothing.

"I am Larna, Alpha of the Farseer pack. Will anyone challenge me?"

This time, a cry of triumph erupted from the waiting circle. As one, all of the wolves raised their heads to the sky and howled, opening their throats until the air was filled with their song. A smile broke across my face. Farseer would have been pleased.

The brief moment of joy did not last. Larna stumbled, and I hurried to stand beside her, ignoring the lines of fire that raced along my back and through my torn shoulder. I was just in time. She fell, collapsing against my side as I wrapped my good arm around her. "Cate," she murmured, "please..." The rest of her words trailed off as I lowered her back to the ground. There was more blood around her neck than before, and my stomach lurched when I saw her limp, broken forearm.

All around us, the pack began changing back. They shed their other-skins and stood up on two legs, hurrying over to us. Several of them looked at me, and I realized with some surprise that they expected me to do something. My new power surprised me, but I had no time to think about it. "Find Seppea. She needs a healer, quickly!"

CHAPTER NINE

THE NEXT MORNING DAWNED grey and cold. Mist lingered over the mountains, and a fine layer of frost covered the dry brown grass. Icy wind blew between the tents, a swirling breath from the north. Several dead rebels and Wyr were stretched out on the ground, blood outlining the shapes of their bodies. These poor souls had been blotted out like the dying flames of the fire pit. They would never see the sky and grass again.

I sat outside with the rest of the pack, waiting to hear news from Seppea. She had whisked Larna away into one of the tents and ordered all of us to keep out. Thankfully, the battle around us had nearly finished by the time she arrived to help. I wanted to go with her, but she had shaken her head and urged me to stay outside in a low whisper. "You will be seeing her later, once I am stopping the bleeding. Stay with the pack. They need you."

I still did not understand why the pack suddenly treated me with such reverence, but it was clear that my banishment was over. As we watched the tent, Goran, Kera, and several of the others gathered around me. Perhaps a few days ago, I would have been too bitter to accept their change of heart, but after what all of us had endured, I was relieved to be part of the pack again. For now, we were joined by our concern for Larna.

Larna. Just thinking her name made me shudder as I took in sharp, burning breaths of cold air. Emptiness clawed out a hollow place within my chest. She had almost died. The last time I had seen her, blood had covered her neck and arm, and the skin beneath had been a frightening, yellow-grey color where it wasn't stained crimson. Her soft brown eyes had been dull and glassy with pain.

I closed my eyes and tried to force the memories from my mind. With the rest of the pack surrounding me, I could not show weakness. Several of them were still watching me, even a few that had taken their wolf-forms to protect them from the chill. All of us waited in silence, pressed into a close group as the sky above the mountains began to glow behind its lingering mask of grey. I was still not sure whether their presence comforted me, or frightened me. Waiting as part of a crowd reminded me of our vigil outside of Farseer's tent, and that had ended with his death.

Farseer, Kalwyn, Hosta, and Yerta. And now, perhaps Larna. There had been so much death that I could not process anything clearly. Had it really been just last night that Larna had kissed me and wiped away my tears? Had it truly been less than a day since she had driven away my fears with her hands and lips? She had been so full of life then, so warm and strong in my arms. I bit down on my lower lip and tried not to think about it. The memories would only make me cry.

I blinked back the sting in my eyes and tried to control my breathing, forcing myself to think of nothing until the first sliver of pale sunlight rose over the black silhouette of the Rengast and broke through the fading mist. At last, Seppea emerged from the tent and stepped out into the open. I stood to meet her, ignoring the pain in my back. My wounds had been bandaged, but it still hurt to move.

"Well? How is she?"

"She is not bad off. She will be getting better."

I did not respond at first. Everything that had happened after the fight felt like a dream. I had spent the past several weeks watching Larna die over and over again in my mind, and it was difficult for me to believe Seppea's words. I needed to see her. Touch her. Hear her breathing. Until I saw the rise and fall of her chest and felt her heartbeat, I would not be able to trust that she was alive. "Please," I begged, staring over her shoulder at the tent, "I need to see her…"

Seppea turned and motioned for me to follow her. "Come with me. She is waiting for you."

I pushed aside the flap and stepped through. The tent was dark, although several candles cast their weak, flickering light over a small cot. When I saw Larna, I let out a gasp. She was resting on her back, breathing shallowly but steadily. Her eyes were closed, and her face did not show any pain. There was no blood around her throat, only a pile of used bandages waiting to be thrown out.

Relief rushed in to replace the numbness. I hurried forward and knelt beside her, reaching out to cup one of her cheeks. Larna still looked like herself, and she smelled the same as always. The burning scent of blood mixed with magic and death was gone. She stirred when I touched her, and her eyes fluttered open as my fingertips trailed over the familiar curve of her face. Her mouth pulled into a weak smile. "Cate…"

"Larna…"

I could not stop myself. I bent down to kiss her. Her lips were rough and dry as paper, but I did not care. It was overwhelming to see her, to feel her. I stroked her hair, her face, the smooth arch of her forehead, listening for each breath. She was alive. She was truly alive. "I almost lost you," I whispered, mouthing more than speaking. We were so close that Larna could feel the words against her mouth.

"You will never be losing me. You saved me."

The knot within my chest finally unraveled. My vision had come true, but not in the way I expected. I did not remain frozen, unable to do anything as the life bled from Larna's throat. I moved. I came between her and Yerta's teeth. I had saved her, and she had saved all of us. My cheeks ached with smiling, and I barely noticed that they were also wet with tears. It was finally over.

**

The funeral began just after nightfall. As soon as the sun's last rays disappeared over the western edge of the mountains, the rebels brought a great fire to life. Instead of using the cooking pit, they cleared several tents away from the center of camp, placing down a circle of small stones and stretching large beams of wood between the edges. Next came the kindling: chunks of coarse mountain grass, thin sticks, and oil filled the empty spaces. Amendyrri had burned their dead for thousands of years. It was tradition. Maybe that was one reason the kerak seemed so monstrous to us. Using the ashes of the dead for dark magic was a terrible crime.

Larna watched the rebels work as we made our way around the fire, where the rest of the Farseer pack was waiting for us. Seppea had not wanted her to leave the tent, and even I was worried that going outside would be too much for her, but she was determined. Some of the dead were Wyr, part of our pack, and it was her duty as the new

Alpha to attend the funeral and pay her respects. Once she had circled the tent several times without help, Seppea had reluctantly granted her permission to come outside with the rest of us.

The pack was relieved to see her, and smiles broke across their somber faces as we joined them. Several looked as though they wanted to speak, but Larna raised her good hand to silence them. "Later," she said in a low voice. "Our brothers and sisters were giving their lives to fight the witch. This is their time, not mine." She took my arm in hers and led me to stand at the front of the group.

The brief surge of happiness faded quickly once the pyre was finished. One by one, bodies were stretched out on top of the wood. After a little while, I stopped counting. I did not want to think about how many faces I would recognize. Some of them had belonged to the Farseer pack, and even more were rebels that I had spoken to over the past several weeks. It was a small miracle that Larna had not been one of them.

The flame came last. Jett Bahari stepped forward from the crowd of men and women. He held a torch in his giant hand, and the dancing flicker of light made his skin look even darker than usual. With one smooth motion, he tossed the torch onto the funeral pyre. It landed in a shower of sparks, and the fire quickly caught. The flames soon reached high above our heads. Tongues of red and white lashed over the velvety black sheet of the sky, stretching up toward the crescent moon. Smoke rose into the air, swirling beneath the stars. It carried our grief, our prayers, and our hopes with it.

At first, the large tower of flame made loud popping noises, but they grew quieter, or we grew used to them. "I want us to die at the same time," Larna said, only just loud enough for me to hear. She wrapped an arm around my shoulder, pulling me against her side as she stared up at the giant column of flame. "We should be burned together."

I smiled. For the first time in a long time, I was no longer afraid. I turned to look up at Larna, studying her through the darkness. The firelight brought out the hollows of her cheeks, painting her skin in hues of brown and gold. Her hair mixed with the dark sky. "I'm not so scared of death anymore," I told her. "I know that I will always be with you, even through whatever comes after."

Larna's lips parted as though she wanted to answer me, but she could not find her words. Instead, she smiled. Her fingers found mine, squeezing tight around my hand. Her palm was warm, and once more, I realized how lucky she had been to survive. How lucky we both were. Just because death and I had started to make peace did not mean that I was ready to find out what waited for us beyond this life any time soon.

We looked up as Jett Bahari stepped out from the circle of people around the pyre. The whites of his eyes stood out eerily until he stepped closer to the firelight, the dancing yellow flame bringing color back to his face.

"Alaram irini. To honor the fallen."

"To the fallen," we said. It was like a toast, but no one raised a glass to drink.

"Alaram enias. To honor their memory."

"To their memory."

"Alaram abios. To honor life."

"To life."

All around us, the crowd started singing. It was such an old song that no one remembered when it was written, or who first sang the words. For once, I was not embarrassed to raise my voice. In fact, I hoped that it would carry up into the sky along with the smoke of the pyre.

To those who have fallen asleep, you will not be forgotten.
Body and flesh are passing, but the spirit is eternal.

***

"Why do you think Yerta betrayed us?" I asked Larna as the two of us made our way through the darkness, heading back toward our tent. It was a question that had been bothering me for the whole day, tickling at the back of my thoughts, but I had not found the right moment to voice it. Now that we were alone, without Seppea or the pack hovering over us, it pushed to the front of my mind again.

Larna shrugged, then winced as the motion put pressure on her injured neck. She flinched, and I grabbed her arm in case her balance faltered. After a moment, she turned to look at me. "I'm fine, little bird. You can let go. But I am not knowing why Yerta betrayed us. I dinna think we will ever know for certain now that he is dead."

I relaxed my hold on Larna's arm and waited for her to start walking again. I had my own opinions about why Yerta had turned on the pack, but Larna was right. There was no way to know without talking to him. "I wonder why I didn't see it," I said, staring up at the stars. The sky was clear, although the air was still spiced with smoke from the fire. "He was my friend...or at least, I thought he was. If I had been paying more attention, could I have seen that he was lying to us?"

"Yerta was clever. He tricked all of us, not just you. Perhaps he was tired of being the *Pekah*."

I was glad that Larna had voiced what I was thinking without being prompted, but also surprised. "I thought you said that without a last, there could be no first?"

Larna nodded her head. "Aye. I still believe that. But maybe you were right as well. If we had been treating Yerta with more respect, honoring him for what the *Pekah* gives to the pack, maybe he wouldna have grown so bitter. It is not a mistake I will be forgetting."

"And the rest of the pack? Have you forgiven them for what they did to you?" Being part of the group had been a relief while Larna lingered on the brink of death, but part of me was still hurt by what they had done to her. The pack had rejected her when she needed them most, and even if she forgave them, I was not sure that my own forgiveness would come so easily.

"Hosta was their Alpha. What else could they do? He was the one who banished us, and he was doing it to keep us away from Yerta. I wonder how long he knew his brother was a traitor..."

I thought for a moment. "Probably a long time. It explains why I thought he was always following me. I spent a lot of time with Yerta once I joined the pack. Hosta was probably trying to keep an eye on him." I sighed with regret. Despite the power of my visions, my judgment couldn't have been worse. "If I had just paid more attention..."

Larna stopped again and turned to face me. She reached out with her right hand and cupped my cheek, brushing my hair away from my face. "'If' is a silly word. If Hosta had come to Farseer and told him about Yerta, maybe no one would have died. If we had all been kinder to Yerta, maybe he wouldna have turned on us. And if you were not joining the pack..."

I smiled, standing on tip-toe to bring my face closer to Larna's. "And if I never joined the pack, I wouldn't be able to do this..." My lips met hers, and warmth pulsed over my skin, driving away the cold. Carefully, I let my body melt into hers, making sure not to touch her arm or her throat. Despite her injuries, we were still a perfect fit.

Larna wrapped her arm around my waist, squeezing tight until our mouths finally broke apart. "And you can be doing that whenever you like." She rested her forehead against mine and cupped the side of my hip. "Every time you think of if...think that if anything had been different, I might not have been meeting you."

I let my own hand cup the back of her neck, preparing to draw her in for another kiss. "Well, when you put it that way, I wouldn't change a thing."

CHAPTER TEN

SEVERAL NIGHTS LATER, LARNA entered our tent as I was reading my journal. Her shape and smell were familiar, so I did not look up right away. Instead, I continued scanning Ellie's most recent letter. She was worried, and rightfully so, after hearing of my recent adventures. Even I had a hard time believing everything that had happened to me since leaving Baxstresse.

"Ellie is horrified at what I am doing with myself," I told Larna as I set my quill aside. "She demands to know where I am so that she can come take me home. I don't have the heart to tell her that Seria isn't home anymore. I think hearing about how Yerta almost killed both of us was too much for her. Maybe I should have skipped that part."

Larna did not answer. There was an alluring, heavy spice around the edges of her scent that distracted me. I looked up. Her brown eyes were intently focused, and the tip of her tongue outlined her soft lips. She looked hungry. My own eyes grew wider. "Oh!" I let out a soft, startled gasp as she knelt beside me and pulled me into her arms, nuzzling my hair. Her nails scraped against the fabric of my shirt, wanting to feel skin.

My journal dropped onto the floor beside me, completely forgotten. "Hello," I purred, running my fingers through Larna's dark hair. The pads of my fingers brushed her warm cheeks. She shivered in my arms, letting out a low growl that vibrated beside my ear. She nipped the lobe, causing me to fall backwards onto our sleeping pallet. "I see you're feeling better," I teased, smiling up at her as she hovered over me.

"Aye. Much better." She gave her injured hand a flex to show me that it was starting to heal. "This might not be good for much, but I have another one..."

"And what are you going to do with it?" I whispered.

Larna decided to show me instead. She struggled out of her shirt, tearing it over her head and tossing it into a corner of the room. She wore nothing underneath, and the heat of her skin burned through my clothes as she lowered herself on top of me. My lips found her naked shoulder, drawing up to the place where her pulse pounded along her neck, just below the edge of her bandage. She gasped as the edges of my teeth teased her throat. "Tell me," I murmured.

"I...I want..." Larna stammered, but her words were lost in a sharp hiss when I bit down just above her collarbone. I soothed the sore spot with my tongue, proud of the fact that I could render her speechless so easily.

I worked my way across the smooth slope of her chest, kissing down along her collarbone until my lips were hovering an inch away from the hard tip of her breast. "Tell me what you want..."

Larna's muscles seized as I caught her nipple between my lips. She arched above me, asking for more contact without words. My hands left her hair and wandered across the broad, smooth muscles of her back, running down along her shuddering sides until I found her hips. When she gave me a pleading look, I reached around her front to undo the ties on her pants. She kicked them off clumsily, trembling all over again as I switched over to her other breast. "You, Catie." Her voice cracked with need. "I want you. Just you."

I pulled my mouth away, blowing a stream of cool air over the hard, wet point of her nipple. This time, I decided, Larna was not going to take me until I could barely walk. She had already given me a great deal of attention over the past several weeks, and I had hardly done anything for her in return. But I knew that Larna would not simply lie back and let me take care of her. So, I thought of a compromise. I pressed my thigh between her legs, smiling when I felt wetness against my skin. Larna was more than ready for me.

I let her pull off my shirt and leggings, but when she tried to reach between my legs, I caught her hand. She looked down at me with sad brown eyes and a pouting lower lip. I caught the lip between my teeth and pulled her tight against me. "I want you over me," I breathed in between kisses, trying not to let the dizzying taste of her lips distract me from my goal.

"Over you?" Larna repeated. It took her several moments to process the words even as she said them. When she finally did, her dark eyes grew wide with surprise, and a flush spread across her tanned cheeks, creeping all the way down to the edge of the bandage around her neck.

I lifted my knee higher, pressing deliberately against her. At the same time, I let my hands wander down to the firm swell of her backside, urging her to shift forward. She took the invitation and bucked against me, shuddering when she found a motion she liked. I felt the throbbing point of her clit as it caught against my thigh, and another pulse of wetness ran along my skin. "Yes. You heard what I said, didn't you?"

"But..." Larna gave me a hesitant look. For some reason, it made me want her even more. Her strange mixture of dominance and shyness was captivating. Desire sliced through my lower belly, and it was all I could do to keep from shaking. I loved her, all of her, and I wanted her terribly.

"Please?"

Larna moved until she was kneeling over me, using her hands to brace herself. "You will be telling me if you want to stop?"

I stared back up along the tight plane of her stomach. The powerful muscles there twitched with desire. "Trust me, I don't want to stop." To prove it, I pulled her hips down until she was hovering just above my mouth. A gasp caught in her throat, and she held perfectly still. I examined her carefully, taking in all of the soft parts, colors, and textures. Her outer lips were already parted, and the slick, heavy folds between them were swollen-red. Everything was covered in a clear, shimmering coat of wetness. The proud bud of her clit stood out from beneath its hood, pleading for attention. I lifted my head just enough to take it between my lips.

Larna's hips jerked forward at the first slow swipe of my tongue. She tried to keep still as I pulled her deeper, tugging the swollen shaft and circling the sensitive tip, but soon, instinct got the better of her. She forgot her shyness and relaxed her legs, spreading them further apart and offering me everything she had. Her fingers threaded through my hair, pulling me tight against her. She raked her nails along my scalp, just hard enough to send a tingle shooting down the middle of my back. "Cate, please..."

I could not deny her. I shifted down, ignoring her whimpers of protest. As I moved lower, more salt and sweetness spilled into my mouth. Her taste was intoxicating, and I wanted more. I circled the tight ring of muscle at her entrance, teasing her until I could slip inside. She fluttered around me, and I pushed as deep as I could, ignoring the ache in my jaw. I let her guide me to the spots that made her gasp and shudder, the places that made her rock harder against my mouth. Her warmth spilled over my cheeks and covered my chin, but I was past caring.

Desperate for more than I could give her, Larna moved her own hand down along her stomach and between her legs. If her thighs had not been clamped tight against my cheeks, I would have shaken my head. That was my job. The flat of my tongue pushed her fingers away. I replaced my mouth with my hand, sliding inside of her and taking the tight bundle of her clit back between my lips.

One forward curl of my fingers, one last flutter of my tongue, and she was lost. She tossed her head back as a flood of warmth poured across my cheeks. I wanted to move down and taste as much as I could, but I caught her wetness in my palm instead, sealing my lips tighter around her. She throbbed against my tongue, crying out something that sounded almost like my name. The velvet heat around my fingers pulled impossibly tight, and Larna's hands twisted through the tangle of my hair, but I barely noticed. I was too enthralled by how handsome she looked arching above me.

Larna's hips finally stopped jerking against my mouth. Her chest rose and fell with rapid pants, and the sleek muscles of her abdomen twitched with aftershocks. She kept fluttering around my fingers until I pulled out of her, but I was able to coax several more ripples from her exhausted body by teasing the hard shaft of her clit through its hood and kissing the tip. At last, she fell forward and released the back of my head. Regretfully, I let her pull away. To make up for the loss, I brought my wrist to my mouth and cleaned the shimmering trails of wetness beneath the heel of my hand.

"I...I canna begin to guess how you learned to do that," Larna mumbled, collapsing back down on the sleeping pallet beside me. "Are you wanting..."

"No," I whispered, gathering her limp body in her arms. I pulled her close and snuggled against her side. "That was for you."

Larna's breathing slowed, and her warm skin began to cool as the light sheen of sweat covering it disappeared. "You smell like me," she whispered as she tucked her head under my chin. "I like having my scent on you."

Perhaps if we had been human, her words would have seemed strange, but a smile broke across my face. "I like it, too."

***

Alone, I stared out over the mountaintops and the Forest. The branches of the trees below were mostly bare, but I could see a line of green along the horizon where the plains began. Sitting on the side of the mountain, the world below me felt very big, and I felt very small. The wind wove through my hair, sending it spilling back behind my shoulders and drawing a few tears from my eyes, but I relished the cold bite because I was alive to feel it.

Death was never far from my mind. The battle had ended five days ago now, but it was still vivid in my memory. Sometimes, I woke up shaking in Larna's arms. She told me I did not struggle or cry out, but I heard screams in my sleep. The screams of men and Wyr as they fell before Mogra's demons, and the screams of Elaran, Kalwyn, and Farseer. I had seen so many die, but for some reason, Larna and I were still alive, despite my visions.

Even though she had been the one to almost lose her life, Larna handled her fears with more grace than me. She did not have nightmares. But once in a while, usually before we fell asleep, I noticed a sad look on her face in the firelight. When I saw that look, I held her hand and stroked her hair, but neither of us spoke. There was nothing to say.

The wind died down, and I sensed someone behind me on the mountain's edge. My nose told me who it was. A human's scent was as unique and easy to recognize as a face for me. This scent carried herbs and ash and the wind. "Auriye?" I called out, turning to look over my shoulder.

I was right. Auriye approached me slowly, with just a trace of a limp. Perhaps her joints were stiff from the cold. "Arim dei, young shaman," she said, standing beside me to gaze down the side of the mountain. The Forest stretched out below us, an ocean of bare branches. The color was strange mixture of mottled brown and green, since some of the trees had lost their leaves, but the pines had kept their needles. "The traitor is gone, but I sense that you are still not at peace."

I lowered my head in shame. Even though Larna had killed him, I felt responsible for bringing the Farseer pack and Yerta to the rebel camp. In a way, the deaths were our fault. "I wish that no one had died," I whispered. But wishing could not change the past. If only things had been different…I tore my eyes away from the great Forest and looked at Auriye. "Maybe if Kalwyn had finished teaching me, I could have done something to stop it."

"I am not a shaman," Auriye said, "but I do know something about visions. They are unpredictable. Even the wisest of us can fail to understand them. But making a mistake doesn't mean you failed. You are alive, and so is your mate. It is not such a bad ending. Kalwyn would have been proud of you."

My view of Auriye and the Forest faded as my thoughts turned inward, remembering. "In Kalwyn's house, I saw the moving energy of a person that was gone. Do you think that I will ever speak to her again?"

Auriye shrugged. "We still don't know what happens to the soul after death. Many believe that the Maker takes them to a place of rest. But perhaps through the gifts she has given you, Kalwyn will remain with you still."

For a while, we were content to sit in silence together. The wind died, and the sun rose higher in the sky, casting golden beams down over us. I wrapped my fingers around the Deadeye. It was warm in my hand…

The sun was just rising above the mountains, so I knew that this was a different place, a different time. Larna approached me from behind and sat beside me. She opened her arm, and I rested my head against her shoulder, closing my eyes as she pressed a kiss to my temple. Her arm found itself in a familiar position, wrapped around my belly, which had grown too large to hide beneath my clothes.

"I wish I could be feeling them," she said, letting her hand roam across my swollen stomach.

I shifted my head against her shoulder, looking up at Larna's pointed chin. There was a relaxed smile on her face, although the sense of strength that was her core remained. The proud angle of her head and the set of her shoulders clearly said that I was her mate, and these were our pups. "You will," I said, resting my hand on top of hers. Our fingers linked. "I only started feeling them a few days ago."

Larna remained silent and thoughtful for a few moments. I was content to rest against her side. To me, the most perfect place in the world was in her arms. "We should start thinking of names. I wonder how many we will be needing," she said, almost shyly. The streak of timidity in my proud Larna made my lips turn up in a small smile. Even though she would never admit it, she was a little frightened at the prospect of having children.

"We need three." I could not explain how I knew, but I was carrying three children. Wyr rarely had just one pup at a time.

"You said that they looked like me?" Larna asked, even though I had already answered that question at least a hundred times.

I indulged her. "Yes, Tuathe. All three of them will look just like you. They will be handsome and strong, and you will teach them to be kind and good."

Larna looked pleased and a little disappointed at the same time. "I wanted them to look like you," she said, kissing my hair. "You are so beautiful..."

"I'm sure they will look a little like me," I said, trying to appease her. "Ellie keeps asking me when I will come visit. I know that she and Belle want to be there for the birth of their Godchildren."

At the mention of a visit, Larna frowned. A worry wrinkle creased her smooth forehead. "We canna go back to Seria right now."

"I told them that. Ellie says they'll come here anyway, but I can't believe they're serious."

Larna snorted. "Little bird, your friends are delusional. Are all Serians like that?"

I smiled, shaking my head against Larna's chest. "No, only Ellie and Belle. The rest of them are usually normal."

"Maybe living in Seria left you a little crazy," she teased.

I lifted my head up, nipping affectionately at a tempting ear. "Maybe. And maybe I should show you just how crazy I am..."

"Cate?" I blinked. Auriye was looking at me curiously, but she did not seem worried. "Cate, what did you see?"

I smiled. "Nothing," I said, leaning back and staring up at the sky. "At least, nothing dangerous this time."

Auriye smiled. "Not all visions are great, important messages for the kingdom."

"Not this one." But it was a great, important message to me. I wondered if I should tell Larna about the vision. No, I decided. I wanted to keep this to myself for a while longer.

The End

About the Author

Rae D. Magdon

Rae D. Magdon is a writer living and working in the state of Alaska. Over the past few years, she has written several lesbian-themed novels, including Dark Horizons, The Second Sister, and her first published work, All The Pretty Things. She enjoys writing fantasy and science fiction, in addition to modern-day romances. When she is not writing original fiction, she ~~wastes~~ spends her time dabbling in ~~unapologetically smutty~~ romantic lesbian fanfiction. Her favorite fandoms are Law & Order: SVU and Mass Effect. In her free moments, which are few and far between, she enjoys spending time with Tory, her wonderful spouse, and their two cats.

Connect with Rae online

Website - http://raedmagdon.com/
Facebook - https://www.facebook.com/RaeDMagdon
Tumblr - http://raedmagdon.tumblr.com/
Email - rdmagdon@desertpalmpress.com

Cover Design By : Rachel George
www.rachelgeorgeillustration.com

Other books from Desert Palm Press

The Guardian Series by Stein Willard
A Guardian's Touch – Book 1
A Guardian's Love – Book 2
A Guardian's Passion – Book 3

Scarred for Life by S.L. Kassidy

Please Baby by S.L. Kassidy

Friends Series by AJ Adaire
Sunset Island — Book 1
The Interim — a novelette
Awaiting My Assignment — Book 2
Anything Your Heart Desires — Book 3

One Day Longer Than Forever by AJ Adaire

Dark Horizons by Rae D. Magdon & Michelle Magly

Amydyr Series by Rae D. Magdon
The Second Sister — Book 1

Available from Smashwords, Amazon, and CreateSpace

Coming in 2014

Amydyr Series by Rae D. Magdon
The Witch's Daughter — Book 3

It's Complicated by AJ Adaire

Dark Horizons Series by Rae D. Magdon & Michelle Magly
Starless Night — Book 2

CPSIA information can be obtained at www.ICGtesting.com
Printed in the USA
BVOW06s0057070715

407376BV00018B/40/P

9 781500 828707